IN SAFE HANDS

IVY NGEOW

Penguin
Random House
SEA

Title: In Safe Hands
Author: Ivy Ngeow
Price: SGD26.90
Publisher/Imprint: Penguin Random House SEA/Penguin Books
Category: Fiction
Format: Paperback
Pages: 384
Publication: October 2025
Distribution: In United States, United Kingdom, and Europe:
Independent Publishers Group
In Southeast Asia: Times Distributions and Alkem,
In India: Penguin Random House India/Repro India

NOTE FOR THE READER

Do not quote for publication until verified with finished books. This advance uncorrected reader's proof is the property of Penguin Random House SEA. It is being loaned for promotional purposes and review by the recipient and may not be used for any other purpose or transferred to any third party. Penguin Random House SEA reserves the right to cancel the loan and recall possession of the proof at any time. Any duplication, sale, or distribution to the public is a violation of law.

Please send all queries for this book to our team below:

Publicity & Marketing: Chaitanya Srivastava,
csrivastava@penguinrandomhouse.in

Digital Marketing: Simran Singh, ssingh3@penguinrandomhouse.in

Sales & Distribution: Almira Ebio Manduriao,
Aemanduriao@penguinrandomhouse.sg

Editorial: Swadha Singh, Ssingh4@penguinrandomhouse.in

PART ONE

1

GENEVIEVE

Thursday 29th December

By the early morning winter light, Fulham seems older, tighter, busier: the rows of houses like a grey perm. Rumbold Road comes into view from the Uber window. I remove my earring and poke the stem into the tiny hole at the side of the phone. When the SIM drawer slides out, I remove the SIM card and drop it into the slot on the lid of my airport Caffe Nero cup. I will get a UK phone number that no one knows.

'Mummy, help me,' says Jasper, handing me his Lego Star Wars backpack when he could have just put it on.

'I need to get the luggage out first,' I mutter. The expressionless Uber driver gives us a hand, robotic and mechanical in his action. He can't wait to drive away. Soon, all our possessions within the 45 kg luggage allowance are sitting on the pavement outside my childhood home. The boxes and cases seem enormous now, more like furniture than luggage. I only now see that I don't know or care what's in them.

'Mummy, is Gung Gung in?' says Jasper, assisting me with the smaller items of luggage. This *hand luggage,* within cabin guidelines, is not for my hand. It's a misnomer.

'I'm sure he is, yup.' I don't add that my father didn't pick up when I called.

My head throbs as my eyes take in the three-storey, double-fronted Victorian detached home, with a pair of classical white columns that frame the entrance steps, Welsh black slate roof and filigree railings of the first floor Juliet balcony. That had been my favourite street-watching place as a child, my fingers gripping the intricate iron lace. I had played with a dollhouse replica of the house made for my sister and me.

Small-paned symmetrical sash windows form the canted shape of the bay window. The curtains are shut. On each of the ground floor sills sits a trendy stainless-steel tub of white cyclamen and ivy. My father is the least green-fingered man I know. He has no interest in art or design. Has he got a landscape gardener now? Since my mother's passing, the house's upkeep has been neglected. But he, like anyone successful, hires someone if he wants something done. He does not make any creative decisions and will not attempt DIY. Judging from the spotless black-and-white chequerboard front path, it's likely that someone else has taken charge. I have tried to find out how he is coping during our weekly calls, and his reply is always 'I've eaten.'

I had not been back since my mother's passing four years ago. I should have come sooner, but first there was the business, then the pandemic, and later, the business again. Now it's finished.

Memories arrive in chunks as I move the luggage piece by piece up the front steps, admiring the brass knocker's high shine. The newly-painted green door is smooth as the skin of a ripe olive. Everything seems a little too slick for Daddy. We are not refined. My family is from the Hakka dialect group, Chinese peasant stock known for the nomadic life and gruelling labour. He likes things rustic, flyblown, reminiscent of his life back home and the hardship he went through as a child in Singapore during the war. He finds comfort in the old and worn. Is this even the right house?

Jasper interrupts my thoughts. 'Can I, please? Can I?' he asks eagerly. His little hand is outstretched, ready to grab the gold ring bitten by a lion's mouth. On the last visit he was too little to reach the knocker. He has grown, and I've aged so much since I have been away from London.

'Yes, of course,' I laugh a little. He goes for it. The clank is hard and resonant.

I look straight at the olive-green door, ready to face my father. I worry that he will ask me, 'Have you eaten?', which in Chinese is the informal way of saying 'Hello, how are you?', a greeting of familiarity rather than formality. I prepare to say 'I've eaten,;I've had tons to eat on the plane,' being how you say 'I'm fine'.

The door opens and my words catch in my throat like a bone. Before me stands a tall, radiant middle-aged woman in a high-collared sweater and fine gold necklaces, elegant as those 1930s paintings of chiselled, fair Shanghai socialites. Her eyes are lively and charming. Even I find it hard to tell the age of Asians, despite being Asian and living in Asia for years. Our skincare secrets are our heirloom. I see her cat-eye eyeliner and am reminded of cruises, old-fashioned cars, good hair.

'Hello,' she says, with a small formal smile. 'May I help you?'

Could I have the wrong house? My eyes dart around: the polished-brass house number is correct. Her voice is high-pitched like a girl's, and her accent is Singaporean or Malaysian, with an ersatz Americanised TV twang.

'I-I am Genevieve,' I stammer. 'Genevieve Ho. My father... Is my father here... Richie Ho?'

She presses her palms to her cheeks in that dramatic 'what was I thinking' *Vogue*-magazine way. 'Of course. Richard has mentioned you.'

Richard? What the—? Nobody calls my father that, absolutely no one. He was born Ho Keong in Singapore. He chose the nickname Richie, because it sounded 'rich', when we emigrated to the UK. It stuck. And it's not short for Richard.

'Please come in,' she smiles.

Conscious that I am muppet-like now, frizzy-haired and frazzled, not just from the twelve-hour flight but from the business, the separation, life – I just want her to disappear so that I can see my father. That has been the objective since I booked the plane tickets. I am not in the mood for small talk.

My mouth is dry. I ask as clearly as possible, 'And who are you?'

'Stella,' she says, her eyes wide as if surprised that I have no idea who she is. Her name means 'star', and that's rubbing it in.

'You'll call her Auntie Stella.'

'Daddy!' I call out to the darkened hall, thrilled to hear his familiar voice.

'Gung Gung!' shouts Jasper. He runs in and I follow him, ignoring the woman. I almost trip over her embroidered velvet Chinese pumps.

'Are you there, Daddy?' I repeat, removing my grubby

gold Converse high-tops, the starter uniform of mums. They look scuffed, shabby and old.

'I am, I am,' comes my father's reply. 'Gen, where have you been?' It seems less a question than a lament.

'Let me help you with the luggage,' says Stella.

'No, thank you, I can do it,' I say, then reply in a louder voice to my dad, 'I'm here now, Daddy!'

The woman ignores me and we take the luggage in, piece by piece. I am obliged to put up with her assistance because it's quicker and Jasper has lost interest in everything but seeing his grandfather.

'Hey, little monkey!' Dad cries. My father sounds like he did when I was a child, though a little weaker. For those seconds, he could have been young. 'Punky monkey!'

To me he repeats, 'You need to call her Auntie Stella.' Daddy's voice is frail, coming from the front reception room, where the grand piano was... is. I notice its high shine as I turn towards the impressive double-panelled doors to the hallway, through which Jasper has just run.

'Shoes off!' I remind Jasper.

'Oh, never mind the shoes! Give Gung Gung a big hug!' announces my father. He is smaller and more hunched than a few years ago. He's in the armchair with his copy of the *Times,* which he flings on the floor the moment Jasper runs into his arms.

He tilts his chin moments later when he lets go of Jasper, then, in a rapper's gesture, points with both hands at the wheelchair beside the sofa. 'I don't really need it. It's just much... much—,'

'Easier,' the woman says.

'I get tired. I can still get up and down—,'

'The stairs,' she turns to me in a faux-conspiratorial

manner and says in a low voice, 'We are getting a stairlift fitted.'

'Aiyah! I don't n—'

'Richard, I know you don't. But you will be so pleased when it arrives.'

She is finishing his sentences for him. Mummy used to do it and it drove Daddy nuts. Now he does not seem to mind, and even enjoys the attention. He's grinning, which makes my skin prickle.

'Coffee? Tea?' The strange woman looks at me. 'Let me get you something.'

'Oh, all right. Coffee, thank you,' I blurt out. "Auntie" Stella disappears like a gust of wind into the kitchen. Once it was Cassie's and my domain: we were interested in cooking and baking from a young age. My sister is now a professional chef in Riyadh and works long shifts in a grand hotel for some sultan's private suites. I have not told her that I have returned to our family home.

I am astonished when Stella returns. She is wearing Cassie's deep royal blue training apron, embroidered in gold with her initials C.H., and the hotel and catering school crest. My sister left it here for my mother when she went abroad a decade ago.

Why can't Stella wear it, after all? Am I being unreasonable? My mother is dead and Cassie is abroad, and will never wear it again. When my mother passed away, I could still smell her cooking on the apron. I didn't have the heart to wash away her lingering scent and kept it folded in one of the drawers. Now it's been laundered and starched to perfection, so neatly ironed that I can see the sharp creases. Each one cuts into me.

My coffee is lukewarm.

Jasper is showing my father how to play *Yeti in my Spaghetti*, a game on his phone that he likes. That's right, he's six and has an iPhone. Not the latest, but pretty new. I had to get him one as the business was taking up at least six days of my week. Jasper spends all his time in school, in after-school club, or with Asunción, our Filipino live-in help. It looks like Stella *is* hired help like Asun.

I take my coffee mug into the kitchen. 'Excuse me,' I mutter.

'It's Stella.' She misunderstands my uncertain tone for forgetting her name. *Not* likely.

'I know you're Stella. Did my dad hire you from the agency?'

She clams up. Have I asked the right question? Or wrong? Then Stella bursts out laughing. 'Yes, he hired me,' she says. I know I should relax, but I can't.

'Not from the agency,' she adds, after a pause.

I have more questions to ask her, like, if not the agency, then where on earth did Daddy hire her from? There will be more time for all that. I have only just arrived and my mind is still on my business. It was my baby. I dwell on it too much and it makes me riled. I have to focus on the here and now.

'Jasper, let's think which room you will have. You're going to be staying here with Gung Gung. Do you want to see your room?' I hear my dad saying.

'Oh yes, please,' Jasper says, casting an *is that OK?* look at me. I tilt my head towards the staircase. 'Go on, then,' I say. 'Auntie Stella will take you upstairs.'

I watch them while she takes his hand and his Star Wars backpack. When they are out of sight, I ask my father if I can see the garden. He gets up with relative ease, which makes me wonder if the wheelchair is redundant and for convenience only. Someone else's convenience. I must admit that my father looks better than the last time I saw him. He is wearing one of those fine-knit jumpers with an alligator logo embroidered on the left breast pocket and casual navy trousers. He could be going to work with a smart outfit like that. Since when did he start paying attention to what he wears?

He puts his tortoiseshell glasses down.

'Oof,' he says, with affected difficulty, and then gives me a big smile to show me he's only joking. He seems to walk fine, and I follow him into the garden. It's not as overgrown as I'd expected. I am surprised by the clematis, mahonia, and ornamental grasses in the beds. A Fulham garden, compact, but traditional.

'What exactly is she doing here?'

'Who?'

'You know who.'

'Gen, you only just got here. Give it some time.'

'That's why I want to know.'

'She is here to look after me, obviously.'

'But *I* am here to look after you.'

'No, you're not.'

'Daddy, I couldn't travel for the last few years.'

'Who is going to look after all this?' He waves vaguely at the garden and the house, like a conductor.

'You said you never wanted a carer,' I say. 'All those people hired for you either left or were asked to go.'

'You should know better than to use agencies, Gen. You're too blind to see that they just want your money.'

'That's not true.'

'It's true. I am your father. I am not an employer or

someone who needs an uneducated matron moron coming in here to reheat some Tesco TV dinner for me.'

'Dad!' I am perplexed by the image of the staff who had been carefully selected but I have nothing to add to his one-liner Trustpilot review.

'Anyway, that's all before Stella arrived,' he adds. 'I'm in safe hands.'

'You never mention this whenever I call,' I say. 'I didn't know you were trying to find someone.'

'I had some mobility issues and needed some help after my fall.'

'You had a fall? You said nothing about that.'

'There's nothing to say. You're ever so busy with your work, Gen. Speaking of which, how's business?'

'Fine.' I change the subject. 'How old is she?'

'I have no idea,' he mumbles.

'You have no idea.'

'All right, I forgot. Gen. You cannot expect me to remember a woman's age,' he chuckled. 'That would be rude, wouldn't it?'

'She's an employee.' Her mannerisms, wasp-waist and height make it difficult for me to have guessed. She does not look like someone who would even own a hoodie, sweatpants or anything elasticated. Her cheekbones glow like two lightbulb moments.

'Yes, I know, and, she's perfect,' he repeats irritably, enunciating each word like I am hard of hearing. He pronounces *fect* as fact. Per-*fact*.

'She's very experienced,' confirms my dad, tilting his head side to side, as if weighing her qualifications up, 'in case that is what you are worried about.'

'I don't doubt it,' I shake my head. 'Did you check her references?'

'Of course. She comes highly recommended from *back home*. She knows my routine, my meds, my likes and dislikes. She fixes my meals, appointments, the whole house. I mean just look at it now,' he points at the garden with a grand sweep of his arm. 'And wait for this: it is clearly an advantage that she can cook me all my favourite traditional meals. From my childhood and youth, ok? Hainanese chicken rice. Kway teow soup. Lontong.' He beams while he reminisces. I roll my eyes, turning my head first towards the garden wall so that he cannot see them.

Back home meaning Singapore. 'So, she's fresh off the boat? Or plane, rather?'

He ignores me. 'You'll like her. She is a terrific cook.' He nods sagely, his eyes shut with conviction.

I don't dare to add, *so was Mummy*.

'Gen,' he runs a shaky hand over his sparse fine, white hair, not looking at me. 'We're going away in two days.'

'You are?' I look at him, perplexed.

'Yes. It's all booked,' he nods, with the smugness of smiling eyes. 'Just a three-day trip.'

'But...*we*?'

'Well, Auntie Stella and I,' he explains, then protests. 'We would have booked for you, but you never said you were coming home. Now that you're here, surely, you and my dear grandson will not remain at home? I will get her to add you to the booking.'

'But where are we going?'

My father breaks into a grin. 'On a family trip! Just what the doctoress ordered.'

Our little in-joke. He calls any female doctor a doctoress. A lady carer is a caress. Ugh. Is Stella in on the in-jokes, too?

2

MARCUS

Bethnal Green, East London

Marcus runs, but he skids on the uneven cobbles, feet first. His arms turn like windmills while he tried to steady himself. He loses control and trips. The dark, wintry rain is icy and has made the alleyway slippery. He feels light as a paper plane, shooting off in a random direction before plunging into the paving stones. It is like being a preschooler again, falling over in the playground, when a sudden intake of breath seemed to stop time before he'd burst out screaming and an adult would run over to pick him up.

It's nearly midnight. There is no adult now. *He* is adulting. Between his teeth, blood mixes with the bitterly pungent odour of mud and drains. He lands in the gutter, staring at the black sludge. His neck is cranked at an odd angle from the rough gradient of the gutter. He wants to retch and the acid burns his throat.

His mouth has filled with the cocktail of filth, rain and his vomit. He can't breathe through his nose.

Seconds later, the thug catches up with him. His voice explodes. 'I knew it! It's you.'

An East London voice. *Knew* is 'noo' and *you* is 'yew'. Inexplicable, unidentifiable. He's never seen this person or heard the voice before. *What* does he know, and why Marcus? At first, Marcus assumes he is being attacked because of his ethnicity. It would not be the first time: he had been mocked during his school days for the 'slit' eyes and being asked if he was from ching-chong Chingford.

Wrong assumption: the thug is also Chinese, or at least, East Asian.

The thug pulls at his feet and Marcus attempts to kick him away, but like an octopus, none of his tentacles make any difference. The assailant thumps down on his shin to keep him still. Marcus screams. Those steel-reinforced boots with lugged soles clamp him with the weight of concrete blocks. The rain beats down and it is hard to tell: Is the man sawing his feet off? Marcus cannot stop panic screaming until he feels a boot in his jaw to shut him up. His ears ring and for a second he sees sparkling lights, so white he knows he will black out from the pain. Marcus's mouth forced shut, the mugger removes the £450 Hanwag workboots Marcus wears on site.

What *does* the thug know? Why does he say "I knew it; it's you"? Those nails tear into the skin of Marcus's legs, sharp as an animal's claws. They work away at him until his feet are free of the boots.

That oversized hoodie, the young mannerisms. Marcus

can tell the thug is heavy set. Built like a cupboard. There is no way Marcus can match him in weight, height or strength. One blow from him is all it would take. Marcus does not want the thug to follow him to where he lives. He lies low and listens to the high pitch ringing in his head.

Marcus does not know how long it has been. When he opens his eyes, he is still flat on his belly. He tries to raise his left wrist like Superman but the pain is searing. His watch is gone. It is only a Wahk Rahk, thirty-five quid from Amazon. Indestructible but not unstealable. His glasses have flown off long ago. It seems like decades but it might have only been minutes. Nothing is clear. His eyes, like time, have gone funny, dream-like. He touches his pocket for his phone, feeling for its rigid rectangular bulk. It isn't there. Disastrous. Is it in the van? No matter. Wallet? Lost. All of it is gone. He is left with a broken nose, jaw, whatever else.

When he gets to his apartment on Corfield Street, Marcus does *not* want anybody to see him. He has one sock on, soaked. How will he get to work the next day? He hasn't been with the new agency that long and he's never been late or missed a day because he really needs the income.

He would have to find spare shoes. In his imbalance, he trips up the steps to the front door. He lurches. Only five steps but he feels as mushy as a piece of fruit falling from lap to floor, his nose and teeth kissing the worn out stone bull-nose of the treads. He runs his tongue over the top and bottom row feeling for wobbly or missing teeth.

His hard gums, icy and bleeding, grin through his

swollen jaw and mouth. If the neighbours see him there will be whispers and questions he himself does not know the answer to.

'Is that you? Oh my god. What's happened?'

It is bloody Angela from upstairs, Flat 3. She is the last person you'd want to encounter when you're coming *or* going. She worked as a legal secretary at one point in a suburban firm in Finchley, a dancer in some West End show, Downing Street in an event management type position and then retired early. She had volunteered all that information before in an attempt to make conversation, not that he had ever asked her. Who cares about her CV; who can keep up?

He wants to break down, tell her everything and be hugged like a colleague, a friend, a fellow East Ender. He misses that kinship, the closeness of strangers, being assured that "everything would be all right" even if it isn't.

Angela is on her way out with the bin bags. Oh that's right, it is Thursday night.

He calls her bloody Angela because she always seems to appear then and there like a ghost when he is in the hall. She always wants to chat, and he never has the urge, being too busy or tired from work. Plus she owes him a lot of money for building work he's done over the last few months, probably exceeding the £2000 mark now, but she keeps saying that she's waiting for funds. The fuck does that mean? Who has the time to exchange pleasantries with her? Not he.

Marcus does not dislike her, despite everything. She *will* pay. She *has* made late payments before. Angela always says *You OK?* rather than *hello*, which makes him think of her as a maternal figure. Why is she always there? Doesn't she want to go back quickly to catch the latest episode of whatever series she's following?

But this time she says, 'Is that you?' Like she's already decided to skip the *You OK*?

The irony is pulling overtime. Someone he doesn't know at all, had said 'It's you,' and now someone whom he *does* know, asks, *Is that you?*

He just wants to be teleported into his own flat from the entrance hall with its build-up of mail in white, black and brown packages. Amazon delivery, red outlined Royal Mail We-Tried-to-Deliver-Your-Package cards, pizza, We-Are-Working-In-Your-Area-Right-Now roofing repairs and kebab leaflets.

'You're covered in blood,' she states, with confusion more than concern. He has no reply to that, yet, he disagrees with her out of habit. *I'm fine*, he mutters, but it comes out as *Ah fah*. He ignores the intense pain from his jaw as he pushes the two slurred words out. She offers to help him up, and he winces. He wants her to disappear. She's not even a doctor or a nurse.

The relief of being home is so great he is unable to move: slumping against the back of his flat's entrance door, he stays there for minutes or hours.

Marcus falls into a semi-sleep.

It's suddenly bright.

Someone has switched the lights on.

3

GENEVIEVE

'So what brings you home, Gen?' My father asks. 'It's all so sudden.'

We turn around and walk into the house as it is too chilly to stay in the garden for that long. He is in a jumper and I in my Hoodrich hoodie.

I have a job interview in a week on 5th January. I want to simply say that, but I don't want to jinx it. I've been applying for a couple of months. It is my first job interview in years. Also, I can't say all this while we are going inside, as I don't want *her* to hear.

My father leads the way into the kitchen. I shut the French doors behind me. He picks up and puts down the cup of tea he's sipped from. He says, absent-mindedly to himself more than me, 'I don't want that now. I want to sleep.' He looks suddenly vulnerable, old, changed. He never used to say these things to himself. And in English too.

· · ·

He wanders back into the living room. Its proportion seems more generous than I remember, the sofa, chairs and grand piano don't dent the space at all. There is now less clutter. That's what's changed. The *objets*, newspapers, books lying around when my mother was alive have been removed. My mother, a paediatrician, enjoyed picking up different things to read in the house, and her multiple pairs of reading glasses were either missing or everywhere in the house. They, too, have gone. Definitely missing now. And I am missing her very much too while I look around at this modernised smartened-up grand old-new home.

Jasper is upstairs shrieking with delight. Either he's sharing a joke with Stella or he's watching something on his phone.

I want to go back to that time when we had everything just after Jasper was born. I had a family, a business and a car. We did not know it wasn't to last and that my husband was busy spending the money that my mother gave me to start the wine merchant business. I don't know how my husband got us into this much trouble when *he* has a degree in business. This is why I can't tell my father we've blown it.

The last days were hellish. My car was towed away. Black BMW Z4. Cost $99,000 in Singapore. I think of the black BMW like an ancient legend that I vaguely adored. Yet at some point it was no fantasy. I knew it well for 2 years. Asun polished it twice a week. I dropped off and picked up Jasper in it. A head turner that someone else will be enjoying now.

Asun has gone back to her town in the Philippines; she has to look after her ailing mother. Unless she comes back to work in Singapore, I doubt she will see another black BMW

Z4. That whole life will be a dream for her, just like it was for me.

My father is snoring in his winged reclining armchair with his navy and red checked tartan blanket over his legs, oblivious to me being in the room. My mother, not my dad, always gave all her children more credit than deserved. She made me think that I could do anything I wanted. What would you think of me now, Mummy?

My Singaporean boyfriend, as he was then, got me into his burning passion, wine. I associate it with the high life. I didn't want to meet someone from here, from the UK. That would have been way too boring. I would have been just like my classmates with their dull local boyfriends. He convinced me to move to Singapore after UCL, where we met. 'Do you always want to feel like a second class citizen here?' He'd asked me.

'What do you mean?' I said.

'In Singapore, you will make it in any industry. You'll smash it. They have the highest admiration and respect for anyone with a qualification from the West. And UCL, too! That means you are the crème de la crème. Plus you are a BBC, that will get their attention. Top class, innit!'

I sit on the leather sofa next to my dad, equally drowsy, though not elderly. British-born Chinese. Sure. I am a class act now.

Being home feels soporific, like being medicated. Home is a drug. I shut my eyes.

. . .

My then boyfriend was an overseas student who was simply returning home after studying in the UK. We got married in Bali. We had the best time. It was so exciting to move abroad after Uni. I remember how I longed to start something new, anything, live in a condo and swim every day to cool down in the tropical heat, drink buckets of cocktails, attend rooftop parties.

We researched the businesses that would do well in Singapore based on supply and demand and the economic market. A profession where I could drink wine for free and swan around in top restaurants and high society parties? Help rich people spend money? Yes, please.

I trained as a sommelier, did the exams, swigged the Sauv. I worked in top restaurants for 10 years before my husband had his terrible idea of owning and running a wine retail business. 'Imagine,' he said, 'No more late nights in wine bars, no more 6-day weeks. You will be your own boss!'

The reality was much worse. It was 7-day weeks and early starts. The manuals tell you that running a business will be flexible: work at your own pace and decide your own hours. There's no such thing. No one could have predicted the downturn over the last few years, not just in the luxury industry, which wine obviously is. Other luxury businesses seemed to thrive and boom in bad times. So what happened to ours?

It's too early to think about wine.

When I wake up, I forget where I am. It's still Thursday, 29th December, the day we arrive, but it feels like we have been here a long time. That is the trouble with winter. It's bleak.

My brain is fogged up and I wait a few seconds for my eyelids to open fully. I leave my father to his nap.

Stella has come downstairs with Jasper. His hand makes a squeaky sliding sound on the polished wood handrail. 'I'm hungry,' he says.

'Already?' I ask.

'We've had nothing to eat since the plane, mummy.'

Stella says, 'Come into the kitchen, Ah Boy. I'll get you something.'

She does not ask me if I want anything.

'Auntie Stella, my dad says we're going away. Do you know where?'

'We?' She raises her eyebrows, and puts a hand on her throat like I've choked her. 'It's just Richard and I.'

'My dad says he'd like Jasper and I to come too.'

'Oh,' she pauses at first. 'Fine!' She nods and gives that smile that does not reach her eyes.

'So... do you know where we are going?'

'Paris,' she replies. *Pairs.*

It's me who has the raised eyebrows and the dropped jaw.

4

SAHIL

Sahil hurries towards someone crouching low on the paving stones. The rain is feathery, like icy lines being drawn all over him. He recognises the Decathlon waterproof jacket, teal blue with reflective stripes on the sleeves, raised as the figure protects himself. Sahil skids on the cobbles and stops. *It's Marcus.*

'Hey,' Sahil shouts, audibly but tentatively. His glasses are fogged up and streaked with rain. Someone seems to be striking Marcus over and over, shouting, but Sahil couldn't hear what it is.

'Stop!' Sahil cries, approaching, but the thug does not. 'Hey! Stop!'

Sahil hurls himself at the thug and grabs his thick fur-lined hood with his long fingers. The thug is broad, bulky as a fridge. His chiselled and distinctive superhero villain features are somewhat unsettling, like a comic strip come to life.

Sahil has the advantage of height. He flings the fridge-like man at the brick wall of the alleyway. 'I said stop,' he repeats.

'Stay out of it, you fag,' the thug snarls.

Who is Yuffag? Whoever it is doesn't sound good to Sahil. He whips his neck round to check if Marcus is OK. But in that half a second, the thug grabs the chance to lunge back, gain momentum and shoot a fist out at him. It knocks Sahil senseless and his glasses go flying. Everything becomes out of focus and he could only randomly strike back at the thug. He catches one of those gorilla arms and twists it all the way behind. The bastard screams.

Sahil doesn't let go and when he does the man springs back, hitting his head hard on the sharp corner on a rough stone wall in the alleyway. Sahil heard a sharp tap despite the sizzling white noise of the rain.

He stops.

All he could do is stare at the fuzzy scene, panting. He can't breathe. Sahil must be stronger than he thinks, as everything has happened easily. The fridge-like man-child flies like a log. He swings wildly, staggering and falling over to the ground.

Sahil tosses a lightning glance over. Marcus is not moving. He must be unconscious. Sahil crawls on his hands and knees over the wet and filthy cobbles looking for his glasses. At least they are getting washed by the rain. Everything is. He could not even take his phone out to use the torch as it does not have a waterproof case.

Sahil has been strong from his building work sideline with Marcus, and before that, from back home in Surajkhund, a small town 2 hours from Delhi. The Raibeshe martial arts training he had since childhood has come in handy. He only learned it with his sisters because his uncle had been an instructor. Martial arts and dance seemed the only solution for those who are not keen on sports but have too much energy. Even now watching action movies are his only way of sitting still.

He breathes in shallow breaths, his eyes darting around. All he could think of is, *are there cameras? Is anyone around?* Thursday night. Almost Friday. What are the chances of being seen? His hopes fall. This is a high density area. They are near home and he knows all the streets well.

He leans over the man-child. Sweat pours when Sahil shakes his head in disbelief. *Nooooo*, he whispers, *ho gaya hoon*, his voice a high tremor. What has he done? Oh fuck.

The thug looks like a big Chinese baby, but his circular face, hooded eyes and the protruding forehead are far from cherubic. He is more like a sleeping neanderthal.

Sahil checks his pulse. He does not see any blood; the rain must be washing everything away. All the evidence.

The thug's resting expression reminds him of Marcus and Marcus is no oil painting. Sahil wonders if he is seeing things.

Marcus, as his employer, flatmate and landlord, has been good to Sahil. When he couldn't pay the rent twice, Marcus said it was OK. He could pay anytime he was ready. He also charges Sahil a reasonable rent, something not to be sniffed at in London, where unscrupulous rent raising is rife. Not that he cares, but Marcus doesn't have a mortgage. The flat was Marcus's mother's. Since he had been at Uni, he had been working with Marcus. Sahil has finished his final year at Queen Mary doing Engineering, and is now on a Graduate Visa.

Marcus also sometimes buys Chinese takeaway meals and shares them with Sahil. He says it isn't real Chinese food, and grins, 'But it's East London.' Marcus is Chinese so he *would* know, wouldn't he? Why would Sahil mind anyway? He could step out and get Indian food on Commercial Street. It isn't Indian food either but it would do. It has to.

'Not Far East but Near East,' said Sahil. And they had laughed.

A female classmate X has mentioned to him that with his Chalamet mass of hair, Sahil resembles a younger, bespectacled and curly-haired version of the movie star, Arhaan Khan. Two months ago, he started seeing a classmate, Anjali. She had been a friend since first year. She had not liked that other Classmate X since day one. They were all doing Engineering and came on the same scheme that he did. Anjali and Sahil had had 8 dates. Sahil was keeping count. When that number got to around 60, his parents would bring up the question as to when he will pop THE question. He is concerned about the inevitability.

Sahil has been working out since having a girlfriend. He senses a kind of pressure building. Even if his parents are not the totally traditional kind, they would still have some expectations of him.

He has been unaware of his resemblance to Arhaan Khan before, because of how his bespectacled appearance defines him. The bigger the glasses the more you could hide and just let the glasses do the talking. But once he considered Classmate X's comment, a strange vanity grew on him, like a plant he is obliged to tend. He has been gradually moving onto wearing contact lenses on and off and bulking up in the few months since term started in September. It isn't just joining a gym. He has been taking supplements. He does not aim to be inflated to near-explosion but it has gone way too fast, and he only notices when his clothes are tight and become what is known as "muscle fit".

He finds his glasses and it is another of God's miracles. The right lens is worse than the left, being scratched and cracked but it is better than to have no glasses. With his eyesight half improved, Sahil fishes the keys from Marcus's pocket. He walks to the lock up garage in the next block. He starts the engine and drives the van to the body. He could definitely move a fridge and has done it many times on building sites where they have to store appliances before a job began. He stops himself from vomiting but he can't. At the bottom of a hedge lining the dark driveway to the garages, he empties the contents of his stomach, two pints of Camden pale ale and a very huge chilli con carne from a student bar near LSE where he had attended a lecture earlier.

It is so awful it takes him some moments to recover and to take a few deep breaths.

Once he has dragged the body into the grey van whose side doors open easily and provide a wide access not too high from the ground level, he checks the giant's pockets and shoves the few items into his own. He covers the body with one of the neatly-folded dust sheets in the van. For now, he must take care of Marcus. When he has driven back to the garage, and walked back to the flat block entrance, Marcus is gone.

He can't believe it. He looks around. Marcus must have got up. He has only been a few minutes. Would he have gone home?

Sahil shivers. *This must be a terrible, visceral dream. It's not even very clear. It's a Renoir. All those lines of freezing misty rain. No need to worry about things that didn't happen, right? Check the van tomorrow.* His heavy eyelids sag as he ascends the stairs.

5

GENEVIEVE

My father wakes up from his nap. My face reddens at the thought of the Paris jaunt when I see his eyes blink unsteadily. I scratch at my temple in disbelief. Yet he speaks first.

'Gen, how long are you here for?' No words come. He misunderstands my speechlessness. 'OK. Then, you'll see,' he adds, 'We don't need to go to a restaurant again.'

I reply dutifully: 'I am actually here to spend some time with you, so long as that's OK—,'

'Aiyah, my brain is not what it used to be. I don't know what day it is, on any day. Let's talk about this trip!'

'Trip. Yes.' I reply, taking a deep breath, grateful for the change of subject.

'Stella and I have a list of the sights we'd like to see. Leave it to her. I tell you, she's brilliant.' He shakes his head, in wonder, like he's never met anyone like her.

I keep hearing it but can't get comfortable with the use of the royal *we*.

'Why don't you go and unpack now?' He says this more

as an *I've had enough, do you mind* dismissal rather than a helpful suggestion. 'And by the way, Stella is in your old room.'

This. Is. Great.

'Why? Why is she in my room?'

'I didn't know you're coming back, Gen. We are getting the place redecorated, room by room. You know that we have not decorated for at least 21 years, right? Yours has been done. The room she was in, which was Cassie's, is a bit small. She hardly complains but I offered to move her. We only have five rooms, dear, please understand.'

Only.

'Where will I go?' I squeak.

'Why not Cassie's? It's going to be a bit *musical chairs* now,' he guffaws theatrically. 'Jasper will be in Alistair's room, you'll be in Cassie's and Stella is in your room.' Anyway, it's only temporary, so I am sure you don't mind. At your next whim, you will be leaving London.'

Right. My oldest brother has been in Dubai working in a start-up tech firm in construction management for the past 12 years. He left London just before I moved to Singapore. Cassie was last to leave home.

'Daddy, it's not temporary,' I say, unable to hold it any longer.

'What do you mean?' He asks without irony.

'I mean it's not temporary, it's permanent, I'm here to stay. And Jasper too.'

'I don't understand, Gen, what about... er...,' my dad searches, his eyes squinting at his bony knees.

I am not going to fill in my father's memory gaps. I don't even want to speak of my husband's name ever again.

My rosy plan to find work in the UK, live in my original

home and look after my dad and son has been ruined. Am I
being made redundant? I back pedal and think how to ad lib
here. To my dad, it's *she* who's staying, not me. That's what
he means by *temporary*. It's temporary for me, not for her.

'There you are,' announces a feminine high-pitched voice.
Really? Is she a full-grown woman or is she not? With my
hoodie, greasy hair and every inch of my confidence sliced
off, who should I dislike more at this moment, myself or this
woman?

Stella floats in from the French windows with a pleasant
wide smile and takes Daddy by the elbow to lead him back
outdoors. They walk through the kitchen with an easy closeness, as though they are old pals. 'It's not very warm,
Richard, but after naps we have fresh air, remember? Before
it gets too late. Come on, Ah Boy, have a look at the garden,'
she says to Jasper. She ignores me, like I am see-through.

Jasper runs out, looks over his shoulder at me and says,
'It's not cold! Mummy! Where's the snow? Will it snow?'

Jasper has had a quick snack of crackers and cheese to which
he says yuck. She hasn't offered any lunch to me.

I take my son out all afternoon to get out of their hair.
We need to wear ourselves out with being outdoors (not
sunlight since there is not much of it) to counteract jet lag of
8 hours' time difference. If you can't make money, make
melatonin. I'm already weary and ready to crash in my
"new" room, Cassie's, but I still have to wait until it's night.

Today I have a secret mission, which is to take Jasper on

a dummy run to the local school where he will start the following week. It is not my old primary school as my siblings and I had gone to a £28.5K-a-year school. I need to familiarise him.

After we take a walk around Fulham and the school where I point through the metal fence railings, he seems excited. He says *wow* more than once. 'You mean we are not going back to Singapore?' He manages in a little voice.

'Not for some time, no,' I reply in honesty. 'Let's take a look at dinosaurs.'

'Cool! There are dinosaurs?'

We take the tube into South Kensington so we can get out of the cold and into the Natural History Museum. It gives me a jolt to find out that public transport fares have gone up so much. How will I afford to live here? How does anyone live in London? Getting work will ease my settling back into the UK after a decade of high life in Singapore. Just a quick walk along Fulham Road earlier has restored my confidence. There are plenty of Positions Vacant A4 printouts taped to restaurant windows, although these are minimum wage positions, none suited to me.

With a detached nonchalance, I remember that 3 weeks ago, I sold my BMW, Choos, Louboutins, Cartiers to some dealer to recoup assets. I did not get as much as I had thought, because I reek of desperation. I don't even have my Tory Burch laptop bag anymore for this trip. Although my interview is coming up, it's not a bird in hand.

Once British, always British. I have come home, haven't I? How hard can it be? Work is the great leveller. Immigrants get work here. And I'm not an immigrant. I am articulate. I should be able to find work, shouldn't I? *Shouldn't I?* I shudder.

With lunch for Jasper and I at the V&A museum cafe, treats and so on, it's set me back almost £30, and that's without alcohol. I have no heart to buy myself a glass of wine. I am teetotal not by preference but by purse restrictions. A meal without wine is like a day without sun, said someone famous. In good times back in Singapore, if I was out at lunch in a gallery somewhere, I would have invited friends and ordered an ice bucket filled with bubbly, as though looking at art is a cause celebre in itself. *When life gives you lemons...* someone would start tittering as soon as the vodkas arrived, followed by huge roars of laughter. Where are these friends now?

'Let's go home. Gung Gung will be waiting for us. I told him we'll be home for dinner.'

'Is Auntie Stella my auntie?"

'No.'

'Is she *your* Auntie?

'Most definitely not.'

'Is she like Asun Jie Jie?'

I hesitate, my mouth moulding into a false Buddha smile. 'No,' then I add, 'Here in the UK, we don't call people who work for us Jie Jie or Auntie or anything resembling family.'

'What is zembling? Is Auntie Stella going to cook for us or are you? Mummy? Mummy?'

'No,' I say, numb from the cold, 'I don't mean no; I mean I am not sure if she is cooking for us or just Gung Gung.' Not in the mood for splitting hairs, I grip his hand a little too tightly. Jasper has only known living in Asia. The polite term *Auntie* is reserved for domestic helpers, real aunties and close family friends. This period will be a transition for both him and I since he already started school there and has to go into a higher form here. In Singapore, he had started year 1 at the eye-wateringly expensive international school for expat children, United World College, but in the UK education system he has to go according to the year and month of birth, so he has to start year 2.

'C'mon then,' I say, sick of my own circulatory thoughts, 'Let's go.'

It is already dark, at 4:25pm when we arrive back home. There is a van outside with the sign printed on its side,

FORTHRIGHT MOBILITY SOLUTIONS (ESTD. 1999)
- Installed within 4 hours
- New and reconditioned stairlifts
- FREE survey and quotation
- In-house service engineers
- Private homes or care homes
- Accredited with NAEP, CERA and *Which?*
- Buy-back guarantee

This is followed by all their usual social media handles, direct hotline and email.

Even the side of a van is now like its web home page and company CV. Looking for work has opened my eyes to how I have to market myself just to face the competition. If I was a van, my body would carry the sign:

- Qualified sommelier
- Wine tours and private tour guiding (Aust, NZ, Chile)

- Food and wine pairing events, workshops, talks
- Author of food and wine pairings manuals
- TV host of food and wine shows

The last two are not true but they may as well be. If I say something enough, it will become true. Stella is not family. She is not.

6

STELLA

The child has mastered the few buttons on the stairlift's remote control. He has gone up and down six times like it's his new toy when it really should not be abused. He's also put his toy grey Labrador plush toy, Ranger, on it. Ranger has had three rides. At last, when I cannot hold it in any longer, I firmly ask: 'Ah Boy, please could you stop? This is Gung Gung's mobility solution.'

'No, let him, let him,' waves Richard dismissively, holding onto the handrail at the bottom of the stairs. 'Can't stop him learning to use it, heh heh, he may even have to teach *me*!'

'The technicians have already gone through the instruction before they left when I signed the papers and guarantee,' I protest. 'Also, what about the waste of electricity?'

'It's only £10 a year, the man said,' Jasper says, not looking at me once.

Richard puts up with the comments and titters, covering his mouth to suppress himself when he spots my expression. Jasper has now loaded more items on the chairlift seat. A

Ninjago lego kit with Kai on a motorcycle, a plate with breadcrumbs and a Marvel water bottle are being sent up. It's like a dumb waiter for him.

I remember now why I don't have kids. I put up with his antics for a few more seconds. It's only a novelty. He will be sick of it. I can see discipline will be a bone of contention. His mother does not tell him off at all. She just stares at the stair-lift mechanism, blinking, mortified. Why does she not do anything?

7
GENEVIEVE

6:25pm.

My eyelids droop. In Singapore time it would be 2:25 am already. I fight sleep. Be gone, jet lag. I watch the stairlift suppliers pack up their van and leave.

"Auntie" Stella is in the kitchen preparing dinner so I do not attempt conversation. "Auntie" Stella is always busy. If she is not, she pretends to be. Moving stuff, wiping surfaces, picking up a plant pot and putting it back down, opening and shutting curtains. Yeah, yeah, I know all those tricks. I used to do them too when my husband was in the room and I was monitoring what he was doing.

'I guess the stairlift was your idea?' I ask timidly, though I am not sure why I feel so fearful.

'Very reasonable price,' she adds, tossing a glance at my father. She grins at him sheepishly like he's just bought her a necklace.

The stairlift is inevitable, or Daddy will have to live on the ground floor, where there are no bedrooms. He would have to turn the living room into a bedroom and he always said he would never want to. 'What about the damned grand piano?' He could not possibly sleep next to it like some tramp. He always referred to it as *the damned*, because it's like a boon to be able to play but also a beast. I mean, just the size alone commands your attention and focus. We can't ignore it.

Daddy was the only one in our family who was a gifted and versatile musician. He knew every song that ever existed. We do not know where this has come from. That was how he charmed my mother. He has not played for a long time, since his children left home. We took the music away. We took a part of him with us and he is no longer interested in music.

Dinner looks and smells delicious. Hakka pork rib followed by lotus root and black bean soup, prawn omelette and steamed pak choy. Brown rice. In Chinese meals, the soup is *after* or *with* the meal, which is the opposite in Western cuisine. 'Very healthy,' confirms Stella. 'We eat a low fat, high fibre diet.'

'Yuck,' says Jasper sticking his tongue out.

'Jas! Say sorry!' I bark instinctively.

Stella bleats out a weak laugh. 'It's okay, Jasper. Gung Gung also says yuck!'

Daddy makes a funny face of being choked and revolted, eyes rolling high as a helium balloon, and Jasper cackles like Bart Simpson before apologising to his grandfather.

'Your father needs a better diet, that's all,' Stella says to me picking up her chopsticks. 'He can't live on those ready meals from supermarkets. No good.'

I listen, my mouth a flat line. Stella does not need to give me a lecture on nutrition. My sister is a qualified chef to Saudi royalty.

'Aiyah, enough, enough. Let's eat,' announces my dad. He doesn't ask me anything about the business and I haven't been alone with him yet. There's plenty of time for all that, and it suits me to be able to conceal the news.

I observe Stella from every angle while she eats so delicately and neatly, her chopsticks articulating with grace. She silently puts the blue and white porcelain rice bowl down, unlike mine, which lands with a thump. No wonder she's slim. I feel self-conscious that I am "wolfing" my dinner down in huge gulps like I am a street dog who's never seen a meal in its appalling life. I am starving. Homeless. And hopeless.

'We are going to watch Netflix after dinner. Stella has found this fantastic series. What is it, again? What is the series name?'

'Firefly Lane, Season 2, Richard.'

I prickle. *Richard*. That's not daddy, that strange word in the house. Why won't he correct her? He has never been known by that name.

I haven't watched any TV, except with Jasper so I am unable to contribute to their excitement when they bring up the previous episodes and the characters they have invested in.

Jasper pipes up, 'What's for dessert?'

'No, no, Ah Boy, dessert is only for special occasions. We have cut out sugar in this house,' smiles Stella with a firm nod. 'Your Gung Gung is pre-diabetic.'

'What is pretty Betty?'

'It means too much sugar makes him ill, Jas,' I mutter. Not an ideal explanation, but it'll do.

Mummy had been a baking whizz. I remember coming home from school to the aroma of a freshly baked cake from the street. From all of Fulham, I dare say. Thanks to my mum, Cassie had been inspired to train as a chef. In those days, my dad indulged not only in English teatime treats like apple tea cake (my mum's speciality), brownies, jam cookies, but also Asian delicacies like pandan cake, Nyonya tapioca steamed puddings, pastries like curry puffs and pineapple tarts during the festive seasons. My mouth salivates at the dusty, distant memory.

'Aww, shucks,' says Jasper. 'What about fruit?'

'No fruit after dinner,' Stella waves her pointer finger in a cautionary way. 'Bad habit. The acid and the fibre make it hard to digest. No raw after four.'

Who is this nutritionist? What are these rules? I bite my tongue.

'Oh, c'mon, Stella,' my dad implores in a mock-irritable way, 'Let the boy have something. Don't we have bananas, or I don't know, berries?'

The *we* again.

'All right, then,' she gives him a big smile and agrees. 'Let me find you some cookies. Or why don't you come with me?' She holds her hand out and Jasper takes it. They go into the kitchen and my dad says, 'Gen, are you here for work?'

'No. Yes.' I most definitely am. Just not the work he thinks I am doing.

He is surprisingly lucid. He keeps remembering to ask the difficult questions. 'What are you up to tonight? Are you going out?'

'No, I am not, Daddy. Should I be?' That tug of guilt.

'Gen, you always go out when you are in London.'

Always. I feel Stella's mocking eyes on me and I keep

mine fixed on my rice bowl, which is painfully ironic, since the Chinese saying is that the iron rice bowl means stable employment in a secure industry, both of which are now out of my reach.

I grew up here and know plenty of people. But I don't want anyone to know I am back.

'Are we ready to watch the next episode?' Stella comes back in with Jasper who holds two choc chip cookies on a little Pooh bear saucer I recognise from my childhood.

'Oh yes, what a splendid idea,' my father concurs.

'I am going to bed, daddy,' I say, excruciated.

'Wah! So soon!' My dad interjects.

'Jet lag,' I explain. 'Such a long day too.'

'You came today?' He says, his eyes narrowed and chin lifted.

This is the first time I experience his confusion.

'Yes, she did; this morning, Richard,' interjects Stella.

She gets the remote, as if it's a wand to shoo me and Jasper off. 'Goodnight, Ah Boy,' she chimes. She looks at me icily. 'Goodnight, Jean-Viv.'

I collapse into bed and I remember my hand luggage is still on the entry hall table where my book and my painkillers are. When I creep downstairs to retrieve it, I see that she is behind him, her hands kneading his neck and shoulders, stroking him while they watch the screen. My blood rises.

'You... you're...,' I stammer.

'Y-your father needs a... massage. To stimulate circulation and muscle strength.'

At the sound of the word *stimulate* I feel sick. My father is 76 years old and this woman has no right to be here in this intimate situation or even in this house. I feel protective and want to run up to my father, but he is nodding off. Reluctantly, I go back upstairs.

I check on Jasper and he is sound asleep in Alistair's room. I can't read a word tonight as my head hurts. I need a massage too, but maybe not from *her*. I decide not to take the prescription sleeping tablets because I have to be more vigilant. I'm in a new place. A new old place.

An old man with someone new.

I almost drift off before I remember something. She called me Jean-Viv. I did not twig before. It is the name I called myself when I was little. How does she know this?

8

MARCUS

Friday 30th December

Marcus cringes. Suddenly it's bright and the light stabs his pupils. He cowers, holds his breath. He fears another blow, not knowing what the "clack" is, a heel or a weapon. He put his arms across his face to protect himself.

'Marcus. Marcus. It is fine. Hey. Shhhh. It is only me. Hey.' The gentle familiar voice brings relief and his breathing slows. He drops his arms and strains to look. The clack is Sahil switching on the four LED downlights, which flooding the room, assault his senses.

His flatmate's bearded bespectacled face is a relief. He remembers in flickering slices what has happened, like a movie that is constantly being interrupted by ads.

He remembers bloody Angela. The irony is that it's *his* face that's bloody not Angela's. He had felt his chin being sticky and slimy.

'He's been following you. He must have been,' says Sahil.

'Who?' Whispers Marcus. It comes out like a cough.

'The...'

Sahil doesn't finish. Marcus shut his eyes from exhaustion. He knows what Sahil Maitreya was about to say and he does not want to hear it.

Marcus prises his eyes open with sheer effort. He wants to sleep for a million years, like sleeping beauty apart from the fact that he is not as much of a princess as he is a middle-aged jobbing builder with a small paunch and a huge fore-head. The days when girls would look at him in a bar even when he was young never existed. His father always said he looked like his mother, which was cruel in a way that was kind.

'He doesn't want money,' Marcus mumbled. Each word burns his throat. He needs water, or whiskey or a wee. Something beginning with W.

'What did he want? Why didn't you give it? Whatever he wanted?' Sahil asks crisply, in a curious but not demanding way. His eyes narrow, but he could never sound hard even when he is being direct.

Sahil has a kind and soft voice, like you would expect of a classical musician or a dancer. His glasses are black, TV-shaped and huge, the trendy kind you see on young people in Shoreditch. The thick lenses, both now very scuffed, and one lightning-cracked, reduce the size of his eyes as he is very short-sighted. That would cost him. The fine lines across the expensive thinning lenses make him look like a victim, not an attacker.

'Drink this,' Sahil holds out a mug. Marcus accepts it and inhales the aroma of fresh coffee.

'You want Anadin Extra?' Asks Sahil.

Marcus looks at him at last, now being able to focus. His

glasses were flung during the attack. He has no idea where they are now or how he is going to drive, get to work or do anything in his current state. Like Sahil, his eyesight is not great.

They are the bespectacled boys. That could be a good company name, Marcus has thought. Gets the middle class clientele, or rather, the middle class clientele will *get it*.

They could be a mismatched gay couple. Marcus had assumed he was been beaten up for his ethnicity but now his opinion has shifted. It could be for his boots or for being gay, or both. He is not gay; at least he does *not* think he is, but try telling that to someone who is a bit busy punching your lights out. Why can't he be left alone for being asexual?

He can't remember the evening apart from the fact that it was bin night and that was why bloody Angela was in the hall rummaging about with the recycling bags and organic waste as per Tower Hamlets's strict rules before depositing them in the huge purple wheelie bins.

'You... you...,' Marcus couldn't find the words. His mind moved like crunchy peanut butter across untoasted bread, ripping it. He wants to know if Sahil had had a fall. He is not interested in himself at all, even if he could remember everything.

'Yes,' Sahil put his hand on his glasses unconsciously or habitually as if to readjust. 'I've taken care of it.'

'Taken care... of?' Marcus's heart skips a beat. He does not understand. What is Sahil talking about?

'It.'

'What?' Marcus quizzes again.

'Nevermind. You were mugged. You need to rest.'

'I...,' Marcus immediately reaches out, patting his tummy, thighs and bottom subconsciously. 'My watch, boots, wallet! I don't know what else I could give him,' Marcus slurs. 'You... saw...?' Marcus swallows, thinking that Sahil must be rephrasing or recounting the evening's activities in a digested and simplified format. 'I saw he jumped on you,' Sahil explains, his eyes downcast, unfocussed. 'He would not stop. He would have killed you.'

'But he didn't,' Marcus says.

'How would you know?' He sounds defiant. 'You lost consciousness. He thought he killed you. He ran off.'

'And you...? You were there?'

'I was coming home from the pub myself.'

Sahil was out with his classmates. He had pocket money to spend, thanks to Marcus getting him the side hustle of building work on days when he is not in college. His undergraduate course at Queen Mary is very prestigious. Next he would be doing his Masters in International Relations. His aim is to go into project management in international software businesses and earn a six-figure income.

Marcus understands all that. He knows *his* is a minuscule business. Marcus found him jobs and a roof over his head when Sahil's previous landlord kicked him out. Pig of a landlord. Marcus could never do that to anyone. Sahil lost half of his £2000 deposit too in repairs and replacements which were not even Sahil's fault, like the broken boiler which had to be fixed. Carbon monoxide had been detected. The landlord claimed that the parts cost him half the deposit and that it was because Sahil did not use the central heating properly.

Builders are in serious shortage in the UK. The local English builders still exist, but in a parallel universe alongside the Eastern Europeans. The English also become the directors and managers. Marcus had met lots of workers from Eastern Europe. Quite a few had "gone home": when they want to start a family where they are from, or if there are family business opportunities back home which have come up or if they are simply just sick of London. It is after all very expensive and competitive here, with most workers living in old, cramped flats in an unsalubrious suburb. Oddly enough none of them were builders back home. They were students or people doing other jobs such as admin or accounting. It is hard to say no to £250 a day for basic handyman jobs or assisting a skilled craftsman like an electrician or a plumber.

Marcus sometimes refers to Sahil by his full name as it sounds famous. After Sahil Maitreya arrived from Delhi, he found building work easy money, or rather, Marcus found him easy money in building work. Sahil's whole family has dabbled in construction and manufacturing back home so in that sense it is an ideal match.

They remain quiet for a while.

'What do you remember?' Says Sahil, breaking the silence.

Marcus needs his meds. He could not work in this state.

'Could you get me my pills?' He asks Sahil, helplessly, like a child asking for cereal. 'I don't mean painkillers.'

'Of course. What colour are they?'

'Yellow and white,' he replies, knowing that Sahil has seen them in the kitchen before, and would be able to easily find them in the spartan, practically male kitchen, devoid of a single piece of decoration, not even a clock.

'You want them now?'

'Yes, now please.'

. . .

Sahil comes back with a garish little box, pulls the blister pack out and pops the caplets for Marcus, who swallows them with the coffee.

'You can't go into work looking like this,' Sahil rearranges the duvet even though Marcus has been lying on the floor with its trendy woven wool carpet Marcus had salvaged from an office job he was doing up. They would have thrown it out if not for him taking it home.

Marcus feels an unfamiliar weightlessness. His head is being tenderly lifted by Sahil's hand which supports his neck before placing a pillow under his head, like sliding a letter into an envelope. 'You sleep,' Sahil says in his soothing vampire voice. 'We can take you to the doctor's if you don't feel better.'

Marcus is drowsy again. His head is banging.

'We can talk when you wake up,' says Sahil. 'Nothing to worry about.'

Sahil snaps the lights off. That clack again. The hallmark of cheap electrical work. The cover plates which make that plasticky sound. Marcus did the rewiring of the flat himself. He could not complain when that is the satisfying on-off sound he wants to hear to allay his OCD. Everything should either be on or off, black or white. He wishes he also has an on-off switch right then. Instead, he is a dial that goes down to 2 but never zero.

Marcus goes alone to the minor injuries unit as Sahil is at his classes. He does not want a chaperone. As he leaves the building, Angela is mounting the entrance steps, one at a time, laden with two Sainsbury's bags of shopping. This time she goes back to her usual greeting, 'Good afternoon. You OK?'

Marcus bites his lower lip. 'Yep, fine, and you?' He holds the self-closing entrance door open for her. Now obliged to help her with her shopping, his "minor injuries" can wait. 'Ahhhh, could be better,' she chuckles absent-mindedly. She's had her hair done, he notices. He can't tell what exactly, but it's dark and has been blowdried into a feathery layered bob like Chrissie Hynde. When a man notices something like that it means she has *really* changed her hairstyle. What was it even before?

She's struggling as she is huffing and dragging the bags in. Tossing a glance into the bags, there seems to be a lot for one person. 'Let me give you a hand with them,' he offers.

'You sure?'

'Yeah, course'm sure,' he replies without sounding too impatient. They ascend the stairs and he limps with pain from having his feet and shins clobbered.

'Expecting guests?' He pushes the boundaries a bit and asks her.

'Oooh, yes, a special friend is coming for a visit,' she says coyly. Marcus is piqued by her discretion. It is like some Victorian melodrama.

'Oh yeah?' He goads, his eyes remaining downcast. Two more flights. He grunts as he starts to sweat from his pain and intense headache.

She turns red. 'Don't worry, I know I owe ya. He'll sort it out. But first you've gotta finish all those tasks. He says the shelves are not quite right,' she says.

She says *he* like this mystery man is in charge of her and her apartment, and now it also seems, the payment for building work that is due to Marcus. He can't bear to think about it. It must be well over two thousand pounds. He is not thick-skinned. He is sick of asking her repeatedly. The Chinese embarrassment kicks in and his face turns red.

'You OK?' She asks again. Does she actually care? Marcus nods.

'And you know,' she lowers her voice as they reach her front door and she gets her keys out. 'I saw what happened.'

Marcus's ears are pricked. He blinks at her. 'What happened?'

'Last night. You were duffed up, weren't ya. Lucky for you. Your flatmate, whatsisname—,'

'Sahil.'

'Sa-heel, that's right. You're lucky Sa-heel got your back.' She makes an irritatingly big deal of the name pronunciation.

'Is that what you saw?' He prods.

'Oh no. There's more.'

Marcus pauses. *More?* He wonders what she will say next.

'He put the huge man in your van and drove it away, to that street next door!'

'What were you doing out late last night?' Marcus stops on the landing, puffing from exertion and discomfort.

'Well, I followed the voices, didn't I? I heard a commotion from my back window. You forgot. That lane backs onto the dog park which backs onto our gardens. And I went downstairs and round the block, to see what was going on behind that high wall.'

'Thanks for that,' Marcus blurts out sarcastically, putting the bags down after the final flight of stairs. 'Here's your shopping.'

'You look awful,' she says, glancing at him, trying not to make it obvious.

'Cheers.'

'No, I don't mean that. I mean, was there a fight?'

'No! I mean, I don't know! He just jumped on me!' Marcus snaps, but she keeps interrogating. Must be terrible being married to her. He's not, fortunately, but he's already getting deafened by the incessant questioning.

'What you gonna do about it?'

'About what?' He lifts his palms in desperation.

'The guy! The bloke in the back of the van.'

'D-don't worry,' Marcus gesticulates with his raised palms to reassure her, though what he really wants to do is to shake her. 'He's fine.'

'He's *fine*? Don't look at me like that. Are you saying he's fine?'

'Yeah,' Marcus stares at her, his jaw dropping. 'Sahil took him in for treatment.'

'What was it all about?'

This is getting too much for Marcus. Why is he replying to her third degree? What does she want? Does she want to get out of paying him?

'Look, I've got to go. Here's your shopping and I hope you have a lovely day ahead with your friend who's visiting.'

'Why, thank you so much, Marcus. I really appreciate your help. I can't wait to—,'

Yeah, and he can't wait to get the hell out of there. He does not wait for her to finish as he gallops down like a broken chair: 3 flights of stairs, 2 steps at a time. Every joint in him hurt.

· · ·

Whitechapel Hospital was within walking distance anyway. He wouldn't want Sahil with him. That would be way too weird. What if he is in a state of despair or undress or something? He has mental health issues and they could suddenly escalate despite the meds. He is a bunch of flowers. One minute he looks fine, all bolstered by life and newness, and the next he sagged, stank and was ready to drop. Sometimes he would clam up without warning, a sense of panic crawling over him like insects.

Marcus is sure, from his first aid training when he was working with a firm, that he would not need a scan. The doctor seems to concur after doing a few tests. 'I fell over and I went flying...,' he explains. Facts are facts. 'Due to the wet cobbles, I lost my... er... footing.'

He omits the bit about being chased and pummelled by someone. He does not want to recount what he could recall of the attack and he's put it in a locked drawer in his mind. He did pass out on the bench in the alleyway which, thinking about it, was not a bench but those boulders which stopped trucks from driving into the alleyway. All of the details are lost on him. They appear filtered like someone had given him a long lost photo album but the pictures are disconnected.

'My glasses... they're gone,' he admits. New ones are on order. 'I fell on my face on a concrete bench, one of those modern designs,' he tries to smile. The doctor does not smile back.

Sahil has made himself scarce but obviously he is busy with his college assignments. He is under a lot of pressure, not just pressure-pressure, but Asian family pressure, and Marcus only knows it too well himself. Firstly, Sahil is already a slight disappointment to his family for not getting into medicine so he had to "settle for" computer systems engineering instead. Secondly, according to Sahil, relatives from something like 8 villages and towns had to put money together to send him abroad. He could not let them down, apart from which, all these people have to be paid back (except one very wealthy philanthropist uncle who has a hand in the transportation business). To his family, Sahil is indebted forever. He has a part scholarship to Queen Mary, which helps tremendously, and is the reason why he is abroad in the first place. Sahil is always grateful for any work. Hence they started working together on building jobs.

When he gets home, Marcus gets WhatsApp photos and the good news from the agency that he would be doing up a nice raised ground floor flat in Chelsea. He has 2 to 3 months to do the job in. That would make a change from the awful piecemeal labouring that he had been doing, digging, moving rubbish from sites, carrying bricks in buckets to the top floor.

He couldn't wait to celebrate with Sahil, and maybe even offer him the opportunity to work together again on a classy number. Now that was the type of connection they had, an easiness, a camaraderie, an understanding.

Marcus watches TV and falls asleep on the sunken threadbare sofa. When he wakes up, it is already afternoon and he is still tired but hungry. The room is dark apart from the piercing glow of the TV. He suddenly has a flash of the assailant: the teeth, the huge forehead not unlike his, and hooded menacing eyes where you could not see the pupils as they were so dark. Why does he say *It's you*? What does he want?

There is the clang of keys and the door is flung open. Sahil snaps the switch on. In pours the light from the entrance hall, like a jug of yellow sauce. Marcus wired four LEDs on the same circuit, to save on costs, so they all come on at the same time. 'I'm... I'm resting,' says Marcus. 'Sleeping.'

'OK, good...,' Sahil mutters. His face is downcast and his eyes dart from side to side.

'I saw Angela today,' Marcus grunts. 'She says she saw you put the thug in the van. *My* van! The hell is going on?'

'Look, I must tell you something,' Sahil says. Marcus can't see his expression but his voice sounds strained. Sahil comes out of the shadows and under the eerie yellow light, he looks grim as he finally looks Marcus in the eye.

9
SAHIL

Sahil tells Marcus everything that he can remember, in the right order. He confirms that the thug is in Marcus's van. It comes out mechanically. Sahil has practised his telling and retelling in order to avoid emotional input. It is like he's explaining how to re-code an app. His breath is laboured and his head starts to spin. He waits.

'THEN WHAT?' Marcus shouts, prompting him. Sahil does *not* like that raised voice, so comically tense in its falsetto. At the same time, there are silences in between where the thoughts between the two shoot around the room like arrows.

Sahil lowers his eyes, feverish, all of a sudden like the boyish big boy that he is. They both tremble, almost on cue.

Marcus repeats, this time in a hoarse whisper, 'After. That. What?' His hands are raised in confrontation towards the ceiling, above his shoulders. He looks up, as if in prayer.

Sahil weeps. His shoulders quake and he covers his face with his palms. 'And then nothing,' he splutters. 'I don't know what to do now! I was waiting for you to get well!'

'Shit. You fucking killed him. You killed him,' Marcus whispers, head in hands.

'Oh, SHUT UP,' Sahil roars, the veins in his temples bulging. 'It was an accident. I came to stop him. You were going to die. He kept going. He meant to kill you. I just wanted to stop him. He fell and hit his head. It was an accident. You don't expect me to do nothing while you were getting beaten to a pulp?'

'No! Jesus!' Marcus swears.

'Fuck. FUCK!' Sahil tears at his hair. There is so much of it, thick, glossy, Indian hair. He hates all of it. What is it there for apart for being ripped out? 'What did he want? What?'

'You didn't find my glasses, did you?' Marcus bleats. What the actual...? Is he changing the subject? If he is, Sahil isn't going to be fooled. Everything is now relevant.

'Fuck the glasses. I found mine. I moved the body. What did you want me to do?' Sahil cries, hot tears flying from him. 'What DO you want me to do? Tell me.'

Marcus shakes his head so rapidly everything appears blurry, his fingers gripping his head, eyes wide, jaw dropped.

'TELL ME,' Sahil screams.

'Jesus,' Marcus growls. 'Shut up. Shut up. Shut up. For fuck's sake, do you want the neighbours to hear you? Are you insane?'

They stay silent. Sahil gets up, goes to his room and shuts the door, leaving Marcus for minutes or maybe an hour.

When he opens his eyes, a small chink of grey daylight enters the window through the curtain cracks.

There is a tap on Sahil's door and he doesn't answer. When he hears the door open, Sahil pretends to be fast asleep. Even with his eyes shut, he feels a sense of comfort that Marcus is in the room. After a while, he must have dozed off.

Marcus is still sitting next to his bed hours later, as silent and shaky as a grandfather when Sahil wakes up and pulls out of his pocket a phone.

'Oh, for God's sake, don't turn it on,' Marcus immediately warns before Sahil could even consider it.

'I wasn't going to,' Sahil asserts. 'I am not *that* stupid. It's already on!' He turns it around to show the screen to Marcus.

The picture is of the thug and a middle-aged Chinese woman, both smiling, in the middle of a restaurant: roast duck is on the table, with a stack of pancakes, a dish of spring onions, a dip. Surreal.

Marcus gasps. 'Turn it off,' Marcus commands like he is a captain on some sinking ship. 'They can track a phone that's on. Might even be too bloody late.'

Sahil presses a button for a few seconds to turn it off.

'We don't even know who he is,' says Marcus, biting his thumbnail and pulling what seemed like slivers of skin off. 'What else did you find?'

Sahil reaches over to his bedside and points to a key ring with two keys: a brass mortice key and a Yale lever key in silver. Marcus picks them up as if he was able to get some identification communication out of them by magic.

'Useless,' Marcus snaps and throws them back onto the bedside cabinet where they land with an impossibly loud ringing crash. 'What else?'

'I found his wallet. It has nothing in it. Only one thing. A card.'

'A card?' Quizzes Marcus.

'Yes.'

Marcus looks at the name.

'Ring any bells?' Asks Sahil.

'Of course not,' says Marcus.

It is a Barclays Bank card in the name of Barry O'Keefe.

10

STELLA

My wrists and shoulders ache. I am twisting my neck left and right, arching my back to stretch.

I'm in my Ralph Lauren "uniform" — a wool skirt and ironed shirt, wearing Estee Lauder matte lipstick in *Fearless* shade, and a navy apron. The others are relaxing in their fleece "loungewear" ready for bed. I look professional because I *am* professional. Being a live-in carer is better paid than my previous job for good reason: back-breaking, long hours. While everyone is chilling, I am still working. I guess I always knew that but now I am living it.

I've given Richard his thrice-weekly massage therapy while he watches TV. My fingers and eyes burn with exhaustion. I don't enjoy the boring lifestyle or reality shows Richard feasts on, about cooking, hotels and train journeys, involving rich people on yachts or hotel palaces enjoying themselves. But watching TV *is* part of my job description. At least it involves sitting down. Firefly Lane 2 is some sickly sweet American drama that Richard is fond of. He can't read very much due to his failing eyesight so he'd rather watch the 60" screen.

I'm not allowed to snooze through these interminable shows. Richard expects thoughtful, amusing conversation. What do I know about American small towns, luxury cruises and top restaurants? He can't understand that I've nothing in common with him or his family. He talks about them like they are right here on the sofa with us. I make some fake and fairly pleasant convincing comments (I can't even remember what they are, I am *that* tired) and he nods.

Tonight I'm up later than usual because Richard has casually mentioned in the course of the day that his daughter and grandson are coming to Paris too. Though I imagine my ears emitting steady streams of hot steam, I swallow and answer, 'Certainly, that sounds— very— lovely, indeed.' The words do not seem to come from my smiling mouth and nodding head.

My fingers stay poised and unmoving on the keyboard and my eyelids are shutting. Sitting at the keyboard makes my aches worse. *I* am the one in need of a massage. I have already worked 14 hours today. I'm beginning to feel too old for this job, and as far as I understand, the winter is very long in the UK.

I have only just cleaned the whole kitchen after dinner, after massage and TV time. Jean-Viv doesn't offer to help, assuming that there is a dishwasher. She should be aware that in an Asian household, the dishwasher is a *person*, and in this household, it's me. I am of that class of Asians who avoid the dishwasher as it's not as clean as handwashing. Jean-Viv is in her own self-absorbed bubble, spoilt first by her mum and then by domestic maids.

Every extra person in the house adds a layer of admin. She's that layer. I'm going to do this booking very quickly so that I can get to bed. There is no point me wasting time or looking at recommendations. I just book the choices he's made. Richard will always know where he wants to stay, as someone who has come from the hotel industry. He knows which hotels he is going to be comfortable with, and that's where we're going. I open the tabs for both the Eurostar and the hotel booking and I key in the 3-digit on the back of the card to confirm the amendments.

Richard used to own and manage The Peony, a boutique hotel and upmarket B and B in London's Farringdon for a decades before the business and the building were sold for a handsome sum. It's a favourite with the press, marketing and publicity folk. On the same hotel booking platform that I had just booked the Hotel du Quai Voltaire, out of curiosity I search and click on The Peony to check out the pictures.

I have been to the Peony before, in my youth as a nursing student. It's absolutely beautiful. The restaurant and bar area is in pink, black and gold colour scheme, with marble table tops and feature wall papered in a tropical jungle print. The bar is lined in mirror with thin gilt frames. Photos show some handsome bloke in a black apron polishing glasses and grinning. A couple are perched at the bar on velvet stools enjoying their tête-à-tête. Grinning. Everyone is always grinning insanely or laughing with open mouths in these ads: the couple, the kids, the bartender.

The Hotel du Quai Voltaire is as chic as The Peony, with its plush linen beige and black curtains. The rooms look small but well-positioned. I've had to make sure Richard and I would get interconnecting rooms and I would pack the baby monitor. I get very little sleep as it is; Jean-Viv has no understanding how exhausting and demanding it is being on high alert all the time living with an elderly person. It is just like having a newborn, so I've heard.

I must have nodded off. Going deeper into sleep, I have rotated in Richard's leather office chair and I knock something with my elbow or the chair's armrest. I hear a thump. My eyes pop open. I blink rapidly and re-focus. For a second I think I am back in my parents' old house on Singapore's East Coast, before I reorientate myself. I look down at the floor around me. Richard's big coffee table hotel book, the title of which I fail to notice as it's in German, has slid and fallen to the floor along with the mousemat.

I am post-drooling. Ugh. My fingers grip onto the hard armrests like they are grab rails. I uncurl my fingers and wipe at my wet spit with the back of my hand. How long have I been asleep? Could be an hour. I wake the screen up and log in using Richard's ID. It is almost 2 in the morning.

I hear footsteps in the corridor.

11

GENEVIEVE

I wander down the landing and push the slightly ajar door, a little worried that my father is awake at this time. My eyes can't be lying. I blink to make sure. Stella is sitting at his desk.

'Where is my father?' I ask.

She swivels around. 'He's asleep, of course.'

Why does she say *of course*?

'Umm. I heard a thump...,' I mumble, 'And I saw light coming in from the corridor. What are you doing in here?' I ask. I glance down but there is nothing on the floor. She must have either picked it up or it had been *her* who fell over.

'I am paying his bills, booking the trip, downloading his health reports.'

'And you're allowed to use his laptop?'

'Of course. How else can I book his appointments and health checks? You know that since the pandemic you can only do online bookings. No one will answer and there is no number to ring unless it's an emergency. And you? What are *you* doing in here?' Stella asks. It sounds like she's accusing me of something rather than the other way round.

'I heard a sound,' I reply. I am guilty as a schoolgirl caught out for snooping around in a staff room.

'Your father asked me to book the trip to Paris.'

'Oh.' I utter. 'Fine.'

She takes her hands off my dad's keyboard and rotates in his office chair to look at me. Her hands on her thighs, her fingers move on the skirt like a piano she is playing.

'OK,' she says. She stands up, shutting the laptop.

'You're done with the booking?' I blurt out, eyes on the card. She nods and shows me the debit card like a passenger to a bus driver. It's my dad's card.

'Where did you get that from?'

'From your father,' she replies with a little smile.

'And h-he gives you his card to pay?'

'Your dad asked me to book it,' she adds, 'So obviously, he's paying for it.' Her voice is raised, defensive.

I stare. I can't seem to think faster. Of course I want to go with Daddy and Jasper. At the same time, we've only just arrived, so, no, we don't want to leave for somewhere else. And besides, it's winter. But because I haven't been articulate enough to reply promptly, she has mistaken my hesitation for reticence. She adds, 'Look, Jean-Viv. I booked this trip before you arrived. I'm just amending it to include you and Jasper.'

Daddy and her *were* planning to go away together, like they are on some romantic break. I really have no choice but to agree. I wonder if it is Daddy's idea or hers? At the same time I'm not sure my mind will be at ease if she goes with my dad without me and Jasper. We are a family, are we not?

If it had been up to me, I wouldn't go. Jasper needs to settle in. The moment he comes back, he starts school.

After she leaves Daddy's office, I hear her shut her room door. Previously known as *my* room door.

12

GENEVIEVE

Friday 30th December

I wake with the pale grey northern light. When I remember where I am, I open Jasper's door and check on him. He's asleep. According to the clock on the landing it is just after 6 am. So I must have slept since the night awakening and that strange encounter with Stella in my dad's office.

I descend the stairs to the kitchen to get coffee. I need something to wash the meds down. I always have had to make sure I was eating and drinking at the right times to trigger remembering to take them. All this will change *when* I get a job here. I'm not asking my father for money. *Yet*. I'm not here for his help. I'm here to help *him*.

I've come home to London start anew and not to give up, pathetic though I may sound. Am I not a Londoner? Are we not known for our resilience? I shudder because I'm not myself right now. *It's a wake-up call, that's all*. A sharp lemony spray of positivity never harmed anyone.

'What are you doing up so early?' The girlish voice chimes.

'Good morning to you, too,' I spin around to where the voice is coming from. 'I-- I'm jet-lagged.'

'Where are you off to today? Anywhere nice?'

'No. I got your WhatsApp last night,' I bleat mechanically. 'The itinerary you sent.'

'Oh, good. You're welcome.'

I ignore her sarcasm. 'We're staying at the Hotel du Quai Voltaire?' I ask incredulously, my eyes now widened from being awake.

'That's right. Richard likes the place. Looks very smart. Do you have any problem with it? I got you and Boy a room—'

'It's fine,' I close on it. 'You say you're from Singapore.'

She nods. She does not look at me, but at the mugs she is busy putting away, from the draining rack back into the wall cabinets. 'Yes.'

'How did you...how did you get this job?' I blurt out.

Stella puts the last mug away and stares into the cupboard for a second before she shuts the door and replies.

'Are you trying to find out if I'm an illegal immigrant?' Her hands now free, she folds her arms and tilts her head back peering down at me, allowing me the underside view of her straight and aquiline nose.

'What?' I reply, a little weirded out. 'No.'

'Then?'

'What visa are you on?' I press on.

'Your father has sorted it out; don't worry.'

'Your family... they know you are here?'

'Of course they know.'

'But who— who are your family?' I turn red. I do what all Chinese people do when embarrassed: laugh. We have a laugh for every loss-of-words moment. There is a contextual and separate laugh for being nervous, anxious, appalled, derisive and more.

As she doesn't answer, I wonder if I'm being insolent, as a child would be to an adult. Or perhaps, an employee to an employer, yet she and I are none of the above roles. Her eyes widen as though *family* is a foreign term.

'My father says you have references, I—,'

'Yes,' she cuts in, 'Check them if you want, but he's already followed through on them.'

Follow through. She makes it sound like we're playing tennis. Deuce!

'Fine. Please.'

'You want to see them?'

'Yes,' I reply, with held breath. She storms off.

When she goes to her room, or should I say *my* room, I look at the fridge organisation and fling open the kitchen cabinets, unsure what I will find. I'm not hungry. I feel full just looking at food. She has rearranged the insides of the cupboards. The wine racks have gone. My mother used to enjoy wine and cheese evenings with her book club or when her colleagues came round. The tinned fruit, dried fruit and nuts in a basket in what my mother called her "baking corner" have been replaced by unrecognisable herbs and spices which look like twigs, leaves and bark: traditional Chinese herbs, powders and remedies, each jar or packet carefully labelled in Chinese like in an old apothecary.

I find little handwritten post-it notes Auntie Stella has

left for herself, a journal, a recipe book. I flip open the latter two briskly but alas, they are in Chinese. She's written down recipes, ingredients in one and in the other, the routine of the housekeeping and caregiving, including my father's medication eg 25mg, 125g and so on.

I wish I did not rebel against Chinese school when I was little, as I now can't read any characters. I decultured myself. Years of going to Chinese school on a Saturday have given me a complex. Other kids did sport or drama, whereas my siblings and I sat down at wooden desks writing rows upon rows of characters on gridded paper. I recognise a handful of simple words and am surprised by my memory. 1杯 is one cup. This is frustrating as I would love to know what my father's needs are in the event that I have to take over the caregiving.

A breeze enters the kitchen from the speed at which she returns. She hands me a plastic see-through folder. She says nothing. I take it without looking at it.

'You've changed the things in the cabinets,' I mention.

'Naturally!' She puts her hands on her hips. 'All that stuff has been out of date for years. The wine has been given away. I don't do any baking or drink any alcohol.'

Well, Saint Stella, how lovely for you, Patron Saint of the Apostleship of the Sea.

'Wine is your business, isn't it?' She says, suddenly, as if reading my thoughts.

Was, I think. 'I like wine, yes,' I say non-commitally, hoping to halt the topic of discussion. 'Where are my mother's recipe books?'

'Your mother's?' She says incredulously. 'I don't know.'

'She wrote down our family's Hakka recipes.'

'I'm sorry I have not seen them in this house since I got here,' she shakes her head slowly. 'Don't need them. I cook traditional Hakka meals.'

I feel a small prick of disappointment. I wanted very much to find something of my mother's. That is what I must have been looking for when I open the kitchen cabinets. Her favourite mug or wine glass. Her apron, now starched and worn by Auntie Stella, does not inspire hope.

'I've cleaned everything in the cupboards,' she adds. 'Filthy. Old. Dust is no good for old people. All this stuff is hard to clean. Your mother had too much rubbish.'

My mum kept all our painted cups and bowls that we made in school, saving them whether they were chipped and cracked or perfect. Pictures we painted and drew in our childhood adorned the fronts of the kitchen cabinets well into our adulthood. Photos of us as a family sat on our fridge until they were faded ghostly imprints. All that "rubbish" has been removed. At the same time I understand why she has had to clear and clean. It's time for my father to move on too.

'I'm a nurse by training. Cleanliness is routine and routine is cleanliness. Everything must have its place and time. That is how I organise his medication.'

I nod but I'm glazed over, like the faded home-painted cracked ceramics. Surrounded by our appalling clutter, my siblings and I sat here around the pine table waiting for my mum to come home from work while the nanny served us our meals. I miss that time, bickering with my siblings, snatching Lego bricks, listening to the radio.

'Excuse me, I have to get ready your father's breakfast,'

she says, interrupting my memory. 'He'll be awake in half an hour.'

As it's still early and therefore it's afternoon in Singapore time, I creep back into the bedroom.

I sit on the floor next to the bed and flip open the file to the first name and number: Dover Heights Elderly Care Home. A Filipina voice answers after I go on hold. I am put through to her manager, also a Filipina.

'I am ringing to check a reference,' I say. 'Stella Choi, who is now employed by my father.'

'Of course, mam. Yes. Stella Choi.'

'Can you tell me what Stella was employed to do?'

'Miss Choi is a geriatric nurse, who ran the coffee mornings and mahjong nights, gave patients haircuts, organised birthday parties and took them on outings. She volunteered in the land-scaping and care of the grounds as her interest lay in main-taining koi ponds and gardens. We were surprised that she was naturally good at gardening. She moved on to shadowing and assisting one of the senior nurses here in the inhouse daycare for a year, then homecare for patients with advanced dementia to help them get comfortable at home in their end-of-life care.'

'Does she have the qualifications?'

'Oh, sure. She qualified in London. She has done the necessary training here too. We are a training centre too. Is there anything else?'

'Yes,' I say. 'How do you find her work?'

'Very good, mam. Conscientious, careful.'

You mean calculating, cunning.

I know the building. Dover Heights is a handsome curved

brick building with metal railings. But the koi ponds – that makes me ponder. Is that why Daddy's garden is now looking like a House and Garden magazine shoot?

'Can I help you with anything else?'

'No. Thank you.'

After the call, I try the second number: Khoo Medical Centre in Bukit Timah, near the Jacob Ballas Children's Garden. This is where Auntie Stella worked before she went to Dover Heights.

The manager says, 'Can't complain. She's well-spoken and smart. *Very* charming. The patients like that. You know, I think she rejuvenates them. Makes them young again.'

Rejuvenate, very charming, young again.

I can hear voices. My dad is up. I hang up and go downstairs, leaving the file in the bedroom, not wanting it back into the kitchen, where my father may see it and be upset by the fact that I have been checking up on her references and therefore not believing him.

Am I being unreasonable to suspect an articulate stranger when we hear it on the news all the time? Old people get scammed by well-meaning "neighbours", new "internet lovers from abroad" or calls from "the bank" demanding the closure of accounts and large sums being transferred to a holding account.

This macabre story in particular plays over and over in my mind like a bad smell: I'd read in the Evening Standard, a lonely Malaysian elderly retired nurse in East London, whose family are all back home, is befriended by a "kind and helpful" neighbour using emotional bullying over months to get her to change her Will. When she finally did, she was murdered, the parts of her body found 300 miles away.

Builders who lay a new driveway, a cleaning "team" who don't leave, all prey on the vulnerable. She gives the impression of professionalism and thereby, trust. But this Stella Choi may as well be a slick con artist in a three-piece suit pounding on the door of Rumbold Road.

When I hear the doorbell downstairs, I descend to the front door to open it. An attractive mixed race man stands before me. He is younger than my 32 years, but it's hard to tell. His smile is straight and he has laughing amber eyes. His green polo sweatshirt has a logo embroidered on the left breast.

'Hi! You must be Genevieve?'

I don't reply.

'Good to meet ya,' he says, holding his hand out. 'I'm Qamal. I come once a week, on Stella's day off.'

'Oh! You— you cover for her?'

'Yup.'

'Come on in,' I say. I swing the door open and wave him in.

13
MARCUS

Marcus whizzes off. Three doors slam: Sahil's, the flat's door, and the entrance door of the block. Each makes a bigger impact than the last, like thunder claps.

Marcus walks to his lock-up garage. While Sahil goes into shock and dozes, it is time to do something with the problem at hand— the body, lying there being preserved while Marcus is busy *not* working, namby-pambying at the hospital, drinking coffee, arguing with Sahil, who keeps falling asleep like Princess Aurora. Fortunately, winter temperatures have been below 5 deg at night. Time seems to have stretched, a portal they've entered but can't leave.

Marcus unlocks the van and slides the door open with a flourish, like some bad-tempered tyrant. His mouth falls open from which a sickly taste arises. His hand flies to his receding hairline and he runs it over the shiny sweat on his forehead, blinking. He slides the door like a magic show and it flings shut with a dissatisfying clunk. He's seen enough. He hopes it's enough.

14
SAHIL

S ahil has been left with the blue Barclays card, before
Marcus storms off.

He's never seen Marcus in this kind of mood
before. He would no longer be able to speak easily to his
landlord, who has turned from a mild and depressed loner to
an alligator on speed. Sahil is not upset at Marcus. No.

Sahil is terrified of being thrown out of the country and
going to jail. No one in his family would be able to afford a
lawyer and he does not even know if he is entitled to one.
The uncle who donated money he did not want back, who
put his hands on Sahil's shoulders when he left for
Heathrow, would be devastated. He was blinded by tears at
the family goodbye and send-off at Indira Gandhi
International Airport in Delhi. He had said to Sahil, 'Just
make us all proud, leave here, leave everything and leave
everyone, do whatever you have to do. Just make us proud.'

You reap what you sow, goes the Bengali proverb.

. . .

Sahil means 'the shore'. He is so named because his destiny is to find success abroad.

He is abroad all right. But the success part is questionable.

He is lying on the floor and crawls up to the window. Looking outside at the dark wintry rain, just like the night before, and the night before that, confirms that it is the night of the same day.

Since the incident, Sahil has gone into lockdown and it would look to Marcus like Sahil is busy with Uni work. His phone shows 8 missed calls. All from Anjali. There are fewer text messages. He sees the preview to at least one of them:

> Y r u not calling me back :-(

And another:

> W r we doing f NYE?

Oh God, yes. That is the most ridiculous timing. Is it really New Year's Eve tomorrow? What. A. Pain. He does not want to see her. He'll tell her he has the flu.

You don't want to mess around with Anjali. She is like a one-in-a-million Indian girl and her parents brought her up to be on a pedestal. Even her name means 'divine offering'. She is from a middle class family in a leafy Gurgaon suburb with a house that has a pool and a roof terrace with potted trees. Everybody in her family had gone to University though she is the first to go to the UK. By comparison, Sahil's entire family had never been to University, local or abroad.

Anjali is the least of his concerns.

. . .

What should Sahil do now? He had killed someone. It is an *unfinished* job. The body is in the van.

He chose to live in Whitechapel because it is very Asian. From the street markets to the restaurants and kurta departmental stores, he felt at home. He misses real street food like bhel puris and little terracotta cups of tea for 7 rupees but most of all he wanted to wake up and smell the frying onions and methi, look out the windows and see a slice of life back home, and now he is unable to look out of the window, because the view only reminds him of one thing. The van. Marcus's van. The thug is in there.

Marcus would assume that Sahil has washed his hands off it, and that the thug's body is there for Marcus to dispose of. This is not true. It is absolutely not true. Sahil would not abandon this job. He caused it after all. Over and over he thought that actually he had done the right thing. The thug was about to clobber Marcus to death or leave him dead or both.

Apart from the fact that Marcus has been so ungrateful for his generous act of kindness, he has been almost pleased with what he had done for who he considers to be his best friend. This pisses him off. He is already punished enough. Couldn't Marcus see that? Fuck this! In Dostoyevsky's words, "The man who has a conscience suffers whilst acknowledging his sin."

Should he look at moving out? He hasn't considered the possibility until now. Rent is sky high and flats are very hard to come by since there has been a housing shortage. Too many bloody people, that's why. He would have to shell out at least £1400 for a one-bed or £1000 for a studio, move further out of London and thus further from Queen Mary. They have become friends, but right now, there is a situation causing the rift —yes, the body.

It's nuts. While trying to Google Barry O' Keefe in incognito mode on a new ominously black browser window, he finds millions with that name. It is just an Irish name. He slams the laptop shut and swivels in his Ikea office chair. He grabs onto a pillow and screams into it. He has shut the curtains because he cannot bear the sight of anything. The vision of the thug's face and hands haunts him, especially the fingers. Stubby sausage fingers, that face smooth and broad as a mirror, that body substantial as a fridge.

Every minute now he is waiting for the flat-footed knock on the door, walkie-talkies spitting and blustering along the corridor, the ID being flashed, the tight may-we-come-in stare.

He lies down and curls like a worm with his eyes shut. Soon he drifts off and dreams of the old life, an event at his local temple where he, his siblings and other children perform martial arts. Bells and gongs deafen him. Smoke and heat fill the air.

15
MARCUS

Marcus pounds up the stairs and flings open Sahil's room door. When he sits next to Sahil, a tenderness comforts him, which he hasn't felt since he last saw his children. He is not old enough to be Sahil's father. But Marcus was, is, a father. His boys also used to act asleep when it was bedtime but their minds were still active. He watches Sahil sleep for a while, or pretending to sleep. How could he protect Sahil who in turn is trying to protect him?

There seemed to be a sense of familiarity between Marcus and the thug, but he couldn't say for sure. It might have been his imagination. Marcus had been mugged before and it was equally unpleasant but over soon enough once he had handed over the phone, wallet, whatever.

The thug could see that Marcus's iPhone was at least 4 years old even in the rainy dimness of the streetlight. They have very sharp eyes and target victims they have been watching or who look ostentatious. There is nothing showy about Marcus. His grey van is old and dented. His glasses are scratched from working on site. His clothes dirty, dusty and mismatched. He looks like his van. Just a worn out, battered piece of kit. What could the assailant have wanted?

He needs Sahil awake, whether he is or not.

He waits 5 minutes and shakes him. Sahil stirs and sits up with a bolt.

16

SAHIL

'What?' Sahil croaks. His eyes squint in the dim lighting.

'Look,' Marcus pants, 'I-I just —'

Sahil waits in the semi-darkness.

'I don't know if it's good or bad,' murmurs Marcus. 'I... went to the van...,'

'And?' Sahil prompts.

'And... oh my god... Sahil. I-I... can't even,' Marcus stammers and there are tears glittering in his eyes, but not of sadness or joy. It's something else. Horror.

Sahil takes several shallow breaths, his eyes as glazed as the winter rain on the sash windows dirty from pollution.

'The body,' says Marcus. 'It's gone.'

Sahil remains silent, his jaw open. Seconds passed. Then he clutches both his hands to the back of his neck. 'Gone? No... noooo...' he breathed. 'It's impossible. He... he's dead. I checked.'

Marcus shakes his head slowly. 'No. You obviously have no idea what you're checking. Did you even have first aid training? Are you a doctor? Look, listen, Sahil. We have to do something.'

'What?'

'I don't know. I can't bear to think. He... we... he has escaped.'

'No!'

'But don't you see? That's the good news. You didn't kill anyone!'

Is that good news? Sahil is in a Greek tragicomedy. He can't believe what he's hearing.

'What's the bad?' Asks Sahil.

'He will be back,' says Marcus.

'Why? Why will he be back?'

Marcus clamps his mouth shut.

Sahil gnaws at his bottom lip. They could not look at each other. Sweat pours down his back. He is shivering; it is a bad dream come true. He starts reciting a Hindu prayer. His eyes, unfocussed, gaze towards an imaginary mid-distance object.

17
MARCUS

Marcus wipes his face over. He exhales a long breath. 'Let's go to the van. I will show you.'

Sahil folds his arms, still not looking at Marcus.

'You will fucking get out of bed, come with me and take a look!' Marcus's finger jabs at the air. 'Don't forget this is *your* doing!' Marcus is losing his patience. His voice rises to a falsetto when he gets like this.

'All right, all right!' Sahil throws his hands in the air. Marcus will need to get to work by 2nd January as every day he doesn't work is a loss of income. The agency and the client will get pissed off. To them, it is "just so typical" and "what you'd expect of these unreliable builders". He's heard those adjectives bandied about. He is not defending himself. Attacked and ill, he is now unable to handle the van situation alone.

'You're coming now,' Marcus growls, his teeth bared.

'I want to move out,' Sahil replies, raising his chin in defiance, looking at Marcus.

'Fine.'

Marcus frogmarches Sahil, now fully dressed in his winter parka, out into the dark wet yard and to the nearby block of the lock-up garages.

'Well, first we need to throw away the dust sheets,' Marcus says, shining his iPhone torch, having calmed down. The interior of the van brings him some solace and comfort in its familiarity. He clears his throat, as though about to address a small audience with a candid anecdote.

'You can see for yourself. It's fucking covered in blood. His DNA, sweat, whatever else.' His voice takes on a formal, low volume tone.

Sahil observes without expression. Surely he sort of already knows the extent to which the evidence is displayed.

'Just needs cleaning, doesn't it,' Sahil offers helpfully.

'You're fucking mental. Don't have a go about cleaning. Don't even go there. You've never cleaned a sink in your whole life. You had servants. I am cleaning shit and muck every day on site while you sit in front of screens in your lab. Look at the state of my hands,' says Marcus, flashing his palms in a mime artist way. He could feel the veins on his throat bulge as he couldn't get any sense out of Sahil. Has he been wrong in considering Sahil, a flatmate, once a stranger, a friend? Sure! If you believe that someone who saves your life is a friend.

'Oh, Christ. I am sorry,' Marcus apologises immediately. He runs his hand over his scant eyebrows. 'What the fuck are we going to do?'

'Clean,' says Sahil, automatically, misinterpreting his rhetorical question.

'Umm. Yessss,' Marcus hisses, 'but then what?'

'I don't fucking know. He would have killed you. He went at you more than 8 times. I swear. I counted. I am not lying to you. I won't lie to you. You are good to me, Marcus. You are. I swear it was an accident.'

Marcus does not answer. Was it really 8 times or more?

'What about the cameras, Marcus? The CCTV,' shudders Sahil. The shakes turn into panic and Sahil starts weeping.

'Sahil. Look. Sahil! Will you fucking look at me?' He grabs Sahil's collar with his left hand and Sahil's chin with his right. It stops Sahil there. 'Do you know that I do the maintenance for this building? I have access to the cameras, inside and out. Nobody even bloody looks at the footage. We're laughing.'

Sahil hugs him. He holds him tight. Marcus remembers his boys again, when they were little and were hugged like teddy bears when they cried and had to be picked up and smoothed. It is not like that anymore.

This is hell, and he knows it. He wants to pass out.

Sahil breaks off from him. 'I will clean for you,' he says. He stops quivering.

'Great.' Marcus blows out a deep resigned sigh. He is like a Pilates ball being deflated by a large hand on him.

Sahil agrees. 'Yes, that's sorted. Don't worry.' He speaks with a new, calm coldness.

Sahil's *don't worry* earnestness grates on Marcus, is wasted on him, depletes him. He does not want any of it. He does not want Sahil. Marcus is punctured and slowly flattening from the immense pressure.

18

ELIJAH

It's pitch dark, dry but bitingly cold. His mother would be waking him soon with breakfast before her shift at the hotel. He wonders vaguely if it would be bao or something special she's made like cheung fun with prawns. His favourite form of cheung fan, drizzled with soy sauce and sesame oil. Hunger carves at him and his stomach growls like a sick animal. Nausea rises. Did he really drink that much again and black out?

How he craves that first cup of chrysanthemum tea. His mum likes some semblance of a Chinese home life. Her homemade char siu baos are cheaper and better than the ones from the Asian supermarket. They would talk through his plans before she would bring up the pesky subjects of his drinking, looking for work, or both, again. They are the same subjects and the only thing he does not like about his mother. Could she not talk about the weather, TV celebs or the local councillor, like a British mum?

The sheets are rough and unkempt. It must have been helluva night. This seems too odd to be his home. He is shivering; his jacket is drenched. He even has shoes on. His mother must have not seen him and dragged his jacket off, and he would not have protested. He would let her do anything to him, even when she was sick. He knows it is for his own good. His fingers do not recognise the uneven hardness of the surface he is lying on. Maybe it isn't even a surface, come to think of it. Pain shoots out from his back, shoulders and most of his head. It is like someone sawing his head up, as uncomfortable and unbearable as he could get in bed. The aches are blinding. Is this a proper killer of a hangover?

He reaches around him for his phone and clock. The Argos bedside table is not around him. His hand cannot find the switch to his lamp. Hard, multi-shaped and cold objects surround him and as his eyes adjust there is only a very weak chink of light from the edges of what must be the door. There are no windows and Elijah could not tell if it is night or day except for the rectangular line of light. He can just tell this isn't his bedroom.

His hand finds around him a zipped bag. He touches the teeth of the zip and follows the seams around. He does not remember the night before. Has he fallen asleep in someone's flat?

He grasps his head with both heads. The pain intensifies as he struggles to sit up, his hands lying flat to push himself up. His right hand lands in some tray-like surface which overturns hundreds of sharp little things. Pins pricks his palms and he retracts his hand, rubbing them to rid them of being stuck to him. With thumb and index finger, he picks one up. It is an iron nail. He checks his arms and feet. He turns his ankles and wrists. He is not bound. He can move, though not easily. Once he is sitting up like a teddy bear, he rubs his eyes and head. Sticky. He is covered in some sauce and putting his fingers in his mouth, tastes the metallic tang of blood. *Oh my god,* he whispers. *Where the hell am I?*

He can't remember how to get home. Well, this is inevitable since he doesn't know where he is. His phone's Google Maps can help him with that. He reaches in his right pocket and it is empty.

Oh fuck. He's lost his phone and slept out like a homeless tramp. Great. His mother would be so cross with him. Though she would not show it. She would smile and probably say, *Rough night?* He's spoilt to death and never had a harsh word even when his behaviour had been appalling, as it would have been the night before.

His hands approach the rectangular slit of light and it is not hard to locate the door handle. From the shape of the ceiling and the door, it is a van.

Why did he do such a stupid thing and sleep in a van? It is not the first time he he'd passed out from drinking... and couldn't remember how he ended up there.

He rotates himself, adjusting to get a grip of the door handle. The van looks old and if he remembers right, it is a safety feature for passengers to open from the inside even if locked, but he would not be able to relock it again, not that he cares. He adjusts his position and presses the door lever. More of the nails scatter and spill around him, the tinkling sounds muffled by the rough thick sheets he's sitting on.

The door slides open. He's indoors, in a garage. Elijah drops onto the concrete floor like a grand piano. Ouch. That fuckin' hurts. He rotates the T-handle and pulls the tambour garage door up. Grey, dull and dirty daylight pours in. What's this? There is wallet on the floor of the garage. He picks it up. There is no cash. He'll try the cards in a minute when he gets out of here. It is drizzling. He shoves the wallet into his pocket. He does not recognise the street or buildings. He pulls the garage door down so no one can see where he's come from.

Elijah's breath is short as he fights with his own limbs to start walking. He sees his new boots. They pinch as he walks; every step is agony. He breaks into a run when he sees that at the end of the street there is a park. He is next to a park. There would be a sign soon. Any sign. His run becomes lopsided and he is light-headed as a child on a swing, his mother pushing him and grinning. If only...

His mother has always...

He remembers that his mother is dead. Oh God, no.

He still thinks of her as being around, waiting for him, or talking to him, and all of it is useless. The doctors, counselling team have tried and all of them are full of bullshit too. He does not want any of them. He wants his mother back.

She passed away 6 months ago. He's been unemployed for more than a year. The reality always hits him. If not for the Barclays Bank card, he would be living on air and water. His grief blocks all of it and the memory only sometimes returns to prick him with pain. When she was sick, a) she was still working and b) she was very good at acting like she was well, in order to take good care of him. She's taught him cooking, washing and cleaning their one-bedroom flat but he's given up on all that. She is not coming home. His childishness fills him with shame.

The thought winds him. If his mother is dead, then

where is he even heading? He staggers into a corner shop at the end of the park. He can't even get a can of Monster. Shit. All useless. Every. Damn. Card. When the shopskeeper sees the state he's in, he's politely requested to leave,

He flings the wallet away into the park. The ache and the too-tight boots are killing him. Flashes of white come to him. The milky grey sky spits on him, the hardly-any-light of day. He slows, stops and floats down, feathery as a sheet of paper. He sees the grainy concrete pockmarks on the pavement with its black circles of gum become larger and larger. His eyelids are heavy like someone is shutting them. It becomes dark as the inside of the van again.

19
STELLA

Saturday 31st December

On the Eurostar, Richard says, 'You know, Stella, I want to show you as much of France, *my* France, as possible in three days,' he bows his head, and I'm not reading his expression right. Is he joking? 'It may be my last chance. This may be my last trip.'

I beam at Richard. Jean-Viv says nothing; she looks as blank as a mask. She is sitting opposite Jasper, and Richard is opposite me. We are separated by an ocean of differences symbolised by a crumb-covered small melamine table. The boy has been taught absolutely no etiquette. Every time he eats, it's like he's feeding the birds. And he only seems to eat crumbly food with zero nutrients.

'Don't say that, Richard,' I say, folding my hands tidily, trying to avoid Jasper's crumbs and empty carton of Yazoo, its straw having anointed the table with sprays of chocolate milk. 'You may still get a chance to return to Singapore, right?' I add.

I peel a wet wipe out from the Little Angels packet, and clean the table. No one notices.

After all these years working in geriatric care, hearing their almost constant refrain doesn't get easier: *I'm dying. Any day now. Clock's ticking. About to meet my maker. My time is almost up. I'll be off soon. End game, guys.* How are you supposed to answer them? These are comforting cliches to remind us of our mortality, repetitive messages telling the truth. So my policy is to ignore them and to change the subject. Some carers may disagree.

Every immigrant's dream is to return to the motherland. France is not quite the same but it is his chance to travel while he can.

'Glad you think so!' He chuckles sadly. He reaches for my folded hands but I withdraw and put them under the table. 'Thank you for coming to me, to Fulham,' he says, looking at me with an earnest sincerity. 'If I can't go to Singapore, then Singapore must come to me! You know, like that saying, 'If Mohammad can't go to the mountain... that one?' He almost applauds with glee.

Jean-Viv ignores her father. She shuts her eyes and leans back on the headrest. Good. She needs... *head... rest.*

'And you're born in Singapore?' Richard asks. He has asked this so many times, and even answered it himself.

I lower my eyes. I shake my head slowly. He really does not remember anything. 'I was born in Malaysia,' I say in a hushed voice like I am ashamed. Malaysia usually gets the sympathy vote. That is where Singapore gets most of its finest workforce. 'Then my dad got a job in Singapore when I was 7 and we moved. I spent all my school years there before I went to the UK to train as a nurse.'

'Look, Stella, France is one of our favourite countries to

go to. It's next door, isn't it? But it's so... foreign!' Richard flicks his palms towards his head like he's Seinfeld.

'Yes!' I laugh but it sounds fake. I want to humour him so that Jean-Viv will see that work is relentless. I am living in Richard's house and working even when I'm not in the house.

Jean-Viv lives and acts like a guest. Last night, she would not have touched the washing up until I asked her to directly. She never took her plate into the kitchen, nor her mug from the living room. If it is her house, she will pull her weight more. She sees me as *her* help.

'My mother loved French cinema, culture and food,' Jean-Viv adds drily. Her eyelids pop open. It's so tiresome. I've heard nothing from Richard about his late wife, and now I must listen to Jean-Viv go on about it every day. It's just us four now, so why does she always have to bring up *my mother this...my mother that*? Can't she just accept that her mother is not here and I'm not her new mother nor am I old enough to be?

'Mummy worked hard, long days at the hospital. Her book and wine club at our home where she could savour literature and French wine became a hotspot for local residents.'

Hmm, yes, yawn. Can't think of anything worse. I am not surprised the woman bored Richard. Middle-class bookishness, wine affectations and fawning over French culture.

Despite his age, Richard is keen on travel. He comments constantly. 'Look at this, Jasper. Look at that, Stella,' he points out of the window. 'I've been to India.' He nods, pleased, and then shares an anecdote or two, totally unrelated to France.

'Wow, they seem to have built too much in Croydon,' he

adds. He jumps from topic to topic. He can no longer hold a thought for long.

Jean-Viv looks down at her phone. 'I don't think it's Croydon. It's Sidcup. We are cutting through Kent to the tunnel.'

'Map reading has always been your strong point,' remarks Richard to his daughter. 'Remember we had to drive through North London. Disaster! Until you took over the navigation with the A to Z. Remember the A to Z? Oh geez!'

There's nothing to navigate now. We have Wayz, Google Maps, Apple Maps. Pretty impossible to be lost. She thinks she's so smart and useful. Jean-Viv smirks now, but she'll see.

20

GENEVIEVE

We arrive at Gare Du Nord in time for a late lunch. 'Your father is allowed to eat anything. It's a break.' Stella smugly pats me on the shoulder. Who's asked her?

'Passeport, madame, s'il vous plait,' the immigration officer says through the glass. Stella is his walking folder, keeping his documents and his wallet "safe".

She's not hands-free, pushing his wheelchair, with the bags hanging on the handles.

'Are you sure you don't want me to hold onto the documents?' I ask.

'No, you have plenty already to do,' she replies. 'Look after your son's things, please.'

We get a cab to the hotel in the 7th arrondissement on the riverfront. In past visits, my mother chose this hotel for its proximity to the Musee d'Orsay, where we will be having lunch after dropping off the luggage and checking in. Stella doesn't know anything about art and is happy to just hang out with the family, drink coffee and eat pastries. Stella mentions Paris as "one of the most romantic cities in the world". Art, processed meat and cheese are part of life here. She is human, after all, and my hopes are momentarily lifted. I do want this trip to be stress-free.

We vie with crowds for the Eiffel Tower lift after we get out of the cab. Tourists move in dense groups and individually. I'm using my card instead of looking for euros. Neither Stella nor my dad has offered to pay, and I have already paid for lunch. It's not their fault. They think I'm a successful Asian tiger hotshot. Meanwhile they are depleting my limited funds.

When I look up, I notice that Jasper isn't behind me. I glance around. Stella is busy buying an ice-cream for my father at the overpriced kiosk, from what I see on the large handwritten chalkboard signs. She has the wheelchair with her. My breathing becomes disconnected, short. I wander over to her, waving, but I know I look very flustered and unpleasant, almost marching in step. 'Where is Jasper?'

'Jasper?' She parrots. 'I beg your pardon. I was busy buying ice-creams. Boy!' She rotates her head this way and that, her curls bouncy and shiny. 'I don't know. I haven't se... Jasper, Jasper?' She calls out, slightly sounding frantic.

'You're supposed to stay with them while I buy the tickets,' I say, trying not to panic.

'I know but he was just behind me. He can't have gone far!' She arches and pokes her neck out, like a goose.

We can only see heads of the crowds in all directions, jostling, shuffling and the screams of toddlers. Eurotechno with South American lyrics is pumping out. It's from the ice-cream kiosk.

'What about your dad? I have to stay with him.'

'What about my ice-cream?' My father suddenly asks in a small voice. The vendor reaches out and hands it to him. 'Thank you, merci,' says my father.

Fuck the ice-cream, is what I want to say but I stop myself. 'OK,' I take a deep breath and act like this is my normal voice, which it isn't as it's all trembly and weak.

We wander off in different directions, calling out to Jasper. We are drifting like tofu cubes in a soup of people. We are pushed and pulled in every direction. An itch of guilt courses over my skin. This is my fault. I should have been holding my son's hand to get to the front to the queue to pay with Stella keeping both hands on the wheelchair, but she insisted that crowds are not good for his respiratory system so she wheeled him away. I thought nothing more of it. Jasper is too old to wander off in a daze and my Daddy is practically chained to Stella.

It must have been only 10 or 15 minutes but suddenly I hear her shriek, 'Oh Jasper! Jasper! You're here! Where you been? Aiyoh! We are so worried, woh!'

I head over to where the voice is coming from. I wrench his hand. 'Mummy, you're hurting me. Ow!' He cries. I have been gripping Jasper's hand so tight I must be crushing his bones. 'I won't let go of you, not after what's happened. No way.' I sound shrill.

'Mummy,' his eyes are screwed tight and his mouth wide open. I hope this is not turning into the terrible sixes which extends from the terrible twos. I don't care about this tantrum right now. He screams in my ear as I hug him tight. I want to cry too. I am never letting go of him again. I completely blame myself.

'OK, OK, Mummy is very sorry, let's get to Gung Gung quick. Where is everybody?' I look around and we've been floated away like driftwood.

'Jasper,' I say, looking back at him. 'What happened?'

'I went to see a clown,' he points at a considerable forest of a crowd at the centre of which was a small clearing for a monkey-suited clown with a ruff collar on a unicycle. Jasper was trying to get to the front of the crowd as at his height, he could not see anything. The monkey clown was the most bizarre sight, and I am transfixed for a split second before I hear his little voice.

I have seen my father oblivious and it scares me. He is slightly deaf too. He can simply disconnect from a situation and reconnect like he's a phone line.

'Jas, why are you upset? What's the matter? I must have dozed off in the ice-cream queue,' my dad says. 'What did I miss?'

I don't reply, but my sigh comes out as a sob.

'This is such a light wheelchair. I feel pushed around, being pushed out of the way, because in truth, I am in everyone's way, am I not?'

'Aren't the brakes on?' I ask Stella.

'No, *I'm* with him,' she replies. 'Don't need brakes; we're on the move.'

We are sullen when we begin queueing again for the tickets. Now we must stay together.

'He used to come here with my mum,' I tell Jasper. 'Your grandmother.'

'Richard?' Stella addresses my father as though I had

been talking to her. 'Have you been up the Eiffel Tower with Mrs Ho?'

'She is not Mrs Ho,' he tells Stella. 'She is a very proud, independent woman who kept her name.'

My father's lined and wizened face is illuminated from within. Those facial massages may have helped, but what startles me is that he is laughing out loud, as a child laughs, because he's happy, because this trip has been his dream before it's too late. That's why we say *do* or *make* a trip, not *have*. It's an action. It requires effort. He doesn't seem tired at all. He looks young again, and I can see him as he was when I was a child.

When it's our turn to go up and see the view, my father looks at Jasper as if astonished that his grandson is here. Then he remembers where we are and what we're doing. His eyes glimmer with pride and nostalgia.

'I am too old to pick you up, cheeky monkey,' he says. 'But you can see the view, can't you?' He puts coins into Jasper's fingers and shuts them. 'There. Go!'

Jasper excitedly feeds the coins into the telescopic viewer and I lift him up. He is almost too heavy now and that brings me a pang of longing. How fast time goes.

'My God, if your Mum was here right now! Look at the low evening sun,' he points to the horizon. 'There is something about the continental light that gives everything a warm glow even on dull days.'

I have never seen my dad happy, not since Cassie left. She had been his favourite, not that I'd care to admit. I am a source of disappointment to him. It stabs me to remember my ex whom I married because it seemed like the right thing to do: he is Chinese, isn't he? He is successful, a professional, a degree holder. A very cool Asian, not an accountant. I met him at the Institute Bar at UCL where he worked as bartender while studying. My siblings and I did not take after my mother to become doctors. This does not speak well of my family.

The Chinese are no good at accepting failures. And mine was the serious lack of success.

'I want to do this, for your mum, for us. How precious is all this?' My father waves in a random direction around him, the light glinting off the metal railings and the glass of the enclosure. We look at Parisian life under us, the traffic, the buildings and the tree-lined avenues.

'Can I tell my friends I'm in Paris?' Asks Jasper.

'Yes, you certainly can!' I forget that Jasper has been using his iPhone to take photos. The irony is that I'm taking none, when I had been taking them nonstop, making marketing reels for my business and creating content. Now I am unemployed, I have not considered recording anything. He's thrilled and is busy sending messages. 'I miss them very much, Mummy.'

'You'll be back there again.'

'Soon? I'll be back soon?'

I bite my lip. 'C'mon, let's go and find Gung Gung. Let's take a family photo.'

I forget about Auntie Stella until then.

We walk round the viewing platform inching along with the crowds. She has her hands on the handrail and she's looking distant. She turns around, sensing I'm behind her. Her dark eyes are cold as the steel and glass on a wintry day.

'Are you... OK?' I ask.

'I'm fine,' she snaps like a tight purse. Auntie Stella speaks almost with her lips shut like a ventriloquist. 'I am sure you're taking care of your son and your father.'

'We are up 276 m in the sky. Neither of them are going anywhere.' I immediately regret saying it because I do not mean any sarcasm.

When we get back to the hotel, Jasper and I head to our room, my dad to his and Auntie Stella to hers. The fact that she's not sharing a room with me or my dad gives me a disproportionately huge sense of exhausted relief. I flop onto the bed, fling my bag at the mirrored dressing table and bury my face in the huge white pillows.

At 6pm my father WhatsApp calls me. He sounds impatient, 'Woay, I am hungry, Gen. It's Saturday night! New Year's Eve, even!'

Someone is in a good mood.

I hope he does not expect us to go clubbing to usher in the new year. We converge downstairs in the lobby. He is not in his wheelchair. 'Do you want me to get your chair?'

'Oh no. A good nap has sorted me out. It's a beautiful evening. We'll walk and if we can't, we'll get a cab.'

I am buoyed that he says *we*, and she's not here, so it must be me and him. 'The hotel will recommend where we can walk to,' I suggest. The city is stuffed to the gills with restaurants, after all.

'Look at this, Gen, dammit, look at it.' He suddenly cries out. A beautiful polished mahogany Bechstein grand stands in the Salon de The in the corner of the reception lounge. 'Oh my!' My father exclaims, over and over.

'Oh, Daddy, this is your dream!' I concur in a voice that

very much believes in what I am saying, and this is something that has been lacking in my life of late.

'I know! They never had one here before.'

'C'mon then!' I goad. 'Dinner can wait a few minutes.'

'What about Stella?' He frowns and looks at me with a squint.

'What about her?' I counter. 'She'll be down very soon, I'm sure.'

My father trembles with excitement. He sits down on the velvet brocade stool without asking permission from the staff and he lifts the lid. He starts playing the songs from his youth. 50s and 60s crooner classics, including his favourite Nat King Cole songs.

Daddy was an accomplished musician in his youth. He was playing bars and hotels in Singapore's Beach Street near the Raffles Hotel where many of his audience came from before he trained in hotel and catering. Once he decided to pursue hospitality as a business move to relocate to the UK, he never played as much again because it's a very demanding industry with little free time. He never lost it. He never forgot how to play.

Song after song he performs with perfect ease and polished confidence, adding flourishes, intros and outs. *Nature Boy*, *Straighten Up and Fly Right*, *Aquellos Ojos Verdes*. When he plays *Mona Lisa*, he draws half a dozen fans. I feel like his tour manager! They applaud. The manager comes over and says, 'Incroyable. We have never had a 76-year-old play here before. We are so privileged to have you.'

'Thanks, merci, tout le monde,' my father says without attempting a passable French accent. 'I have been playing for 70 years. I was a professional.'

That impresses the manager even more. 'I can see that,

Monsieur Ho. Oui, it's our great pleasure to have you stay again.' They chat about how the 1905 piano with the art nouveau detailing ended up here, from a barn in Arles, refurbished at a high cost by Russian technicians in the outskirts of Paris before ending up in the hotel. They talk about my father's gigs as a youth and how he came to play the piano and run a hotel chain. His health and memory have been failing, and his voice croaks like an old hinge, but his piano playing is still sharp as a tack. Daddy cannot wait to share. He has been invisible. Just an elderly man. There is nothing to look at or to listen to. He has not been the star. Stella has been the star. He has been living in obscurity, AKA retirement, never been the centre of attention for decades, and now he is performing to a live audience.

When we were children we were bored by my father's playing. We heard it too often and ran to our rooms to play games or to watch TV while he was banging away. We did not appreciate his skill or talent. Not because we did not like the songs, (OK we did not like the songs) but because we did not understand what the fuss was about. We took it for granted. When my siblings and I had piano lessons we had not taken to the instrument the way my dad had because he has perfect pitch and plays by ear whereas we were just being typical Asian kids: "doing grades", ABRSM, classical syllabus, *do* being the operative word, like ploughing or mowing. A chore.

Whereas Daddy plays for pleasure and always has. He plays anything from the top of his head and improvises. Never done a music exam in his life.

My father is ecstatic, buzzing from the experience. There's no biz like showbiz after all. The feeling you get from performing to a live audience can never be replicated on Zoom, TikTok or YouTube.

Suddenly my father stops playing and say, 'Wait. Where are we?'

'We're in the lobby. The hotel. In Paris.' I'm holding my phone and filming his performance.

'Oh, that's right. I got so lost. Aren't we going somewhere?'

'Yes,' I reply. My father, being transported to his youth, the ghosts of his musical past, Mummy and the golden days of our family when we were children, has completely forgotten the present. It is like being born. He is relying on me to provide the lowdown.

'Why are we here?' Jasper asks. Jasper is unengaged — he is also on his phone as I would have been when I was a child. Young people don't do old people's music.

'We are waiting for... for Auntie Stella,' I smile at him.

'Oh, my,' Dad takes his fingers off the piano keys and slaps his forehead. 'I really forgot about her.' He reorientates himself. 'Let me check my phone.' There is a pause while he leans back, groans and fishes in his pocket. 'Aiyah, she did send a message. Let's see.' Another round of fumbling while he frowns and bites his lip, looking for his glasses this time. He reads out. 'She says she's too tired to come and wishes us a good evening. She'll see us at breakfast tomorrow. Oh well! I think she must be too tired if she says she is.'

I nod, secretly ecstatic this is the first time I am going to be alone with my father and son.

'I don't know what day it is. Every day is the same to me. Either I am still alive or I'm not alive.' He fizzes at his own joke but I don't laugh, and Jasper isn't listening. 'Well, all that playing has made me even hungrier than before.'

'Me too! Where are we going?' Jasper pipes up, half-listening after all.

'We're just going to walk a block to that restaurant that the manager recommended, Le Cinq-Mars,' I reply, and then to my dad, 'An intimate, low-lit bistro. With a robust selection of wines,' I raise my eyebrows at my Dad.

'Sounds good.' Then my father, almost to himself, adds quietly, 'I think it's a good idea to go French tonight.'

'What do you mean?' I ask.

'Well, you see,' he gets up from the stool. I steady him. 'Stella doesn't do European food. She only eats Asian food. She can't stand English cuisine. It's been tough for her. This is a big culture shock. She's never been anywhere so that's probably why she can't face dinner.'

I turn and grab his coat that he has slung on the back of an armchair. I wonder if he forgot it's there. OK. Enough about her. I ask my dad, 'Where's your stick?'

'Don't need one. She makes me use one but look at me. I'm fine.'

I *am* looking at him.

'Why don't we get her a takeaway?' I add. I don't want her to starve. She is working on this trip even if we don't get on. 'There is a Vietnamese that Mummy took us to. Let's think. Tan Binh. It's directly opposite the Cinq-Mars.'

'Let's message her. You do it. Tell her we'll get her something.' He shoves me his phone. I type the message as he dictates.

21

STELLA

I creep behind the huge potted palms in the grand entrance reception lounge. I know the song playing on the piano. It's something I have tried to block out. My mother played it too. There is a small crowd watching and listening. I can't see the piano yet. I hover for a while near the lift lobby, my eyes on the marble floor, my ears tuning in. The song's outro ends with a flourish and a final chord. I wander nearer and peer between the foliage. The applause is loud and the crowd cheers. Through them, I see the pianist. My hand flies to my mouth. *Richard* is performing. This is not good for his blood pressure. All that adrenaline. I go closer and stand behind a tall man in the gathering. They are dispersing now so I tilt my head and shuffle around to get a better look.

Jasper is sitting on an armchair next to the piano, and Jean-Viv holds his hand, beaming. She has tears in her eyes. This brings me back. Jasper's side profile looks just like Jean-Viv when she was his age. She does not remember me at all. Am I so forgettable?

I watch them leave and get their coats on. He is someone else. Thanks to me, he stands tall and proud. His Aquascutum coat is magnificent, or rather it has made *him* look magnificent, invincible, like a movie star. Jean-Viv guides his elbow and I take my place behind the crowd, preparing to disappear. When she asks him where he stick is, he replies, 'I don't need one. She makes me use one but look at me. I'm fine.'

I mean, what the actual—? That is simply offensive, and he has no idea what he's saying. Of course he's just being macho. Of course he feels the need to show off in front of his daughter and grandson. Trust me, I'm a nurse. We will always err on the safe side. Why take risks?

Richard needs his stick and his chair. Jean-Viv is too lazy and ignorant to go and get both. He may have an accident and at his age, a fall is fatal. I don't want to be there when it happens because it's going to be on *me*. As his carer, I'm responsible. I would rather stay in my room all night. I don't care about the city. They see me as a bumpkin who has not been anywhere. Well, I'm not about to tell them I've been to Paris when I was a student in London. I stayed in a lovely hotel near the Sacre Cœur but I have forgotten the name now. I also don't want them to know I was travelling with my parents whom I'd rather not talk about.

22

GENEVIEVE

We walk out of the hotel. My father walks, no, *strides*, without being supported, without a wheelchair or a stick and sure, he's frail and a *lot* slower than I remember, but capable of getting around. He's a different person without her. He's more keen on being seen as independent, not needy and clingy as he is with her. He has been trained to completely rely on her, right down to asking for his money and his passports. She's his stern, censorious nanny. Without her, he's himself.

When we get outside the hotel, Stella has replied to his phone which I am holding onto. 'She doesn't want anything,' I say. 'She's ordered dinner from the room service menu.'

We head for the Seine, and walk down Quai Anatole France. We pass the Bouquinistes du Quai Voltaire, a popup second-hand book kiosk, now shut. The Seine is lit up. We watch the few sparse "practice" fireworks which are leading to the big guns at midnight. Jasper points at the boats while I hold his hand. 'Look, mummy! That one has got a skeleton on it.'

'Oh yes! And flowers. A Halloween boat house.'

'Can we go in a boathouse, Mummy?'

'I would love to! Some day.'

The three of us are interlinked, my arm in my father's. It's the first time I feel his affection since I arrived at Heathrow. After a block we turn left at Carré Rive Gauche and right onto Rue de Verneuil where the restaurant is located. 'It definitely is more than a block!' He moans.

'We can get an Uber back, no problem, Daddy.'

When the wine list arrives, Daddy gestures to me. '*She's* the expert,' he chuckles at the sommelier and I reply in truth, avoiding all eye contact, 'Not really, I just know my New Zealand wines.'

'Nonsense,' he bursts out laughing, and addressing the sommelier, 'She has her own wine business, you know, and she—,' he starts to boast, and I caution my father with a stern, 'Dad, please.'

I fear that I have to make conversation about wine. I am on holiday, not a busman's holiday.

After we order, I wonder when would be a good time to plunge in. But there's no chance. Daddy lists the plans tomorrow. 'We're going to see the Mona Lisa. Did I tell you, Gen, did I tell you... the manager has organised us a VIP family ticket for the Louvre?'

'That's... awesome,' I remark.

'It's the least he can do. Your mother and I were frequent visitors to Paris when I was a hotelier.'

We talk about the old days, my mum, my siblings, Singapore. We mention The Peony, the designers he hired, who's gone where now, and the staff from the bar and restaurant, one or two of whom he is still in touch with.

'There was a lady from the laundry section in house-keeping who was close to our family too. What was her name?' He presses.

I am surprised that I do remember.

'It's Irene,' I prompt him. 'Irene Chan.' She was from Hong Kong. Whenever we popped by at The Peony during the school holidays or weekends, she would always come out in her black and white starched uniform and give us a handful of Flying Saucers and Foam Shrimps. I still light up when I see pastel colours now. They remind me of The Peony, the juicy rubbery blandness of the pink prawn-shaped candy, the fizzy sherbet surprise as the Flying Saucers melted on your tongue. It was like wasabi for beginners.

'Remind me,' he raises his finger. 'What happened to her?'

'She left, dad.' I don't add that he made her redundant along with others, and hired cheaper staff from Eastern Europe combined with outsourcing the laundry and catering.

He hasn't mentioned Stella. We're getting along well now so I don't want the evening spoiled either. 'No one could mix a drink like that... what's his name, that boy who all the guests loved, what's his name?'

'Tom.'

'Ahhh, yes! He looked like Tom Cruise in that movie, Cocktails. Ohhh, *those days*. But now. Everywhere. Across the board. Times are hard,' my dad rattles off some soothing words. He shakes his head. 'The war against Russia, the war against disease, the war against the war, the war against rocketing inflation, war in the Middle East.'

I nod and look around for the waiter. When is this food supposed to get here?

'And how is Shiong?' He suddenly asks.

'Look, the food's arrived,' I say, relieved and genuinely excited. Ah. So he does remember. 'He's fine.' And that is absolutely true. Of course my estranged husband is fine. He couldn't wait to pack up and leave. Being served food seems to distract my father and Jasper and soon our group attention is on eating.

After dinner, my dad is practically snoring as his head tilts back. His eyes are red and he is looks drawn and tired. I call for the bill. My father snatches it and takes a look, 'I can't see a thing. Here. Just take my wallet.' He pats at his pockets. 'Oh no, I don't have my wallet.'

'Oh,' I exclaim, not quite astonished but taken aback.

'Stella must have it.' He says with a shy nod. 'From before.'

'When?'

'I gave it to her when we were at the Eiffel Tower.'

'No problem, Daddy.' I do really want to take my dad out to dinner since he is kindly already paying for this trip for my son and I.

'So sorry, please get it, dear Gen,' says my father, 'and I will get the next one.'

I have a mini heart attack at the bill but there's nothing I can do. It's not MacDonald's. I'm furious that she has to keep hold of his cards and money, not to mention a little fearful that he trusts her like a child trusts his mother to hang on to all his possessions. I want to take his wallet and documents back from her. He doesn't even know her. My poor Daddy. Why is he being so silly?

23
STELLA

In my room, I have called for room service. Three course dinner would do me fine. Hell, yeah. Oh, and, wine too. Make that a full-bodied Cab Sauv. They know me as a non-drinker only because I'm working in Richard's house. Day and night. I only have a day off a week. On my day off, I have been to the pub, Chinatown, the library, the cinema — sometimes alone and sometimes with the one friend from my student days whom I've reconnected with on Meta.

Tonight I'm having a night off and they can't complain. Anyway they need family time together. I'm sure they're relieved I'm not there fussing over Richard. If her face gets any longer, she will be turning into an alligator. It's been *such* an arduous day with Jasper going missing. His mother just does nothing to discipline him. She's not taking care of him or her father. Fact. Yet she keeps interfering with *me* doing *my* job.

I enjoy my dinner in bed in silence. Thank God, no TV tonight, no massage, no dishes, no admin. Just me time.

. . .

By the time they get in, I have placed the tray of empty plates and glasses on the floor near the room door to be cleared by housekeeping at some point. I hear Jean-Viv's and Richard's voices, since I have an interconnecting room with him. Richard protests about something or other, as he does, and then the door shuts. Hope she realises how testing it is looking after old people. Everything you do is always wrong.

She's gone. It's silent.

I slide back into the huge comfortable bed. I open my navy and red striped Tommy Hilfiger bag with our travel documents on my bedside table. I switch off the room lights but snap on the reading lamp. I fish out a faded 4"x6"photo from a Please Do Not Bend envelope in one of the compartments in my hand luggage. I have been holding onto this photo since I left Singapore.

I look at it and it brings me both joy and pain. It's my nightly ritual. The back has an address scribbled. I don't need it. I know it by heart. Of course I do. I look at it every evening. But I just want to see it written and know it's there, waiting for me.

I grab the hotel stationery — crisp, thick cream linen paper. It's like a wedding invitation. I start to write with my gold Parker fountain pen. As the translucent ink flows, so does my head clear.

I know you are not expecting to hear from me. It's New Year's Eve. I'm in Paris now on a work trip, listening to a few starting pops and fizzes of fireworks which I'll watch from the balcony at midnight. I want to say bonjour but that would be pretentious. Now, don't be envious, my darling. I have not been to any bars or restaurants, nor have I been enjoying myself. I'm working hard, night and day. My feet are killing me; you won't believe it. I will buy you something tomorrow. I can't wait to get back...

24

GENEVIEVE

I see my father to his room. I don't know why but I snap on all the lights, and rush inside like a seagull to make sure it is OK, and by OK, I mean that Stella is not in it, tucked into his bed and awaiting him with her glossy curls in rollers. That image certainly will give me nightmares. I make sure he knows where the bathroom light is for those trouble-some calls of nature.

Getting him dressed in his pyjamas is not easy and he is absent-minded on what comes next. Jasper gives me a hand. We get him to the bathroom and I frankly do not have a clue what Stella does for his nighttime routine. I make a mental note that here's where I have to learn some skills and techniques.

'Daddy. Goodnight.' I say softly.

He mutters and sighs as he gets into bed, and wants a hug from Jasper.

'Well, this is Marseille, Alistair. You come to say good night to Daddy.' He calls Jasper by my brother's name, and he has the city wrong. I feel a little sad yet glad that good memories have been triggered by my son's affection. But I don't have the heart to correct him and Jasper looks at me to check if I know what's going on, and I mouth to him, nodding, *say goodnight*.

'Goodnight, Gung Gung,' says Jasper, but Daddy's already snoring.

We leave quietly making sure the door is securely locked behind us.

Outside the booms have begun to intensify and I tell Jasper that if he's good we can stay up to midnight and watch the fireworks from the balcony.

It will be an early start if we want to see the Mona Lisa. Whose smile is more mysterious? Hers or Auntie Stella's?

PART TWO
THEN

25
STELLA

Dover Heights Elderly Care Home, Singapore

Wild Goose

An Ancient Tale from China

Two hunters spotted a flying wild goose. One of the hunters placed an arrow in his bow and took aim.

First hunter: That goose would make a fine stew.

Second hunter: I am thinking more of a roast.

First hunter: Stew, come on. You had a roast last month.

Second: I vote for roast. It's too warm for stew.

First hunter: Let's ask the clan leader for a decision. What about half and half?

They looked up and the goose had long gone.

• • •

There were two or three people whom Madam Lee mistook me for. Her daughter, her nephew and her maid from a long time ago — her nephew, because due to my height and slimness, I could be androgynous-looking. When she thought I was the maid, she'd keep bringing up tasks being done or not being done, or a meal that was particularly inedible or at best a bit bland.

The maid was clearly her favourite amongst those I was mistaken for. It's likely I resembled her, though the maid was from another era, and had long been gone. Madam Lee called me Ah Goh, the maid's name. Or when in an uncharacteristically affectionate mood, the other way round, Goh Ah, which softens the blow of the cruel name.

She was always to be referred to as Madam Lee. All the patients here were Mr or Mrs this or Madam that. No one could be called his or her given names, or 'Uncle', or 'Auntie'. This was particularly important in setting the boundaries. Although the polite term for anyone elderly should be Uncle or Auntie, it would be considered unprofessional here in an exclusive high end care home.

The Hokkiens gave animal nicknames (cow, dog, pig) to children so as to deceive and ward off evil spirits. During the time of high infant death rate due to lack of vaccines and medications, it was believed that the spirits took their children away during the seventh month, the month of the Hungry Ghosts. Things had now changed, but some of those nicknames had stuck to adulthood and in case you were wondering why there were a few middle-aged adults called Cow? That was why.

Goh is Hokkien for goose. It was not a flattering nickname for the maid (or me) and my long neck had an unfortunate resemblance to her and not classic movie stars. I was mocked in school and called Audrey Neckburn. To disguise my awkward bird-like appearance I wore lacy high neck outfits or large show-off long necklaces to take the attention away from my neck and bony collarbone. Ugh.

I had a very small facial mole removed after she had commented about it enough. Madam Lee had shockingly good eyesight for her age.

After I had transferred her to the wheelchair so I could change her sheets, she must have seen me as her care home staff again, because she reminded me to put her glasses back on the side table.

'You know, my maid Ah Go has stolen stuff from me,' she announced. I had heard this story countless times. Time had stood still for the elderly, and there was humility in that. 'A diamond bracelet here, a gold bangle there, a pair of jade earrings from San Francisco. Rings too. Of course. They are so small and portable. She thought I did not notice. You'd better not. Don't you touch my stuff.'

With elderly care there was a lot of patience and resilience involved in not taking everything they say to heart or you would indeed go insane yourself.

In a heartbeat, I would leave this job. I wanted permanent employment with benefits rather than being temporary staff on an hourly rate contract. The salary was poor, you had no chance of promotion, you got accused of theft from time to time, and you had to "volunteer" to run special interest golden oldie clubs for the residents such as music, gardening, book and movie clubs. They could hardly watch a movie to the end. Almost all were snoring within the first half an hour. Call that a movie club?

On top of that, the turnover was high. Most staff were like me, subcontractors or self-employed. I was here for a different reason. Duty of care. I didn't like the place. I had no choice but to stay until a better offer came along.

'Are you listening?'

'Yes, Madam Lee, of course I am.' Actually I *was*, but she *hadn't* said anything. She thought she did, and that I was ignoring her. I patted down her pillow and transferred her to the wheelchair, an act that I found harder as the years passed me by.

'Good morning to you,' said Madam Lee, astonished there was someone in front of her, like she had not noticed me before.

The buzzer sounded and I looked up at the security screen. 'Wait here, Madam Lee,' I said, hands on her shoulder to reassure her, before I went back out to the corridor. I got her attention by looking at her, as one would address a toddler, but I could never tell if the message sunk in or meant anything.

'Your visitor is here to see you,' I said to her when I came back, pressing my back against the glass door so that the man has space to pass.

'Who?'

'Your nephew. Benjamin.'

'I have a nephew? I suppose I must!'

She said this week after week. It didn't matter if he came in more frequently or less.

. . .

Benjamin had regularly been assured that the care home residents were enjoying a wide variety of meals. We had had American, Italian, Thai or Indian food in the staff cafeteria. The residents preferred Chinese food. It was steamed and bland, so nothing offensive to the sensitive tummies here.

I went to the visitor entrance lobby, opened the glass door for the man who was shorter and slighter than me. He was well turned out. It was such a rare occurrence in a home for end-of-life care. Why would any relatives of the patients bother to dress up? Might as well give up. No one was looking at anyone. The elderly held our attention in other ways — they were a constant reminder of our mortality. Glad rags did not protect you from expiring.

He blinked rapidly. The hot aroma of rice porridge hit him like a sauna. It was almost lunchtime and my stomach had started to rumble, as a reaction to the fragrant steam.

'Good morning, Benjamin,' I said, with a firm nod. 'You're early today.'

'Am I?' He glanced at his watch, disproportionately prickled by my comment.

'Come on, I'll take you through,' I tried my wide professional smile on him but he didn't smile back. He looked distracted and distant.

The strong waft of his aftershave nearly knocked me out. What was it? Dior? I could smell orange blossom, the blue Mediterranean, sandalwood. I would have asked him if I knew him well enough. All I ever inhaled in this place was a base note of rice and a faintly lingering top note of Ajax floor bleach.

I swiped the card and we heard the beep unlocking the set of double doors. We walked in silence down a corridor lined with faded paintings of boats and junks in Clarke Quay, and inky sketches of the Singapore skyline. I walked past the cork staff noticeboard, making a mental note that I must return to take a look. It had become a habit.

'Your aunt has been doing well,' I quipped.

'She has?'

'She's played the piano.'

'I didn't know she played the piano. In the past, I mean...'

'Don't worry, I understand what you mean. Muscle memory. They never forget.'

I felt nauseous recalling the old songs she'd played. She was a fan of vaudeville and cabaret numbers. Yellow Rose of Texas and I'll Be Seeing You. I shut my eyes to block the memory.

I waited to the end of my shift when I had got changed into my civilians to return to the noticeboard. Ah yes. A new job post!

Elderly Man Seeks Live-in Carer with a Nursing Background

I am a retired hotelier looking for a housekeeper from Singapore. I have been living in London for decades, so you must be willing to relocate to, work and live in London, UK. I am physically mobile with limitations, a bit forgetful but with plenty of muscle memory! I miss real Asian home-made food. You must be fit, healthy and a good cook, who can make all the classic Chinese, Malaysian or Singaporean nutritious and healthy dishes from back home. I need to be walked like an old dog at least once a day. You should be companionable, someone who enjoys tai chi, TV and listening to me play piano. Very good remuneration and benefits. In addition, I will cover your costs and expenses.

No agents.

Apply in writing to richie_ho497 at gmail dot com

The piano bit would be excruciating, but OK. If that was what it took to clinch the job, then I was prepared to wear ear plugs and think pleasant thoughts.

Naturally at Dover Heights notices should not be moved nor new unauthorised ads put up from small business owners or estate agents. I had to get the key from reception to open the glass cabinet.

I found it in the drawer of the admin room, one accessible by senior staff and that included me. On top of this chest of drawers was a 3-tier basket in-tray tower with other notices to be put up for the next week. I took a similar job ad flyer for a part-time carer to a 16-year-old with cerebral palsy (ability to lift was a requirement).

I carefully removed the thumb tacks and take down the flyer putting it into my satchel style crossbody bag. I put up the new ad, feeling a little sad for the 16-year-old. That was a seriously important ad and I didn't understand why it was in the in-tray waiting to be put up when it should have been immediately put up to find the girl urgent care. I pushed in the tacks with my thumb, locked the cabinet and returned the key.

After work, I trudged for 12 minutes in the early evening to Buona Vista, the nearest MRT station, for the more-than-an-hour-long journey to my HDB local authority flat, or apartment as it's called these days. On the sardine-packed East West line towards Pasir Ris, I took the A4 sheet out of my Zara tote bag and studied each word. I rode 14 stops and alighted at Bedok Station, Exit B. Up and down flights of escalators before I was out of the station. I waited for the connecting bus number 222. I watched the traffic lights and soaring towers of accommodation. I got off opposite Block 180. From the bus-stop, it was another 7 minutes' (10 minutes if I was dog-tired in a fog trance) walk to Block 78, Bedok North. That's me.

I was lucky to still be in the workforce even if my job was a drag. The patients made it unbearable. Sometimes I thought I was going mad. Working with ill patients sent you into an alternate universe. The past, present and future all blended into a weak and tepid cappuccino, without any power to perk you up.

I couldn't wait until I got home and through the front door where I collapsed in a heap on my threadbare sofa.

I pressed the mic icon, and dictated the start of my letter.

Dear Mr Ho,

I am a nurse applying for the position of live-in carer. I believe I have worked for you before, though you may not remember it.

26

STELLA

A week later, I gestured and Benjamin stepped in. The lobby door shut behind him, cutting off the distant rumble of the Buona Vista MRT on elevated tracks heading towards the city.

'Hello Auntie,' he said to Madam Lee.

She stared at him. Madam Lee was one of the most talkative patients, yet she clammed up with her nephew until she had "warmed up" to him.

'I'll leave you,' I said. 'Feel free to come and say hi on the way out. You can take her to the cafeteria for lunch or a coffee,' I suggested.

He took charge of the wheelchair. 'I'll be OK,' he nodded at me. 'See you later.' Thus dismissed, I held the glass doors open again, and watched him push the wheelchair through the grand classical arch, then the corridors leading to the caféteria which had been overhauled to resemble a café. How class, mood, everything changed when the letters *teria* were dropped, and the accent added to the *e*.

I followed them a short distance. Sometimes my heart did not let go of patients. This was end-of-life care after all. What if their life ended while they were not in my hands? This would not do. You could say it was like separation anxiety. I was the one Madam Lee needed and wanted. I was responsible for her. I was a part of her life in a way that he would never be. Who was this Benjamin? He came sporadically. At times he came once a month and at times twice. He would not have a clue how she deteriorated or improved in the times that he did not see her. I could understand that. He was a busy young man. He probably had small children, a wife, a pet to take care of.

When I got to the end of the corridor to the visibility panel of the café's double doors, I peered through and they could not see me. They were caught up in some intense conversation.

Madam Lee looked better than the week before. Nothing had changed in her diet or medication but it might be she had a bit more fresh air. I had taken care to read to her outside in the terraced garden area and she liked that.

Her eyes focussed on Benjamin. She never smiled at him until she was at least halfway through their conversation and even so, she only briefly produced a smile that did not reach the wrinkles of her eyes.

He must have said something that she did not like, because Madam Lee shot a warning finger out at him, wagging, her eyes stuck on him in a cold glare. I pushed the double doors open and went inside. There was no rule about the elderly being aggravated by visitors but both parties often appreciated the intervention to cool things down.

The coffee he ordered had arrived just in time when I

appeared. 'How is everything? Will you be having lunch here?' I asked, maybe too earnestly.

'Ummm, yes. Let's see,' he looked up at the blackboard menu. 'Hainanese Chicken with soup? And side salad? I think I will have that.'

'Sure. Let me order for you,' I said. 'You sit with your aunt.'

He made no attempt to get up or to pay.

'You have to pay at the counter, I am afraid,' I hinted to him, 'They will bring it to you, though.'

'Is Henry here?' Madam Lee suddenly piped up, her voice croaky.

'Who's Henry?' Benjamin said, suspiciously turning his head to her.

'I don't know,' I said. I hoped that he didn't take it too seriously. She always mentioned people past and present.

'Will you be having the same lunch, Auntie?' He asked her.

She did not answer, instead her eyes looked far away as though she was on a cruise liner searching for the horizon.

She answered finally. 'Yes, I will have the same. You should know it is my favourite meal. Maybe not here. The food here is appalling.' She chewed at the word *appalling*, prolonging the gnawing action, her hot pink lipstick lost in the creases of her wrinkled lips. Her fingers kneaded restlessly on her thighs and I was tempted to hold her hands for a second as I could sense her anxiety.

'Let me order your lunch too,' I said instead. 'Chicken rice. Two, please.'

'What about you?' Benjamin asked me.

'I don't eat here. My break is in an hour and I will be having lunch in the staff canteen.'

'Oh. What is that like?'

'Probably more sodium and saturated fats than here,' I rolled my eyes upwards.

Benjamin burst into laughter. It was not meant to be a joke.

I gave him a little nod and left them. I tossed a last glance at my ward and she seemed OK. The food had arrived.

When the visitor's hour was almost over, Benjamin had already left. I got buzzed by the cafe to come and take Madam Lee back as they were shutting it for cleaning. That was so odd that Benjamin left his aunt in there alone. He could have waited for me. Like I suspected, he must be very busy with his own work and family.

'He left me here,' Madam Lee said.

'I know. It's OK. I will take you out now. You'd love it. I have planted some new plants. Oleander. I can't wait to show you.'

'Wait,' said Ah Kai at the till. 'The man did not pay.'

'What? What about the last time?'

'He's never paid on any of the times he had been here. He charged it to her account.'

'You let him?'

'What can I do? I simply told him to pay at the exit, lor. I am sure he did not.'

'Why didn't you mention this before?'

'I can't. Stella. Look. I'm really busy here, serving and cleaning and doing the till too.' She pointed at seemingly every object around her. 'Why don't they hire more staff? They certainly charge the patients enough!'

Each meal must be about $14.95. He had made more than 6 visits if I remembered right. Madam Lee's meals were covered by her fees but his were not.

'Her package doesn't include meals for guests,' I stated, recalling the facts.

'No package includes that.' Ah Kai guffawed and threw her head back showing gold-filled molars. 'Otherwise you would bring your family of 50 and feed them all for free.'

'Shall I call him?'

'Dearie, you do that lah. I have to mop the floor, and my shift is over. I still have a lot to do before I go. The dinner staff will take over soon.' She pulled on the blue gloves.

I hadn't forgotten Madam Lee was sat there in her wheelchair still waiting for me, daydreaming, listening. Just because she wasn't talking didn't mean she hadn't heard the whole conversation.

I wondered what went through her mind. I feared it. Dementia was terrifying for the onlooker. Her lipstick had worn off and her white hair was frizzy and tangled again. She looked like an Eton Mess.

Just having lunch turned her previous focussed and radiant appearance into an unidentifiable vague expression of despair, exhaustion, futility. I felt like how she looked, because she had no idea how she looked. It was degrading. A discarded worn out doll. It was like I never brushed her hair that morning, or painted her furrowed old lips with pink lipstick, Chanel's *Emilienne*.

'When you're young, you don't need much. You don't need money, you don't need makeup;, you have youth,' she had said to me. The only marvel of dementia was time travel. Glittery wit and tidbits resurfaced from ancient history. She was a looker in her day, always vain and attentive to her appearance. After the war in the 1950s as a pre-teen, she had made her own lipstick grounded from wine residue and mulberries. I guess it must have rubbed off on me, because I was just like her. I found myself unable to appear in public without lipstick either.

Occasionally, she would remark on my appearance or outfit after I had changed out of my uniform.

'That skirt,' she pleaded. 'Please. Could you burn it?'

Of course we bantered. We had good days and bad. Sometimes I took her advice and other times I didn't. Sometimes she drove me to tears and vice versa. We had a closeness no outsider would understand. That skirt in question was a favourite windowpane check pleated midi from Zara. It was very good for my height and I was taller than most Asian women. I didn't understand why she hated it.

She also commented on colours which simply made me look sick or which suited me to a tee. 'Really you should be looking only at Chanel. That rubbish from Cover Girl does not look good. *Gipsy Rose* by Chanel. That's a good one. Goes with your peach uniform. Now what do they call that colour that the receptionists wear? Taaa... tawww... that's it, taupe. Thank you.'

'You're welcome.'

She would give a short talk or lecture on style and fashion. She was eagle-eyed even now. I didn't think she needed glasses. They must be for show, as she could see the tiniest, most intimate blemish on my nose or cut on my finger.

'They never give you proper uniforms like the green scrubs or navy. Why do they think pastel suits everyone? They don't. It's like the last thing that I will see on my one-way ticket on the conveyor belt. Macaron colours.'

She continued, grinning at her own imagination. 'Trust me. Red lipstick for you. Pink for me. Stella! Stella, are you listening?' She would suddenly shriek. I wasn't Ah Go the goose girl servant, I wasn't Benjamin. At that moment, she knew it was me.

I tilted and turned the wheelchair around 180 degrees.

'Come on, let's go and take a look at my new oleander,' I repeated like a mantra in a cheery tone. 'Pink and white ones too. You like pink.'

27
STELLA

My HDB local authority flat in Bedok was a daily utilitarian reminder of this life that I needed to escape. My body ached, my jowls sagged, but mostly my legs and sciatica could not take any more standing. I was drenched in sweat by the time I got home. Looking after Madam Lee was a killer but the concrete crate apartment's views were worth the trudge.

I sat patiently in front of the char kway teow vendor. Smoky aromas wafted in front of my face, veiling my hair and uniform with a thick greasy fog. I'm third in line. Couples and singles like me would get a ta-pau or takeaway on a weeknight to save time and cooking. It was a cheap treat. I craved something rich and fried. I'd rather be treated to tea at Claridges in London than wait for a takeaway with my sticky, sweaty ten dollar note, crushed into my fist.

Sometimes people were kind and in Asia there was the advantage of maturity. They took pity on me when they saw I was a middle-aged nurse in my polyester rayon lilac uniform and they let me cut the queue.

. . .

This dirty 3-bedroom apartment was the right size for me. There was only aircon in the main bedroom (mine) and the living room. In some distant fantasy, the spare bedrooms with their solitary spinning ceiling fans, would be for family. I was neither proud nor ashamed of this apartment or as I would like to call it by its proper name, *flat*. It had been home for the last couple of years, and yes, at least it was in my mother's and my name.

Grey dust clung to the window grilles and corners of the floors. The tiles had not been mopped for weeks. I wasn't planning to be here for long. I did not care as I saw this place only as a stepping stone. It was only dirty because I worked all the time. At my age, it was a disgrace. I don't mean the floors, but the all-consuming work. The bills were high. Anyone who lived in Singapore knew the crazy cost of living.

I once lived in a big house, a kind of 80s villa with metal gates, a terracotta tiled patio framed with a pergola of tumbling pink bougainvillea. It had stepping stones, in the koi pond next to the drive. That was how I became an experienced amateur at the art of koi care. A happy koi was one who was in a clean, diverse environment with other koi but without overcrowding. I was not a happy koi.

The waiting time at least gave me a chance to rest. He was very popular. A queue was always a good sign. In fact, any self-respecting Singaporean joins a queue without knowing the reason, even if just to gain the few seconds for finding out what the queue was for.

I inhaled, shut my eyes and thought of my dinner being made.

That night I watched YouTube and copied down recipes in Chinese in a notebook with checked pages like graph paper. What could I say except that I hated cooking. But by the time I got the job I would be very good at it. Even uneducated people could cook; how hard could it be?

It took me a few days before I was happy with my application and email. I made sure I could qualify on every criteria. That was important. A quick search on my phone indicated that the Singapore passport was the number one most powerful in the world, providing visa-free access to 196 countries. I thanked my lucky stars. My passport was going to open doors I did not know existed.

I retrieved a Hong Thai biscuit tin from my kitchen wall cabinet. No, I didn't really enjoy cream crackers. This was my mother's indulgence.

I prised the lid open with the handle of a spoon. Here was my passport and of course, an exquisite pair of jade earrings from San Francisco. I had to be careful not to wear them to work. You didn't wear your best jewellery to work at an Elderly Care home. For a start nobody would notice except for my eagle-eyed ward, and secondly, you would be wearing it with a uniform and look ridiculous.

My wardrobe was filled with Thai silk dresses, gorgeous lace tops, brocade cheongsams. Some were gifts from my mother but I was most proud of those I bought from working in the healthcare service industry. When you spent all day giving, it hardly seemed like there was anything else to give yourself. Oh, but there was. There always was a little drip of kindness for yourself. There was no one else to spend on, not yet. I was looking forward to the day when I could spoil not myself but someone else.

I ran my fingers over the passport's faux leather with the printed gold crest, before I put it back in the tin.

'Good morning, Nurse,' she said the next day.

'Good morning, Madam Lee,' I replied. 'How did we sleep?'

'Ohhh, so-so. In fact, awful,' my ward added.

'Oh no, what happened?' I quizzed, concerned.

'I just kept waking up,' she whined.

'Were you dreaming again?'

'Oh yes. I'm always dreaming, whether I am asleep or awake,' she replied, narrowing her eyes at me.

That might be the sharpest thing she'd ever said. 'Shall we go for breakfast?' I changed the subject. 'They have your favourite dish today. Teochew porridge!'

'I just want some bananas,' she said drily.

'We can do that too,' I conceded, nodding. 'Let's get you out of bed and in the chair.' I said goodbye to the night staff and took over the iPad of the reports. Madam Lee had been awake four times.

'What did you dream about?' I asked.

'Weeeeellll, you know... I...,' she searched, about to say something, her wrists circling the air. Then she snapped shut like a purse.

Her brow furrowed.

'You sit in the chair while I make your bed,' I instructed her, patting the chair. 'Then you can tell me all about it.'

28

STELLA

I saw in the bookings online that Benjamin was coming to visit Madam Lee at tea time. I wanted to finish earlier, quickly get out of my uniform and wear my Zara skirt suit and a cream silk blouse so that when Benjamin Lee left, he could see my outfit.

Benjamin would be taking Madam to the refectory for a quick teatime snack, as per the routine. He had sometimes sat in the garden with her or at the fountain in the courtyard but the weather wasn't great. Predictions or working to routines was part of my job, and usually it would be a combination of both. If the routine was upset, it would be due to an emergency and these were unavoidable in end of life care.

I was a silent engine that moved the wheelchair to the refectory while Benjamin walked alongside. Deus ex machina. 'I come from a rich family,' she told Benjamin even though he already knew as he was her family. He took off his Prada sunglasses and wiped them dry of the rain. He had listened to all this a million times but still managed to act "not bored" and occasionally replied 'Really?' I wondered why he needed sunglasses when it was rainy and a bit grey. A quick thunderstorm in Singapore was followed by sun, even on an overcast day. He grabbed a dining chair for himself.

The speech came again. 'I think of my late friend every day,' Madam addressed me, while he put his glasses down on the table and took his jacket off.

'Who?' I asked.

'The woman I had been telling you about,' she retorted impatiently. 'Have you forgotten?'

'I haven't,' I replied. 'Let's have some curry puffs.' I pushed the chair towards the pastry display and I put a couple on a plate using a pair of stainless steel mini tongs.

'She was my best friend,' she continued. 'Trudie. Very smart. Did you know she was a doctor?'

'Yes, I think you've mentioned,' I replied with a terse smile, turning around to place the plate on the table.

'My maid looked after me,' Madam Lee added, looking at Benjamin as though for the first time. 'Ah Go. Here she is.'

Benjamin looked at me shy, apologetically. 'I am so sorry,' he said.

He was handsome and easily forgiven. I didn't know what he was sorry for. With his whiskery thin moustache, he possessed the old world charm of a film star even though he could be in his thirties. Seeing him in the fountain courtyard often conjured up movie connotations in my mind.

'Sorry for what?' I asked.

'That she called you her maid,' he said. 'The girl called Ah Go.'

I laughed. 'That is quite OK,' I replied. 'She has often mistaken me for more than one person, including you.'

'Me?' He pointed at himself with a thespian open palm, bemused.

'That's just...,' he couldn't find anything to say so he burst out laughing too.

Madam Lee also chuckled good-naturedly. 'Wah, look at you two lovebirds. My boy and my girl. Why don't you please be a dear and pop back to my room? I need you to find my glasses. I want to see the menu. I don't want curry puffs. You think I can't read. But you know I went to school in England, all posh. The bastard.'

Her lips curled. It could be any bastard. Who she was referring to this time didn't matter.

Benjamin said briskly to me, 'Please could you get her glasses.'

I hurriedly left the refectory for her room. I checked her bedside cabinet and they weren't there so I looked in the locker. I tried the handle of her wardrobe. It was locked. I found the glasses kicked under her bed.

'Here you are,' I produced them, and even had a few seconds to rub them clean with my apron. But Benjamin produced his lens cloth from when he dried his sunglasses.

I rubbed them.

Once the visit was over, I made sure I had five minutes to change out of my uniform into my Zara skirt and cream silk blouse. I saw him out to the carpark though he seemed bothered and flustered. He repeatedly told me not to see him off.

But I wanted to see his car. With his Tessuti trouser suits and gold and enamel cufflinks I imagined a BMW or Mercedes. Nothing too ostentatious like a Tesla but still a serious status symbol.

He flagged down and got into a taxi instead.

29
STELLA

'I want you to find the piano score to "You'll Never Walk Alone" from *Carousel*.'

'Very well, I'm trying,' I replied to Madam Lee's whim. I'd prefer to find it now, because Benjamin was coming to take her out to lunch at Goodwood. I was very dubious that he could afford such a luxury venue. Here I was trying to eat meals under $10 with my staff discount. He was also going to take her to Claymore Hill. That rang a bell. Where had I seen that name?

'Now, please could you go and grab my music sheets. Sometimes I feel like... a little... a little Gershwin. But not today. Today... I just think... yes, Rodgers and Hammerstein. Now I remember some of my students simply loved hearing my Rhapsody in Blue. Not everyone in Asia can attempt this piece, Stella! Know why?'

'Yes, you need large hands,' I repeated dully. I had lessons as a child but did not enjoy being rapped on the knuckles with a wooden ruler by my teacher. Mrs Alex Yang was Taiwanese American and my mother thought it was a good idea. It came from the chip on the shoulder standard Asian belief that anyone trained abroad was superior. **外国 的月亮比较圆**. *The foreign moon is rounder* , went the Chinese proverb. Alex Yang moved to Singapore with her US expat husband. She'd trained at the Juilliard and had a Noo Yoik accent. Listening to her was like being spat on. She'd told me that my syncopation was 'Shawwwking... your sense of rhyd'm... simply orrrrful...,' She made me hate Broadway, showchoons, the Great American Sawngbook, and all the things my mother seemed to crave, literally to tears.

I opened her locker, or as she'd like to call it, her *armoire à mystère* and retrieved the heavy metal filing box which I recalled from when she moved in. I rifled through manila folder after folder of sheets. Some were in order and some weren't. Others were yellowed, torn or missing. It was not going to be a quick job to catalogue all this.

The metal box had A to Z divisions including Madam Lee's personal documents and bank stuff mixed up with sheet music. She had moved to Dover Heights in a hurry. Nothing under C for Carousel, or M for musicals. There were a mass of other unclassified or untitled sheet music. I went to R for Rodgers and H for Hammerstein. No luck.

Then I saw it. Under the subdivision for H, the tab folder had been labelled. The branch name was HSBC Claymore Hill. *That* was where I'd seen Claymore Hill. But the documents were missing. There was nothing in the compartment. I knew she had a HSBC Premier account as that was how her bills here were paid.

I kept looking for "You'll Never Walk Alone".

Under the S section, there was an unlabelled creased, slim card envelope. I looked at it curiously. If it had once been one of those 'Please Do Not Bend' envelopes, clearly it was no longer one. It had rounded, ripped corners and was soft from age. There was a small imprint on the back at the top right hand corner of the letter S. It had been marked in a fat soft pencil, and, now faded, was not very legible.

On the back, the envelope had the string ties which was wound multiple times in the figure 8 pattern to keep it shut. I unwound the string that shut the folder. Paper and some pictures fell out.

'Stella? I am waiting. STELLA! Come now. Could you bring the whole box file? Stella, are you listening? Haiyah! You are taking far too long. You have no idea how to look for anything,' Madam Lee started to complain, her croaky voice turning shrill. I shoved all the pictures and paper back in the envelope. My back was turned to her but I could hear the impatient squeak of her wheelchair at the end of the room.

'You don't know any music,' she huffed dismissively. 'Let *me* look. *I* am the musician. Come on lah. The hell is taking you SO long? I am in the mood for a soirée.'

She whined. I did not have time to rewind the string. I would do it later. Instead of replacing it in the metal box, I put the envelope on another shelf with the towels and made a mental note to retrieve it later.

Benjamin did not turn up. He must be busy. It was almost 12 noon and Madam Lee had had to have lunch in the cafeteria. She didn't seem bothered as she claimed not to 'like roast duck that much'. When she mentioned 'roast duck', I asked her where Benjamin was planning on taking her to lunch. It surprised me that she remembered. 'Goodwood Park Hotel,' she said.

When Madam Lee was having her lunch in the cafeteria

and her catch-up with the other residents, I took the opportunity to report the loss of the documents to HSBC. It was a very efficient and quick call.

It was spa afternoon and already 4pm. Benjamin was definitely *not* coming. I finished getting ready Madam Lee for her facial and mixed her *masque* into a paste. The French spelling made it more exotic than it was. Organic serums, oils, sprays and exclusive Korean labels no one had heard of. The amount she spent on her "skincare routine" was more than my food budget.

'I'm sorry to interrupt, but two people are here to see you?' said the Filipina office manager Luisa.

It was like a question.

'Oh?' I said. 'Me?'

'Yes,' said Luisa.

'But who?'

Two uniformed police officers waited in the corridor beyond the glass doors.

30
STELLA

'Thank you for alerting us about this "Benjamin Lee",' said one of the uniformed police officers, showing me his badge. 'Detective Inspector Ismail Ariffin,' he held out his hand. 'Pleased to meet you. This is our fraud squad Investigations Officer, Halizah Awang.'

I beamed. I had saved the world from Benjamin's charms, or rather, claws.

'She had no nephew by that name, but if she did, I wouldn't know as the extended family is quite... extensive,' I said to Detective Inspector Ismail. 'But he'd insisted that he was her relative and had taken on a Christian name in addition to his original Chinese name.'

It was about as eye-rollingly unChristianly as he could get as a con artist. I omitted the fact that I didn't see many attractive men. I allowed his visits for a few months, always watchful. At first he was eye candy and I was curious about him. How foolish was I?

'I followed him outside the building. I just wanted to see what car he drove. He was taking buses and taxis! I knew then he had no car. And he put his lunch on Madam's account.'

Benjamin's status and reputation had plummeted since then, and it wasn't hard to work out what came next.

'We had a call from HSBC when he made an appointment today on Madam Lee's behalf,' IO Halizah said. 'Then you called this afternoon too about the missing documents. We put two and two together. We've been trying to crack down on these scammers who con the wealthy elderly.'

I nodded. 'He was due to visit today to take her on an outing but he failed to turn up so I thought you know what? He was busy with something else. Had my patient not mentioned that he was taking her to Claymore Hill followed by roast duck lunch at the Goodwood Park Hotel, I would *not* have realised he was trying to con her. She has an HSBC Premier account at Claymore Hill.'

'How is Madam Lee's memory given her condition?' Asked IO Halizah.

'She has good and bad days,' I grinned kindly, as I gave the usual expected response.

That evening, I carried the mysterious unlabelled folder with black ties home on the bus. I was impatient with the uncle at the Ocean Curry Fish Head stall in Block 128 on Bedok North Street 2. I almost swore at him. The queue was long and I decided to forgo buying dinner from him. Instead I went to the fruit stall and bought a bag of cut fruit. Pineapple, oranges, melons. I just wanted to get back to my flat. Fast.

. . .

I pulled the ties open, read the entire folder and looked at the pictures. I had lost my appetite. I could not eat. The lurid fruit colours did nothing for me.

I was shaking.

I wept all night. The pillowcase was soaked and I chewed the corners like a dog. I wanted to write it all down, but I couldn't articulate it.

My confusion. My anger.

Friday morning was Madam Lee's physiotherapy and art therapy session. Two things a day usually knocked her out for her afternoon nap. It was really very good that she was still doing all of it at her age. Really good for *her*, not for me.

With puffy eyes and face, I managed some Estée Lauder Stay-in-Place foundation and a deep red lipstick. That always threw off every other flaw. It was a distractingly garish colour I knew she would disapprove of but her approval wasn't something I was seeking that morning. I dressed and went to work as normal, whatever *normal* meant nowadays.

'Good morning Madam... Lee...,' I slurred, my voice mechanical and husky from sobbing. I was still trying to project a professional tone but I sounded like an old hinge. 'Want to talk to you about something.'

'What, goose?'

I winced. I placed the folder with ties in front of her.

Her eyes widened.

'Is everything OK? Irene is here,' Rachel, the part-time receptionist came through the glass doors. 'What's going on?'

'Don't,' Madam Lee held her hands in front of her, as

though protecting herself. 'Please don't.' She shook her head and avoided looking at the folder. 'She will hurt me. Help me. Please,' she said to Rachel.

'She won't hurt you,' Rachel replied drily, glancing at me, her eyes full of questions, then at the folder.

'It's time for your physio, Madam Lee,' she announced. Rachel, then turned to me and said in a concerned low voice, 'Are you feeling well? You look a little... under the weather.'

'I'm fine. Just hormonal, I guess.'

'I know what it's like,' Rachel muttered and nodded briskly in solidarity. 'Hope you feel better.'

Madam Lee's has her two hour "therapy" when I was the one requiring it. My entire neck ached from a night of heaving tears I had not shed for decades. All she did was relax and enjoy her last days on the planet. She yelled at and criticised me all day, and then said *please don't hurt me*.

'You were about to give your money to the conman,' I whispered to her, after her late afternoon nap. This was a time when we would be undisturbed. There would be no appointment or receptionist barging in.

Her eyes popped open.

'I'd rather him than you,' she replied, surprising me. I pressed my fingers on my protection mask to quell my huge gasp.

'You bitch,' I hissed.

'You can't call me that,' she snarled in a low tone. 'Show some respect.'

'You knew all this time. You made me give up my baby in the UK—,' I choked on the words. They were like stones dropped into my throat. 'The doctor and you were in it together.'

'Trudie was my friend! I did it for your own good. I'm very sorry, you were only a young girl then. You didn't want to ruin your life, did you? You were studying nursing. You wouldn't have qualified. You wouldn't be here with a good job.'

'I. Have. A. Shit. Job.'

'Don't you dare. Don't. You. Dare,' she waved a bony finger at me and narrowed her eyes. 'I gave my life to sending you to the UK for your education. I stopped performing and I taught in Yamaha music school 6 days a week. Your father couldn't hold down a job. You have no right to talk to me like this. No right.' Her voice cracked at 'Yamaha'.

After all these years, I was afraid of her. I cowered, frowned, as miserable as I was when I was child being admonished.

'The only reason why you are here is that they don't know who you are,' she grimly announced.

'I *asked* to be your main nurse. I *asked* to care for you.'

'You don't care for anyone,' she said, now turning to look at me with the curiosity and petulance of a child, her wrinkled mouth trying a pout. I could not tell if she really knew who I was or perhaps vaguely recognised me as if in a dream.

I wanted to hit her.

'You put me in here,' she whined.

'We had to sell the house to give you this lifestyle.'

'But why are you here?' she bleated. 'Who are you?'

'I am tired of your games. I am here because I am a nurse. I live in a concrete crate so I can turn up every day.'

'You're the worst nurse. My servant Ah Go was more

caring. You can't lift a finger. Never have. What about that driver? Ah.. Ah what? Ah something. Oh yes. Ah Soon. From Penang. He was far more useful than you'd ever be. He carried me in and out of the house, and then the wheelchair and my bags.'

He did more than carry her. I wanted to throw up.

I looked at her, shaking. She had the power to make me wobble and quake.

'Where is my Louis Vuitton clamshell bag? Where are my jade earrings from California?'

I reached for a tissue in my apron pocket, dabbed my eyes carefully so as not to cause wrinkles, turning my head this way and that to absorb the tears at the ducts before they fell out.

'Why did you put me in here?' She moaned.

'Because. Dad. Died,' I reminded her.

'I am going to call the staff,' she clasped her fingers on the remote with the panic button. I yanked it away.

'I am your daughter. The one you hated so much. You never wanted me.'

'No one will believe you,' she cackled.

'And you can forget about Benjamin too. You're right. You have no nephew with that name. I've turned him in to the cops.'

'What? Who's Benjamin?'

Benjamin, with his Gucci cufflinks. Benjamin with the leather Zegna loafers. He was a loafer all right. 'He was going to take you out on an outing today. To your bank, of course. He visits old people to find his next victim. You have no idea. I protected you.'

'But when? When did he come? Why did you let him visit?'

'Because you don't get any visitors!' A hollow laugh erupts from my throat.

'And you let him play me?'

'Figured you might like some company,' I chuckled absent-mindedly, remembering Benjamin's predecessor, the dashing university-educated Henry, claiming to be a "nephew" once removed. I enjoyed Henry's company more than Benjamin's. He worked in the aviation industry. Aviation, my ass.

'We both could do with it. You might remember Henry? He's gone too, *Mother*.' There was definitely no candy in Dover Heights, nevermind eye candy. 'I saved you and I never got any thanks. After all I've done for you!' I repeated the exact words that she used to say to me throughout my childhood.

My mother clutched at her throat, breathing shallowly. Her eyes bulged like lanterns. I was dry-eyed now. I've shed my tears and dabbed them away. I was done. I did not want to say any of it, yet I did; it was like a river, words that I hated and hurt her flowed and the current was strong.

31

STELLA

Every Singaporean had some interest in working abroad at some point. There was something enticing about escaping the blinding heat, rat race, the concrete crates, block numbers and rigid rules of the nanny state. If you didn't need to see family, or the sun every day, the dark, wintry and grim climate in the UK welcomed you and the chance to bank the money.

I waited for the email from Richie Ho to come, before I could put in my notice. The elastic time gave me a chance to learn Hakka cooking from not cooking anything at all. There were no shortage of qualified nurses who wanted a live-in job in London. But from Singapore and who cooked Hakka food? That was me.

Takeaways paired with ibuprofen and cut fruit was my diet. I was on my feet all day. They were swollen and red. My ugly and ill-fitting shoes which were part of my uniform and my back hurt from bending and lifting.

A job abroad paying in a foreign currency would at least be a decent change of scenery (not to mention free food, uniform and lodging). The high income would be handy for my mother's high expenses. All the additional "lovely things" she enjoyed did not come free. Art therapy, physiotherapy, hydrotherapy. Ayurvedic treatments. Injections. Geriatric shiatsu massage. Even a live piano player to entertain her every once in a while with the show tunes and broadway hits from her youth.

My manager Luisa resented giving me a reference on the account that I had on occasion been surly with the patients. By those she'd meant Madam Lee only. As far as the management knew, we were not related. Even if we were, I was perfectly qualified for the position, was I not?

If only my manager knew what a pain my mother had been throughout my life. I remember standing in the rain as a child while she played mahjong because I did not come in from playing in the street when she had called me to dinner. I had run off to catch the ice cream van but there had been a long queue.

When I got back to the house, I blinked and stared through the iron filigree gates, at her and her so-called friends, heads bent like crows in their silk frilly tops sitting at a table for 4. I called and called my mother. She stayed with her eyes fixed, ignoring me. Her red manicured fingers were too busy to stop. When the storm began, I heard the tiles clacking on the table and counted the minutes to when the game ended.

'That is what happens when you don't come right away. You don't run off and do something else when I call you.'

Ah Go, the servant, wrung her hands in the kitchen when I crept in there. I was handed a bowl of rice. She put her arms around me even though I was drenched. She stank of garlic and sweat and her heat overwhelmed me. I did not want her to hug me yet I did not want her to stop. While I sat down and wolfed down my dinner (and I did not remember what it was), she got me a towel and put it around me like a cape. I felt like a queen.

Later in my nursing student days in London, I partied hard and built my own network of a new life, new people, the silo of local friends and immigrants like myself. I missed my father and Ah Go, her large sad eyes. Like many of the working class in Singapore, she came from Johor. This was a time when there were fewer hired help from Indonesia, the Philippines, Cambodia or Myanmar. She was the goose that I resembled, which was why my mother sometimes mistook me for her.

I dreamt of escaping my mother as I thought surely this was the time. The moment I completed my course I would stay on in the UK and get a job in any of the local hospitals. How hard would it be? I had not only a UK qualification but a London one!

I joined the Singaporean and Malaysian student societies. I got part-time jobs in the hospitality industry. Cleaning, gardening, babysitting. That was when my troubles began.

I held in my hand the folder. Only Ah Go was pleased to see me when I came back from the UK. My parents were deeply ashamed. My father had always been weak. He had middle-class aspirations, hence the house with a koi pond in Katong. It had since been demolished and a monstrosity of an apartment block with underground carparks was where it stood. Sometimes I thought about the koi. As a teenager, I took to looking after them with an amusing seriousness. Other girls were into boys and bands with perms. I became very fond of the koi, and hopefully they, of me.

I gave them all names. Kenji, Kazuo and Kimura. Just like the Kardashians. Later on, the girls joined. Aya, Sumi, Yoko. It was a peaceful time.

When I reminded my manager that I looked after the koi ponds, the habitats (and let's just say it was Zen-like in its backbreaking and character-building nature), she turned red. I cut patients' hair and taught them dancing. I organised movie nights. I did not add that I was only doing all these activities as they were what Madam Lee couldn't stand, so in that way I had managed to avoid my mother.

London, I'd missed you. This was the moment!

PART THREE

32
ELIJAH

Monday 2nd January

When Elijah wakes up, it's so bright and noisy that he knows he's not at home. The bed is high. He's been to a hospital far too many times. Wait, is she here? *Mum?* he whispers. His hands feel around but he's encumbered and restrained by these tubes that connect him to a drip stand and a monitor. Oh no. He *is* in a hospital. From the inside of a van into a ward. How is he here? Someone must have called the ambulance or taken him in a taxi. He has no recollection.

A nurse comes in to take his blood pressure, wheeling in the machine on a trolley.

'I want to go home.' Those five words are all he can manage.

'You have to ask da doctor,' she says in a Nigerian accent. 'You've had a head and neck injury and you've been asleep for days. Do you remember what happened?'

'I fell. Then I... I woke up... in a van.'

'A van?'

'I... I legged it. I opened the van door and I guess I fell.'

'Why were you in a van?' She asks. Her eyes speak more than her voice.

'Jeez. I don't know.'

The nurse seems sympathetic and intelligent. Well, more than him, which is not hard. He's been thick as a wall all his life and all the more now. No wonder he never got anywhere with school or jobs. She nods, like she can read his thoughts.

'What's your name? Do you know?'

'Elijah.'

'Glad you remember! Dat's a very nice name. Unusual nowadays. It means *Jehovah is my God*. Are you a Christian?'

His mum is, he wants to say. And so is the nurse, apparently. Immediately he regrets telling her his name. The fuck has he done that? It's slipped out. She is either curious or plain nosey. What's it to her? He turns a deep red and his head burns, not just with the pain of the injuries but with shame.

He wants to go hom. His clothes are somewhere. In a locker, he imagines. He is wearing a gown and that is the least gown-like garment. It is basically a thin narrow backless dress that's held together by string ties, leaving your front and your back, bum and legs completely exposed.

He gets up the moment she goes. He knows what the NHS is like. They could be gone for minutes, or hours. Before she could get back he would have a look for his clothes.

The sight of the boots brings it back. Couldn't believe he'd stuffed his feet into them. He was very high and probably delusional. They're a size too small. He wants to sell them, by wearing them that night and discarding his own £6.99 trainers from ShoeZone.

He hears his mother's voice saying, *Zai, Shoezone good. Cheap. Last long.* She calls him *Ah Zai* or *Zai*, terms of endearment for *son*.

He is determined not to end up like her. Constrained in a hospital bed, getting institutionalised and sicker and sicker. Now is not the time to have tubes, lines in and out stuck into him like he is an amplifier or mixing desk. He's got to to get out. There's nothing wrong with him. His mother was unvaccinated and so is he. She was only 58. Did they manage to save her? No.

The nurse says she'd go and get his clothes. When she comes back, he gets dressed and lies there looking around at the light green room for a few seconds. He wanders around the ward feeling a little disoriented and light-headed. That'll go, for sure. He notices then that he's wearing the wrong clothes. They're someone else's! No matter; he just needs food. He spies four slices of someone's uneaten bread off a trolley of dishes. They'll do. No one bats an eyelid or even sees him. They're just too busy. Under-staffed and underfunded. Elijah yanks out the tubes and marches out of Royal London Hospital and to the market opposite.

He enjoyed the shopping trips up and down Whitechapel Road looking for bargains with his mother when he was little. The stalls, the sheer variety and colours of vegetables, leggings, plastic sandals and ski pants filled them with inspiration and the buzz of a tight crowd. He'd grown up here. She used to bring home toys, battery-operated furry dogs which barked and had lights for eyes, trucks which had real doors that opened and a tipping tray that tipped.

No toys for him now. He has no money; his card, keys have gone. He has been mugged between the van and the hospital.

Elijah trudges back to his ex-local authority rented 2-bedroom flat in Bullen House, on autopilot. It's dusk and he jostles with commuters and the market stallholders packing up. He moves unsteadily but he knows where he is. By the time he reaches Brady Street, he is limping from the boots. The dusty, acrid traffic fumes make him feel worse. He's got that floating, nauseous feeling when he crosses Merceron Street. A few more minutes, and then he can collapse. The only bad thing is losing the Barclays Card. His neighbour has his spare key so he's all right there.

It's night when he's threaded through the rabbit warren of the estate, knowing it so well he gains pace and momen-tum. The pungent aromas of the tadka dhal floated around him in wafts, smoky corridors, concrete tunnels covered in sprayed-on tagging and the stench of ammonia. Underpaths, urine and graffiti go together like the holy trinity. He is starv-ing. What's even in his fridge? He has not eaten anything but the four stolen white slices and hospital nuggets (three in total on a big white plate like it's some fucking posh restau-rant). Appalling food but beggars could not be complainants. His mother would have concurred. No longer light-headed, he approaches his block with increased optimism.

First he calls on his Bangladeshi neighbour, Nafisah. She lets him in. She is a mum of 4 children under the age of 16.

'Elijah? What's happened?'

'Awful, Naf. Been rolled,' he shakes his head. He doesn't need to say much. He already has her sympathy. His mother was a good friend and neighbour to Nafisah, always stepping in if she needed urgent babysitting. By extension, Nafisah has always looked out for him since the loss of his mother.

'Man. They. Took. Everything. My phone, my card, my keys.'

'You look terrible.'

'Don't feel great, to be honest. Just come back from the 'ospi'al, innit,' Elijah explains.

'Oh no! Please come in. Have something to eat; are you hungry? Or do you want a drink?'

Elijah wants to weep. Yes, he is starving, and yes, he is thirsty. The kindness is killing him. He can't speak but he steps into her tidy home. Toys are stacked against a corner of the cramped room in see-through plastic storage crates, and two of her children are on the sofa gaming.

Nafisah has helped with food and little things like gifts for him during his mother's last days. She's had their spare key since his mother and he had been working in the laundry room of the hotel, in case of emergency.

He looks around the room, at the heavily patterned rugs, gold and black embroidered Islamic inscriptions on the walls and a sewing machine set up on a side table. He takes the Hanwags off and Nafisah glances at them with curiosity. He places them neatly on the doormat and nearly keels over from his exhaustion and pain.

'Did you call the cops?' Asks Nafisah immediately as she sets the table for one.

'You havin' a laugh,' Elijah cackles, tossing his head. 'The cops they don't do nuffin'.'

She gives him a delicious Bengali meal of masoor dahl

and chapatti. She makes him a cup of PG Tips tea with sugar. He dreads asking her for anything more than his spare key. But she already offers to lend him a phone that is her husband's old phone, until he has one. 'Nothing fancy; hope you don't mind,' she says. 'I doubt it can even have apps. Might be an iPhone 5 or 6. He's still out at work, so I can't check with him.' She calls and adds £5 credit. 'Pay me back when you are sorted.'

He almost drops onto his knees. With his phone and his spare key, he limps down the corridor in his Hanwags.

Once inside the flat, Elijah inhales the familiar cheesy scent of stale bedding and rotten pizzas. His mother had been fastidious. The flat used to only smell of Chinese food layered upon detergent, wood polish and incense. It is furnished with various items he'd stolen from the hotels. Just a few. No need to be greedy. Sheets, towels, bath mats, toiletries, slippers. Four white plates, bowls and cutlery sets. Nothing that would raise alarm. He's never taken a TV or an armchair for example. His mum didn't mind. In fact, she'd always taught him to make do with the minimum, and stealing from rich establishments wasn't wrong. They'd never miss it and most importantly, they do *not* need any of this stuff. The guests steal too. And god knows, those kinds of guests definitely don't need any of this stuff. If they can afford the rates, they can afford a bathrobe. Elijah doesn't steal from the poor or needy. He'd be happy to help them. He'd gladly give Nafisah lovely gifts if he has any spare change at all.

There's a comfy luxury leather chair in his flat he and his mother took turns sitting in. It's Herman Miller. That's not stolen. It was a bit broken and his mother fixed it. The management said she could take it home. No guest would want to sit in a once broken chair albeit a designer one.

Everything, especially the sight of that armchair, reminds him of his mum. Her bed is still made up from her last day, untouched, her alarm clock ticks on, the pink fluffy slippers on the floor like she's about to step into them anytime. Even the free Waitrose food and drink magazine she'd been reading (now seven months old), lies next to the clock, open like a bird's wings.

He sleeps on the sofa, next to his "desk" where he is supposed to be looking for work. There's a stack of papers: bills, letters from the local authority about the works being done to the building, notification about the roadworks from Thames Water. He spots letters to oppose some greedy commercial development a block away to demolish and redevelop artisanal industrial works into yet another enormous glittery block. He doesn't even read them. Elijah plans to store the pile for a year before he throws them away into the gigantic purple Tower Hamlets recycling bins.

He takes the phone out and calls the number he knows by heart. It's ringing.

'Barry speaking,' says the voice on the other end, in a clipped and uncertain formal tone due to not recognising Elijah's new number.

'Dad,' he bleats. 'It's me.'

33
SAHIL

Sahil helps Marcus with the van cleaning over the whole long weekend. Everywhere is shut. He drives it to the valet to get it shampooed as a final touch. Sahil wants to do it alone, but relents as they have to be at the new job the next day, and it is quicker if they do it together. Marcus's tools are meticulously stored and he wants things just so. Sahil's had to use the incognito search mode again to find how to remove DNA evidence.

The day after they cleaned the van, Sahil cut the credit card into pieces, took it to Dalston and threw it into a bin in a municipal dog park, along with the phone.

He never hugged Marcus again. It was a horrendous mistake, like an exam in which you've failed but there's no re-sit. He does *not* want a repeat of that evening in the garage next to the van, the witness, the silent beast.

Everything is grey. Every day is now wrong. He endures the bloated ache that would not go away. The awkwardness makes him want to throw up and move out but realistically, he's not going to find anything affordable, or available, and also he doesn't have the time. January is a really important month in the semester. His parents are already freaking out about the £3,000 graduate visa they are forking out for him.

His father: *Find a real job, Sahil. None of this building work lark. Bhagavaan ke lie!*

His mother: *We sent you to England to become a labourer, kya aisa hai? Why are you wasting your life doing construction?*

Nevertheless, because of the £3000 that they keep harping on about, he finds himself agreeing to doing up an office in Clerkenwell. Marcus will pay him almost a thousand. That's pretty good, by any standards. Marcus's work is top class.

Plus the site is not too far from their Bethnal Green flat. *Their.* He kicks himself. He considers it his home too, even if it is Marcus's.

The first sighting of the office space brings sighs of relief... the space, the gigantic French windows. It's a different league to the poky basement 1980s offices or rabbit warren purpose-built interwar commercial units. It will be turned from an HR agency office into shared workspaces. Apparently that's where the money is.

Sahil's first task is to lay protection sheets in the whole floor area and the furniture. After they've moved all the building rubbish into the council skips outside, Marcus hands him a twenty pound note and Sahil is soon on his way to the tube station at Farringdon to get lunch and coffee at Prêt when he picks up the Metro.

His hand starts shaking. The queues to pay are long and

he obediently joins a random queue while he reads the right hand column.

Unidentified man found in East London with head trauma receives treatment at Whitechapel Hospital

His picture has been shared across social media but he has yet to be identified. The patient, a man of East or South East Asian appearance suspected to be in his late-20s to early-30s, was found 6 days ago in the neighbourhood of Buckhurst Street in the residential block between CrossFit Gym and St Bartholomew Gardens in Bethnal Green.

He was found wearing a black puffer jacket, grey tracksuit bottoms and Hanwag work boots.

He suffered a traumatic brain injury, leaving him unconscious. He was intubated and sedated at Royal London Hospital.

A photograph of the victim has been released by the hospital has been viewed by over 7,600 people on X.

Authorities have revealed that the unknown man is 6-feet-2-inches tall and weighs approximately 192 pounds. He has an East Ham tattoo on his calf and a Chinese character on his left forearm. It is unclear how exactly he sustained his intense injuries.

Upon gaining consciousness, the man has been seen on CCTV footage to walk out of the Royal London. Officials fear for his safety. Since he left, many have taken to social media and asked for others to share the man's photo and description to help find him, his family and friends. Officials continue to plead for help in finding and identifying the victim.

'*Behandchod*,' Sahil swears under his breath as the queue

advances. It gets to his turn. He folds the paper into a tight wad. He pays and waits for his change, unable to focus on what the total amount is. The change is only a few coins. Sahil's gobsmacked each time he receives any change at all. How can anyone live in this city? Sandwiches for two with drinks is about 20 pounds now. Not for a restaurant or cooked meal. It literally is just takeaway sandwiches.

The girl hands him the white paper bag, with the inimitable maroon star logo, containing a Bhaji Melt Toastie for him, an Italian-style Chicken and Basil Hot Wrap for Marcus, and their two large cappuccinos, no sugar.

He tucks the metro into the white paper bag and hurries back to the site.

Sooner or later they will find the CCTV footage. Why wouldn't they? The public part of the alleyway is bound to be amped up with cameras, despite Marcus's reassurances. Marcus cannot possibly control every CCTV on the street, only those in and outside their building. Sahil knows there are no cameras in a private alleyway backing onto residential properties. Flytippers come weekly to dump rubbish and nobody finds nor fines them.

Sahil's mind spins with the possibilities. His throat dries as he blinks and re-reads the information.

Marcus stops and takes off his gloves and goggles. They sit down on oak floor planks which have just been delivered and tightly wrapped in plastic sheeting. Marcus stares at the bag and waits to be handed his sandwich like a boy. Sahil distributes and they eat in silence. He wonders when he should bring it up. Should Marcus enjoy his lunch first?

No, he decides. 'Look,' Sahil starts. He removes the

tightly-folded Metro from the bag and throws it on the protection sheets in front of where they sit.

They eat in silence, and Marcus reads the article. Sahil re-reads along with him. Like twins, they are preoccupied in their own thoughts until Sahil suddenly speaks. 'The good news is that the thug would not be coming back anytime soon since he's laid out.'

Marcus snatches the Metro from the floor to get a closer look. 'Oh fuck. He is alive.'

'That's good, right? It means I didn't kill him!' Sahil says hesitantly with a frown. Every time these words are uttered, he becomes less and less sure himself. It has been a case of good and not good since the "incident".

'No!' Explodes Marcus like a hand grenade, jerking his head towards Sahil. 'He'll be back!'

'Why?' Sahil shouts. 'He won't. *Intubated* means nothing. He might still die.'

Marcus does not answer. Sahil bites his lip. Marcus chews noisily and it grates on Sahil.

'Why did you have to wear the Rolls Royce of work boots?' Sahil blurts out. 'Couldn't you have chosen anything from Screwfix?'

'The boots are the least of my worries,' Marcus quietly answers. 'I told you before. They are from my last job. I did not have to pay for them.'

The fucking boots.

'Have you seen the state of my clothes?' Marcus continues in a kind of Asian rhetoric, gesturing to himself using his free hand, from shoulder to knees. 'I think I could live on the boots for a month.'

'Why didn't you? Why didn't you sell them?' Demands Sahil.

'Why sell them? Why not wear them and actually get more work? Look more professional. Look. I am the business. I have been in construction for almost 20 years. I want to get the higher class of customers.'

'And they look at your fucking boots?' Sahil snorts derisively.

'They do.'

The conversation ends as abruptly as it starts. Sahil looks sideways at Marcus. How old is Marcus? He would guess mid-thirties? It is hard to tell from the receding hairline. Is Marcus so vain that he'd wear the Hanwags to work just because they are free?

Marcus crushes his Hot Wrap wrapper into a ball and hurls it into the white bag. 'Time to get back to work,' he announces. 'The heating engineers will be here in a minute to take measurements.'

Sahil follows suit. He gets up, sipping his coffee from the slot of the takeaway lid of the carton, discarding the other rubbish into the bag containing the Metro.

When they get back to Corfield Street and have parked in the lock-up garages around the corner, they each throw a cursory automatic glance again at the space, the ceiling, the van, the floor, in case they had missed anything during the cleaning. He is not sure what, but they can't help looking.

They walk in an uneasy silence to the front of the building. There is a police car waiting.

34
ELIJAH

'I need a new card. Sorry about this,' Elijah gasps into his borrowed iPhone. How he hates grovelling, begging, apologising. He feels a tightness in his throat, and his hand presses down on his chest to steady his breathing. 'Please help me. I have no way of paying for anything or getting around.'

There's a pause.

'You're supposed to be looking for work,' says Barry. His tone starts off terse but softens when he gets to the word *work*.

'I *am* looking for work. Wot'dju expect me to do? Stay in? Please, dad. I have had to borrow Naf's phone to call ya.'

He doesn't know where his father lives. If he did, he would've gone to see him in person a long time ago. A horrible itch of panic crawls over him and he slaps himself on the back of his neck.

Slaphead, they'd laughed at him at work, feeding those stupid sheets into machines, in sauna-hot rooms filled with steam that burned his nostrils and made his eyes stream. Fucking robots are welcome to his job. He can't wait for the day when machines take over machines which take over humans taking over machines.

'I put money on your card so you can live,' Barry splutters. 'I am not paying your rent too!'

His dad nags him all the time to find work but he has no idea that Elijah has had no luck, and is starting to despair. He's on every agency's books now. Every time Elijah takes the card out to pay, he's reminded of his father's name, of who owns him. He won't let his father have the satisfaction! He must find alternative income OR work or both.

His father must have been very guilty. Elijah couldn't work when his head was messed up by his mum's illness and then passing. It was during then that his father sent him a Barclays Card that he had put money on, so that Elijah could make withdrawals and use it to pay for stuff. It was not much in there, usually a float of about five hundred pounds a month. It was certainly more than enough to live on and to buy the odd treat like a pub meal and basic needs like food shopping, phone top-ups and bills. Elijah considers himself the lucky unlucky. It is more than universal credit.

His adoptive parents were a childless couple, Barry O'Keefe and Irene Chan. Elijah looks like his mum, so people had assumed he was hers. Barry really was the best dad. Elijah remembers West Ham matches, hotdogs from the stand at inflated prices (said his mum) and trips to the local shopping centre, Victoria Park on weekends and Hamley's in Regent Street every Christmas.

It was a really big deal for his mother who had come from Hong Kong to marry Barry O'Keefe, a security guard of

Irish descent. He was not surprised that his dad was so taken with this laundry woman. Irene Chan was tall and slim with crystal cut cheekbones. She wore her hair straight and thick, Kabuki-style, with her black eyeliner when everyone else had perms and blue frost eyeshadow as it was the 80s. He worked in the club opposite the hotel where his mother was employed. He is a *gwailo*, white man, devil bloke. She had risked her family's disapproval by not marrying a Chinese man. They cut off all ties with her.

Elijah knows his father left his mum and him for another woman. It has to be. It was very sudden. He hates that woman, whoever she is. He's heard his mother weep enough late at night. At some point during his primary school years, Elijah's dad never came back after popping out to get fags, bread and milk. The fags, bread and milk did not arrive either. His mother had a call shortly after. She hung up without saying goodbye. Her eyes looked dead. *Zai, it's just you and I now*, she'd said. Did his father die? Why wouldn't she talk about him? She clamped up and went all glassy-faced whenever he asked where his father was. Why, where, he kept asking but eventually he gave up and the appearance of his father also faded from memory. Photos of his parents and them as a family in black IKEA frames were removed from their mantelpiece over the fake oak fireplace and pine alcove shelving.

'I am not asking for rent money,' he adds. 'I am still paying that from mum's and my savings. It's going down, Dad.'

Grim, but the grovelling works. After his father has hung up, he takes some painkillers. He can relax now, or try to, for the next couple of days. He has plenty to do. Once he has the new card he will be able to buy a phone, cut a new key and start again.

The bastards! At first Elijah thought Marcus was the ring leader but could easily must be the other one, Hairy Spectacles, the one who duffed him up. Elijah can find out just like that.

35
MARCUS

'Hi! May I help you?' Marcus addresses the two uniformed policemen who are heading out of the car.

His voice sounds falsely courteous and his fake little smile drops as suddenly as it appears. He's trying to look completely blank.

'I am DI Beauchêne-Gill and this is DC Holden,' says the male officer, flashing his identification. He is oddly paternal in the way his forehead is creased when he talks and his earnest eyes widen, though not like Marcus's father's. He imagines that the DI has adult children. 'May we have a word?'

'About what?'

'Please could we get inside the building first?' The DI replies, not smiling.

Marcus swallows. He has no choice. They ascend the three steps up, where he had tripped and knocked his teeth. Each step is closer to closure, or rather, disclosure. His trembling hands unlock the ominous timber and glass front double doors of the flat block and then lead the officers through the dim Victorian hallway to the front door of his raised ground floor flat.

Sahil follows them like a ghost.

'Who are you?' The DI stops and turns around to ask Sahil. Everyone stops. Sahil's voice shakes as he replies that he is Marcus's flatmate. DI Beauchêne-Gill addresses the female cop. 'Jenny, please could you talk to Sahil in the kitchen or something?'

When he says *or something*, Marcus knows there is no escape. Sahil will have to get the story right, and what story is it? Marcus can barely put the bits together. Not to mention the fact that he was indeed unconscious for some of that evening. What the hell is Sahil going to tell DC Holden?

'Please come in,' Marcus announces robotically as they all stand awkwardly in the dim light of the flat. Marcus snaps on the light, briefly satisfied by the loud click of the cheap switch plates. They all want to enter the flat together but the narrowness of the entrance forces them to go in single file. Marcus's throat is tight and his hand flies to his forehead, rubbing it slowly.

'Are you all right?' DI Beauchêne-Gill asks.

In Marcus's head, he is preparing what to say about that evening, in blow by blow detail. He has the broken glasses still, in his bedside drawer. Everything would be OK. Sahil would not be implicated unless he wants to. DC Holden asks Sahil to wait in his room while they talk to Marcus.

'I'm fine. Just knocked out from work.'

'I totally understand,' says the DI nodding. 'This won't

take long. Your wallet. It's been found.' He takes out of his pocket a small brown envelope. 'You might like to check.'

'Oh,' blows out Marcus. 'That's... that's great. I was wondering where it was...er... where was it found?'

'You haven't reported it missing.'

'No,' Marcus says. 'I didn't know it was missing,' he lies.Who found it?'

'We don't know. So you were not at the Novello?

'What? What's the Novello?'

'The West End theatre?' The DI looks more incredulous with each reply from Marcus.

'I've never been to a show since... since never. I can't stand theatre.'

'You didn't watch Mamma Mia last night?'

'Absolutely not. That's just absurd.'

'Why?'

'200 quid for a ticket and I don't like theatre. I don't understand it. Why was it there?'

'The box office staff found it and handed it in to us. From there we took over. I agree that *is* strange, and... you are sure you were not mugged? You look a bit... bruised. What happened to you?'

'OK,' cuts in Marcus, then apologetically, he adds, 'I know I look awful but I'm just knackered and I fell at work. Hope it wasn't too much of an inconvenience to you.'

'No, no, none at all,' the DI reassures, though with a frown. He does not look reassured at all. He knows something is up. 'Glad you got it back.'

'Thank you so much.'

'Goodnight,' says DI Beauchêne-Gill, not leaving for a few seconds.

When the door shuts, Marcus collapses and senses Sahil

peeking out of his door. He creeps out of his room when he's checked the officers had gone. 'What's going on?' He whispers.

'It's... it's not about the assault. They found my wallet. ' He crosses his arms and clutches his shoulders. 'Did you tell them anything?'

'No!' Explodes Sahil. 'Why would I?'

36
GENEVIEVE

Wednesday 4th January

It's the same dream that I've had twice when I lived in Singapore. Everything is in a sepia tinge, so it looks like a long time ago. I have glossy auburn curls stuck like snails to my head. I wear a tweed suit and leather brogues both much too tight. There is a polished wood-panelled wall with a timetable of train arrivals and departures and it's behind glass in a wooden frame screwed to the wall. I study it. It's 1948. Or at least, that's what the timetable says.

I carry too much luggage, someone else's, in garish colours, which I leave on the platform and remember later only to go back and find they have been moved onto the trolleys to the wrong departure lounge. There is much chaos while I try to retrieve these enormous and numerous pieces of luggage in Lego colours from the station master but I am unable to explain why I have them or need to have them back.

When the train comes, I rush onto the right carriage, my

eyes fixed on the tickets. I find my seat and smooth my tweed skirt to sit down. It's far too hot and constrictive. With horror, I see that I am wearing Stella's clothes.

My son has been left behind on the platform. I look up just in time to see through the windows that he is waving and calling out to me. I keep shouting his name, pounding on the glass, but it's too late. The train has pulled out... I cannot hear his words but his eyes look alarmed and then he is running alongside the train as it speeds up...

I wake up sweating and gasping for breath. I must have been shouting in the dream. It's a classic dark, drizzly morning in London. It's like we never went to Paris.

I will have to wear my late mother's clothes for the interview tomorrow. A new outfit will carve a big chunk of what's left on my card. I know it. Thank God Auntie Stella has not donated the contents of my mother's wardrobe. I just know that's next. She has not got around to it because they are out of sight, out of mind.

The house is too big and she is a bit busy with her ward — my father. When I was a child and tried on my mother's Jimmy Choo sandals, it was thrilling. Now it is morbid and upsetting. I know I will break down and cry buckets when I inhale the scent of her clothes and think of her. Life is long, grief is eternal.

My mother once said to me before she got very sick, 'Have no fear, your daddy will not remarry.' She'd laughed then. I didn't. Was that a joke? It sure didn't sound like one. But knowing my mum's twisted sense of humour... 'Do you know what ladies' man means, Gen? Men who *like* women don't remarry. What would be the point?'

My father doesn't like being alone. As a hotelier, he'd meet hundreds of guests a day. Some of the most powerful, attractive and wealthy people too.

For years my parents had slept in separate bedrooms due to the different time zones that they were operating in. My mother had to be at the hospital by 8 am whereas my father arrived at The Peony at 7 am in time for the hotel breakfast shift. He did not finish until 6 pm. His was an 11 hour day, and that was what he expected of everyone else too, including Stella. Hah.

My mother worked until she was too sick. She had wanted to die back home. She never saw her hometown, the historic Joo Chiat Road area in Singapore, ate a char kway teow at a local stall or shopped at Pearl Centre market again. These were on her last wish list.

Was it a myth, a rumour that spread in the silos, the vague unsustainable goal of *go big or go home*. Those who don't go home must have gone big, by elimination. But going big is going home for me. If all immigrants really dream of the final journey, the return with their pile, will they still belong, be welcomed, treated like royalty because they went to the UK and became successful? Or will the original country have far advanced and left them behind? They wouldn't even know anyone anymore. Everyone they once knew would have moved away or passed on. My mother did not have the choice. Looks like daddy would not either. Stella is his little piece of home, his last glimpse of Asia.

I wept at my mother's bedside, not wanting her to see me and my guilt. I flew in to see her but I was not in time. It bothers me that my father was "not very sad" when my mother left this world. Can one be "not very sad"? Yes, totally. My father shed not one tear. At some point, he may even have managed a weak secret smile, like it was a relief she was gone.

It's inset day. School starts tomorrow. This is his "last" day of the holidays and Jasper may not fully grasp it yet. He comes downstairs and asks my father to put the TV on while I get ready breakfast with Auntie Stella in the kitchen. We will be eating in the kitchen, adjacent to the conservatory windows just like we used to as a family, and not the dining room, which is for evenings, for dinner.

As I see what's on the table, it's like a Do's and Don'ts list of healthy eating. Jasper and I will being doing the Don'ts — processed food, and she and my dad will be eating the Do's — a nutritious, fresh, colourful breakfast.

I hear my son's small voice pipe up in the living room.

'What shows are on, Gung Gung? What can I watch?' I peer through the double-doors opening of the dining room to the living room at the front to get a closer look at them. They sit side by side on the sofa with a comfortable and chatty familiarity. The moment is so precious I am unable to tear myself away from watching them. The channels and their deafening noise hop in that irritating non-stop way.

'Those are food shows, monkey.'

'Boring!' Jasper chimes, waving the remote like the TV chef who has just pointed with his wooden spoon.

My dad chuckles at the mimicry and makes a pretend horrified expression with his jaw open and brows knitted. 'What do you watch back home?' My dad asks. Jasper mumbles *Disney Plus* with distant fondness.

'Ah. We don't have that,' says my dad, looking at him and

taking back the remote. 'You have to wait until you go back to Singapore.'

I hear his voice fade as I retreat into the kitchen to get spoons.

We sit and eat breakfast as a family, which we have never done in Singapore. My ex and I would either be lying in, exhausted, eye masks on and ear plugs in, dead to the world as Jasper eats alone in front of the TV the breakfast that Asun has prepared. Occasionally we wake up early and also eat in sequence because Jasper has to get to school and Asun takes him. Sometimes we would have left the condo already, especially if we were travelling for work, which we did often for sales fairs, conferences and trips to find retailers and distributors the neighbouring countries. Asun used to eat after us, in the kitchen. She would never eat at the same table and time, unlike Auntie Stella. Now we have a certain formality. My father and I can't talk about anything private or personal. I find it easier to be silent or to respond to their small talk.

Jasper watches *A Series of Unfortunate Events* on Netflix while Stella clears the table. Then she sets up her mats in the conservatory and calls my dad over to do stretches. My dad follows her like a child. I cannot bear to watch her teaching him tai chi moves like she's Michelle Yeoh. She looks up, suddenly aware that she's forgotten I am there.

'Jean-Viv. Would you like to join us?'

'No, thanks,' I give an over-zealous wave, as though I am saying goodbye on Zoom.

I watch him looking at her doing warm-up stretches. It

makes me blush to see her in the warrior pose, clenching those butt muscles.

Mum used to go for big walks with my dad. That was the extent of his exercise. Parsons Green, Putney Bridge, Bishops Park and all along the river when we had a shiba inu called Edamame, Ed for short. Daddy wouldn't do those walks again because he only liked the dog. He has no actual interest in walking per se.

His eyes are fixed on Auntie Stella. White crane. Single whip move. Snake creeps down, which is like an extended side squat lunge. I observe my dad shadowboxing and... grinning. She's pliable and supple, her skin glowing with middle-aged wisdom and the tropical sunshine that she's brought with her.

I walk upstairs, my feet heavy as two sand bags, to my mother's bedroom on the first floor. It faces the garden and is next to Alistair's. The room is dated, suburban yet relaxing on the eye. The colours have now paled from being south-facing and exposed to harsh sunlight. The wood panelling comes up to dado rail height and over which the walls are papered. The ceilings are yellowed and cracked, the paper peeling. When Stella gets hold of this room, she will turn it into another of her Ralph Lauren striped spa hotel fantasies with potted white hydrangeas.

She's not the only person in the house to have read Condé Nast Traveler. The room was decorated in the 2000s as my mother's combo bedroom, office and dressing room. It's been papered in a Colefax and Fowler Fleur-de-Lys pattern popular then. I remember John Lewis's Furnishings Department sending her samples. She was always sure this could be a spare bedroom for family visiting from Asia. Over the years, we had met cousins we never knew, aunts and uncles and family friends. Members of the extended family in Singapore and Malaysia had stayed.

The two large sash windows have blackout Roman blinds rather than curtains, in a gold and green fabric matching with the wallpaper. Interior decoration had been matchy-matchy then. The bed is stripped, with only a white sheet on it. I am glad the room had not been offered to me when I arrived. Her absence is like her presence, filling the entire grey sky over me.

I fling open my mother's wardrobe doors and bury my head inside. I squeeze my eyes shut in the darkness and denseness in the abundant folds of the hanging clothes. And I inhale my mother's scent.

I hear a rustling from the corridor, and an almost imperceptible footfall. Who's there? I call out. There's no answer. I've left the door open. I thought I had shut it. I turn and walk towards the door, sticking my head outside, left and right. No one is there.

37
GENEVIEVE

I wonder why Daddy has not cleared out my mother's overfilled wardrobe for four years. My poor mummy. I grabbed her cream bathrobe and I can still smell her scent, Chloe by Stella McCartney. It smells fresh and papery, like a new book, brimming with the freshness of ideas. I hold onto her bathrobe, my fingers digging into its thick softness and I fought back the tears. For an "old" person, she had been surprisingly modern. She enjoyed scent-layering. We used to give her "sets" at Christmas, 3-in-1 gifts we bought from Fenwicks which she cherished.

Retiring did not change her into a "retiree". My mother wore hoodies or jeans at home. She wasn't stiff and polished like a movie star on a yacht.

I place the bathrobe back.

I have made 3 possible combinations of outfits from my mother's wardrobe, based on those which look the most contemporary within reason. After all, my mother only bought good quality stuff from Kings Road boutiques or Peter Jones at Sloane Square. Surely the worst I would look is old. I hold a black L K Bennett trouser suit up by the hanger and look in her full length mirror mounted on the inside of the wardrobe doors. I choke back tears. I look just like her, especially now with my big Dior spectacles from Capitol Opticians in Ngee Ann City in Singapore. The huge glasses my mother used to wear are now back in fashion, or maybe they never really went away. It's free to wear glasses (since I already have them from long ago) and I don't have to spend a penny on buying disposable lenses anymore. Anyway I think I now really suit wearing glasses especially as I will be working in top restaurants. I may look like a train wreck, but with lipstick and eyeliner, I will appear groomed for my UK wine debut.

After I have laid them out on the bed to make sure that each one works, I replace the three outfits in the wardrobe. I move towards her desk to see if there is anything I can salvage such as her stationery, accessories, or bags.

'Mummy? Are you free?' Jasper calls out and I hear the thump of his feet running upstairs along the corridor to my mother's room. He bursts in. 'Whose room is this?' He looks around.

'It's Po Po's room,' I reply absent-mindedly. 婆婆 (Po Po) is dialect for maternal granny. It is just an old lady's room, in muted, faded colours. There is nothing to draw his attention.

Jasper will need his school kit and more winter clothes. He's wearing his maroon hoodie from Hong Kong Disneyland, one of two tourist hoodies he owns. The other is from Legoland Malaysia, and they are being alternated. I will do a wash today. I just want school to start so that he can wear his uniform and we can do with fewer clothes.

'What are you doing?' He tugs at my elbow. 'Are we going out? When are we going?'

From downstairs, the TV still blares a theme tune, one I don't recognise.

'When do we feed the ducks?' He demands. Already he has asked about 6 questions and I have not replied to one.

'I'm *hungry*,' he growls as he pulls my hand.

'We'll go out and get some bread,' I reply as I leave the room with him, deliberately shutting the door behind me.

I call out in the hall, 'Daddy?'

'He's here,' her soprano voice comes from the first floor somewhere. 'He's having his medication.'

'I am going out with Jasper now. See you later.'

'See you later,' she chimes.

There is only expensive rye and sourdough seeded loaf in the kitchen's bread bin and it hurt me to waste it on ducks. Auntie Stella would agree, no doubt. All white carbs have been banned from Rumbold Road. Soon there will not be any bread either. I can sense it. Bread is the baddie.

Jasper won't eat anything but white bread, so I'm stuck. I must get to a shop to get some kid-friendly things. Cocopops. Brioche buns. Pain au raisins. Life is uncomfortable enough without cutting out sugar.

After we have checked out the local corner shop and bought the cheapest white sliced loaf at 79p and a packet of chocolate brioches for £1.60 as a stop gap, I take Jasper to Eel

Brook Common and the playground on New Kings Road, where we will be able to sit down and eat the brioches. He can have a play.

We tear and feed the sliced white bread to the ducks in the pond and then we head off for the nearest supermarket. Whole Foods is out of the question for me. I have about £30 pounds on me which will probably buy a bag of potatoes there. Unless I get a job soon, I have to watch what I am spending as all I have now is about £500. I remember that mummy used to spoil us, tiding us over without quibbling or asking the reason for the loan. She trusted us to return it and we did. I settle on the Sainsbury's at Fulham Broadway station. I see a crate of Stella Artois and a bitter laugh escapes me. There will always be a reminder of her.

While I am looking at stacks of things on offer, a shadow passes. I look around. There are a lot of people. There is no one near me. People are queueing, browsing, or lifting things into their trolley. I check over my shoulder and I see no one I know.

It is time for me to lug the Stella-disapproved items back. I pack my backpack on the conveyor belt, pleased I've saved on a 10p bag.

As I turn around, a woman brushes past me.

38

GENEVIEVE

It's Auntie Evie. Mrs Wong. Eva. Fancy bumping into her outside Sainsbury's. Her hair is now completely white and her lipstick redder but it's definitely her from the gait.

She's not a real Auntie. She's an Auntie by definition of Mum's BFF. Mummy first knew and worked with her husband, Dr Robert Wong, a neurologist, for years, well before their family and ours emigrated to the UK. When immigrants arrive in batches, there's safety in numbers. My parents had formed a silo with people of the same origin and class. In our case, my parents and their cohorts were all in healthcare and had arrived to work in the NHS. They became thick as thieves, organising themselves to meet weekly, sharing potluck dinner parties, stories from home, stories of sending money home, exciting gossip on who was going home and who wasn't, money-saving deals at the supermarket, children's school progress or lack of it. All this happened before there was such as thing as Meta, WhatsApp groups or "meet-up events". This was an in-real-life social network for the immigrant class.

No Chinese New Year went by without mahjong nights, a buffet spread of familiar food from home, red packets for the children. Seeing her reminds me of that cherished time of our childhood when our parents were around to organise all the activities, events and festivals. Without them, our silo falls apart and we turn into second generation immigrants.

She doesn't see me, so I call out to her, 'Auntie Evie!'

She turns around, and replies, 'Genevieve Ho, this is crazy! You're here? You're back?'

'Yup,' I confirm with a such a lack of enthusiasm that even I'm unlikely to be convinced.

'For how long?'

'I'm not sure. I have a job interview tomorrow.'

'Congratulations,' she beams. 'That's exciting. Hope you get it.'

'Hope so. Are you heading into Sainsbury's?'

'Yes. Why don't we catch up for a coffee? Come round now. I'm just rushing in to pick up a few things. Are you free?'

'Sure,' I shrug. 'You're still at Bishops Road?'

'That's right,' she says, 'You have a good memory! How's your dad coping?'

'Fine, I guess. You saw him at my mum's funeral.'

'It was very upsetting,' she tilts her head down. 'Your mum was a good friend and colleague. And who's this handsome young man?' Asks Auntie Evie.

'This is Jasper. Say *hello, Auntie*, Jas!' I urge him by tugging at his hand.

'No, not Auntie, lah. Please call me Po Po,' she addresses

him, with a big toothy smile, her chin held back with pride. 'I can be *your* granny here.' I feel choked up.

'I'm sorry, Jasper, I was so busy jibber jabbering with your mum,' she continues. 'Your mum and I know each other from way back in the Victorian times! From when she was born!' Eva puts her arms in a rocking cradle motion. The joke is lost on Jasper.

He stares at her, slack-jawed. After a couple of seconds' delay, he obediently greets her the Asian way, 'Hello, Po Po.'

'Wah, so sweet,' Auntie Evie praises him, pleased with the new title. '乖仔.' *Gwai zai* is "good boy" in Cantonese. The Chinese are fond of children's respect for the elders.

'How's Phoebe doing?' I mention Auntie Evie's daughter, whom I got to know through the arduous Saturday Chinese school, though not well at all, as she is 10 years my senior; she is not my contemporary.

'She's fine, she's fine,' replies Eva. 'She lives in Balham now, has a boyfriend. Aiyah, long story. She may move to the US.'

I stop listening. I glance at the sell-by flowers in the buckets near the tobacco and customer service counter. My mum would have cheered us up in three words, 'Look. Chrysanthemums. Reduced!'

'Meet you out here in 10 minutes!' Auntie Evie says, ready to do her shopping. 'Don't forget. I may have something for you.'

I *do* know someone I consider a friend. She is not my mother, and could never be. But I'm grateful for her right now. 'I won't forget. I have to pick up some stuff too,' I explain.

. . .

After we've done our mini shopping, we meet and chat as we walk back to hers. Jasper saunters across the Fulham Road and nearly gets killed. He's not in a hurry; he's not even aware of where we're heading. His head must be in the clouds as he drifts across. I run. I grab and embrace him. Auntie Evie starts snapping in Cantonese and I can't focus on what she's saying. I shout at him.

'Please don't do that again,' I shout. A motorcycle courier beeps and explodes a monosyllabic expletive.

'It's called jaywalking, mummy.'

'WHAT? You nearly got me, us, run over by that motorcycle. You didn't even look.'

'It's illegal in Singapore but here it isn't, mummy.'

'You haven't even said sorry.'

His lips suddenly tremble. 'Sorry,' he whispers. 'For jaywalking.'

We walk in silence to Bishops Road. If I lose him, I have no one. My mother whom I miss every day, is gone. My siblings are lost in the world of work abroad. I have lost or almost lost my father to that woman. My husband is now an ex. Four years of IVF is a love-killer for him. Our Australian and New Zealand wine business has gone down under. Jasper is all I have left in this world. I exhale slowly to catch my breath on the front steps.

I recognise the front immediately. Eva opens the door and take our shoes off. We go into the front room where there's a large framed picture of a toddler on the alcove bookshelves. 'Phoebe's baby?' I ask, incredulously. She shuts the front door.

'Yep, and JoJo's not a baby now,' she says. 'She's at nursery today. 15 months old.'

'She's adorable,' I say, studying the pretty, dark and curly-haired toddler's photos.

In the old days of IVF rounds, where I would not have been able to look at a baby, I would have to avoid friends with babies and cross the road if I see a group of women with strollers, because of my failure. How I have improved and am pleased I am no longer TTC (the 3-letter abbreviation for trying to conceive) in the Meta support groups. Sometimes it is a lifesaver to have social media for sharing with total strangers you're TTC but it also irks me that those who are no longer TTC (because they have been successful) leave the group with the smug *what a wonderful group so good to have met you all here* announcement. The alacrity that makes you want to throw up. Gimme wine or get lost, according to the wise Rumi.

I settle Jasper in the front room where he goes through a large trug of the baby's toys in case there's anything he can play with. Finding nothing for him, he sits down instead and Auntie Evie grabs the remote to switch on the TV. CBeebies is playing at low volume.

'Let's go into the kitchen,' Eva says, putting the remote down. She fills and puts the kettle on, then spoons scoops of coffee into a Bodum glass cafétiere. I smell the wonderful aroma of ground Lavazza, which always reminds me of my apartment in River Valley, Singapore. It is what gets me out of bed every morning before I face the business, every day steely-eyed and in disbelief that we were getting poorer and poorer.

'So glad you could just pop around, like old days, hah?' Says Eva in her Northern Malaysian Cantonese accent from Ipoh. Despite being in the UK for decades working in intensive care with the NHS, her English is still heavily accented.

'Lei ge daddy, koei dim ah?' *How is your daddy doing*, Auntie Evie asks, a little warily, having switched to Cantonese in a low voice as if anyone else is around. 'I notice he has a... a...'

'He's hired a carer,' I quickly affirm.

She nods. Eva says, 'After your mother's funeral, we've been seeing your dad to keep him company.' When she says *we*, it means she and her husband, Robert. 'We used to take Richie out to lunch, or go on walks with him. But since Stella started working there, maybe more than half a year ago, she's been making it difficult, woh. I call round, but she says he's sleeping, doing exercise, or busy in the garden. Do you believe that? Every time, meh?'

'No, I don't. That's just ridiculous. You and I know that my father does not do gardening or exercise. It's like asking him to go to the moon.'

'Well, guess what, she says he's really into gardening and tai chi. Last week. I brought him a box. Daan tart from Chinatown Bakery, those Macanese egg tarts. You know that one, mah? Newport Place. Malaysian-owned!'

This is part of the silo-speak, of course. Malaysians and Singaporeans prefer to patronise each other's businesses. To announce something was Malaysian or Singaporean was a proud *can you believe it?* exclamation, to which the only justifiable response would be a *Wah!* In recommending and supporting each other, they become close knit in the ethnic community that they founded and formed. It is a smallish world.

'Yes, of course, my mum's favourite,' I recall. 'She used to go in and speak in Hakka to the staff. They're from Ipoh.'

'Aiyah! Can you imagine,' says Eva in a conspiratorial whisper, 'I was asked to take them away as she says he can't have them. Sugar no good for Richard! So who is this *Richard*?' She jokes, breaking into a little laugh.

I purse my lips into a tight line. Eva continues, 'I'm sure that she means well. We all could do with cutting out sugar. I guess,' she adds.

My generation have benefited from the silo. We grew up with a strong sense that we're a part of something huge and yet on the periphery. At heart we identify both as British and Chinese. When you are with Asians, you're Chinese but when you are with your British friends, you're British. You know all the slang, the TV, the political parties and the food. That *is* culture, isn't it? Part of you will always belong here but another will never.

Are we now such harsh gatekeepers that Stella will never be a part of our silo?

I bite my lip. What Eva says concurs with my experience of Stella's censorious attitude towards Daddy's diet. So she is a strict nutritionist. But to control him seeing his oldest friends in the UK? I'm galled. I feel the acridity of the coffee, so warm and fragrant before, now rising up my throat and frothing behind my teeth. I swallow it back down. The Chinese have an expression for withstanding hardship. 吃苦. Sek fu. Eat bitter.

'Well, on the plus side,' gestures Eva with her palms turned upwards. 'The house was getting very run down and filthy. He cannot cope. Frail. Ill. And there's a limit to what I can do for him. I have my own house and granddaughter to look after,' she points to the front room.

'The visits were not enough,' she adds. 'The garden was a mud bath. Now the house looks like a showroom. She got your dad back to good health with diet and exercise. Have some snacks,' says Eva in her heavy accent, so it sounds like *have some snakes*.

She places a tray of shopbought Chinese almond cookies. 'Sorry, hah, sorry. I bought them.'

Auntie Evie is an excellent baker, like my mum. The two always prepared baked goods for our silo's gatherings during festive periods such as Christmas and Chinese New Year, and of course, all our birthday parties. Auntie Evie apologises for shopbought items, as if anyone would be offended by cookies. She has high standards when it comes to Cantonese desserts. My mother and Auntie Evie used to make Hong Kong egg waffles. I remember Mid-Autumn Festival of ridiculous amounts of dumpling and mooncake eating. These would be no-no's in Stella's books.

I look at the time on the kitchen clock, 'Auntie Evie, we'll head back now.'

'Oh! Before I forget, I have something for you. It's upstairs. I'll try not to wake Robert. He's having a nap.'

She takes off like a bird released from a cage.

39
GENEVIEVE

I go into the front room and switch the TV off for Jasper. Auntie Evie comes back with a dark green smart pigskin tote bag.

'A bit heavy; watch out,' she warns.

'What is it?'

'Open it, lor. It's your mum's. She gave it to me when she got very ill.'

I pull out a padded nylon case. 'Oh, is it a laptop?'

'Yes. Your dad will never use one, so your mum thought I should have it. I have no time to even open it. She would never leave it with him. She said that he has his own computer,' she whispers, as though my father can hear.

'Thank you so much!' I finally remember my manners.

'Don't thank me, thank your mum.'

I pull the velcro on the padded case and take the heavy item out. 'A MacBook! It looks brand new!' I exclaim in amazement.

'She did tell me in the last year or so she was trying to write a memoir. That's why she bought it. But I don't know if she started it. Then she thought that *I* might want to write my memoir too,' she chuckles. 'As if! I'm not much of a story-teller, unlike your mum.'

'Probably 16"? A decent size screen.' I comment like I know anything about it.

'Don't know, lah. I am not great with tech. You know more about these things. I can just about go on YouTube to find home hacks and tips, and watch funny dogs on Meta.' She chuckles. 'Oh, wait! I nearly forgot, you see lah, my brain!' She points to her temples. 'The password is some-where else. Wait here.'

I peek back inside the green tote bag and see the power adaptor cable. She comes back with a neon yellow post-it note. 'It was with my address book. Your mum told me to keep the password separate from the laptop, and that's what I did.'

I hug Auntie Evie and reluctantly head back with Jasper to where I now call "home".

When we get back to Rumbold Road, I am reasonably cheered up I have gained a friend, who also is my dad's now-shunned old friend. A heavy feeling settles on my back and tummy. It might still be jetlag which takes a few days to get over, but also it is like I have been here a long time. My dad's not in. The house is silent. The wheelchair has disappeared. He must be out with her.

I cannot bring myself to say her name.

'Mummy, I start school tomorrow?' Jasper checks again. His eyes are wide and vacant, but his thoughts seem clouded.

'Yes. Why?'

Children have a way of starting a conversation abruptly. Small talk is not for small people.

'I— I'm scared.'

'Oh no, my poor baby boy. Don't be scared. Mummy is scared too. Let's do this together. We're in the brave team.' My heart breaks.

'I miss my friends, Mummy. I miss daddy too. Where is daddy? Is he coming?'

Once he starts he will ask at least 5 questions. He sits on the oversized L-shaped sofa and looks terribly alone and almost invisible with his shoulders rounded, oversized maroon Disneyland hoodie and his head hanging down. I sit and put my arms around him but he does not respond.

'Will I see them again?'

'Yes, of course,' I lie, as easily as turning a cushion over. 'Don't you like your room?'

He shrugs. 'I miss my friends,' he repeats.

'You'll make new ones.'

I look at him and cup his face in my hands. 'You're a very grown-up big boy.'

'I'm going to be in Year 2,' he nods, like an old man.

It starts to rain: the sizzle on the patio and crackle hitting the cills, spattering the French windows fill me with nostalgia and dread. I am back in grey, wet, expensive England.

40

ELIJAH

Elijah opens the letter to re-read it. He received it almost 7 months ago. At the time his mother was dying. He had no interest in this woman he doesn't even know writing to him. He'd torn it up once already. It has an earthquake of tape lines where he'd mended it.

Dear Elijah,

I know you will be surprised to receive this letter. I am your birth mother. I have been looking for you for years and I found a box in my mother's care home in Singapore. She's doing well. Still plays the piano. I discovered that your grandmother (my mother) has been sending you money for Christmas, Chinese New Year and your birthday. I had no idea. She has been in touch with Irene Chan all this time. I have your pictures and the letters Irene wrote.

I had you when I was a nursing student in London. I was 21, in my final year. They took you away from me and I had no choice but to agree, as I had to further my studies and not cause my family any more disgrace. I cannot believe I signed you away. I have been living in pain ever since. Not one day passes when I do not think of you. I am reconnecting with you as I am in London. I live and work here now. I have a good job.

My phone number, address and email are on this card. It is the address of my employer where I am a live-in carer.

Some words are illegible from the rips and tape marks. He knows enough from what he can read and what's left of the letter. She signs off as *Mummy*. That's just weird. Elijah did not show his mum the letter, because she had been too ill and bedridden to read anything by then. He simply asked his mum if he was adopted. She said that it was true. He did not want to cause her any pain so he hid his.

He tosses the letter aside to the sofa's armrest but on second thoughts, folds it multiple times and puts it in the pocket of his track pants. He has no choice. She is the only person he could think of.

Since this letter, Stella has written to him many times: what she's up to, what the old man likes and dislikes, his daughter, his grandson. Oh yeah, she even wrote to him from her hotel room in Paris. Like Elijah should be happy for her? *Soooo* boring. Why does he want to know about these rich people? Doesn't she realise she's just rubbing his nose in it?

Every time she writes, she mentions that she wants to meet him on her day off. She has suggested Costa coffee in Whitechapel Station. He's never replied. She must be living a good life, from the postcode, and from the fact that she was "busy all the time". People like him never "go for coffee" or step into a Costa's. A coffee is almost £5 now. He just can't. Why get in touch with him if she was *that* busy? Nobody was *that* busy apart from Nafisah. A full-time mum with piece-meal cottage industry side hustles like sewing and cooking for a few customers, she has 4 kids of school-going age and no help.

Had Elijah been at the same job, he would have borrowed from Ralph, his old boss. Now *he* is a good bloke, an East Londoner like him. Everybody calls him Ralph Lauren as he is very old and tanned, with a million watt smile of huge white teeth. Ralph gave his mother face when she walked in and asked if Elijah could work in the hotel, and he said, 'Bring 'im in.'

Therefore, the only person who could help him was *her*, his birth mother, Stella. He is her child. Barry will never find out. She has an important and secure job. She must have money. She will be able to help tide Elijah over. His rental is due in days and he still owes the landlord company the previous month's, and the month before that.

What will he do? He wrings his hands but they soon loosen and fall at his side on the sofa where he has tucked himself in.

The instant he wakes up, he calls the number. Since she does not have his, and has never heard his voice, she won't recognise who it is. Also she's working, so she may not be able to take calls. He hangs up before it has rung 3 times. *Nah. Just leave it, mate*, he tells himself. He will try again another time. He needs to think exactly what he will say.

Feeling the chill drift into his nostrils, he rubs his palms together. He has to leave the sofa to make himself tea. He chooses chrysanthemum tea. His mum always preferred it and made it for him every morning. He sighs and grabs the loaf of Tesco's White Bread from the fridge, toasting two slices and applying Tesco's 95p margarine, Stockwell & Co Soft Spread. You can live very cheaply if you know how. The bread, at 74p a loaf, lasts a long time for him, at least a few days.

It is freezing and to save on his overdue bills, he won't put on the heating. That's why he sleeps and eats on the sofa wearing 5 blankets. Perfectly OK if you don't mind looking like a mountain. Anyway, there is *some* thermal insulation in these blocks. Not much, but some.

He munches the toast. One thing he is glad for is that he has not told the nurse his last name. That would have been a disaster. He almost did. She seemed maternal.

He doesn't want to be identified. He may get busted. Or if anyone reported the incident, the cops (if they did their job at all) would pin him down about the assault he executed on Marcus. OK, he also robbed the dickhead of those swanky wanker boots. It is not his fault. Bastards. Marcus is a key player in the landlord company which has issued him an eviction notice and where could Elijah go?

41

GENEVIEVE

Dinner is grilled aubergine patties with garlic and mince pork, another Hakka dish my mother had been so fond of. There is brown rice and not one but three plates of different vegetables: courgettes, peppers and spring onions in another, and broccoli in the last. Jasper looks miserable, and I know why.

'What's the matter?' My father asks him in a kind voice.

'I don't like this,' says Jasper with large intakes of breath, trying to hold it in, but he fails. He breaks into a sob.

'You can't be a picky eater, Boy,' Stella shakes her head while looking straight at her rice bowl. She ignores Jasper staring at her with his tears dropping onto the tablecloth. He hasn't touched a thing.

'So sorry,' I find myself apologising. 'Jasper, why don't you have the pork and rice?'

She makes a face and wrinkles her nose. My father looks embarrassed but he's tucking in with verve. He will enjoy himself no matter what. Nothing spoils his appetite.

'How about a fried egg?' I offer.

Jasper says, 'OK,' in a small voice, and concedes to eating the rice and pork first.

'You spoil him,' she says to me, in that special hard low voice reserved for me. 'How can you let him choose what he wants? He's getting no nutrition, ok? And he's at school all day.' She throws a quick glance at me with her reptilian eyes.

My throat is suddenly choked. I can't find anything to say. This woman, this *stranger*, is telling me what to do, what I am doing wrong, what I am not doing right. Is she even a parent? What right has she to talk to me in this way?

My father stops eating, and puts his chopsticks down. A vein in his temple twitches. Stella bites her tongue when she realises she's said too much. 'Eat up, Richard, you've had a long day,' she says coolly.

I get up and head for the kitchen. After some clanging looking for a frying pan and a box of eggs, I somehow succeed in frying one and bringing it on a plate back to the table for Jasper. It's the extent of my cooking.

The moment comes after dinner where I get up and help Stella clear the table. It's almost automatic now. I can hear the wok clattering into the sink and the pressure of tap water running over it. I want to help her. My dad says to me, 'Leave all that, please?'

I stop.

'Leave all that, I said. Come and watch TV with me. It's brilliant,' he grins. '*The White Lotus*. You'll bloody love it. Oh my god, it's so funny.'

'I thought it's not a comedy,' I reply, blinking. I turn to look at the clock on the mantelpiece. 'But no, I should help Stella—'

'Aiyah! You can help her later,' he waves dismissively, eyes already glued on the screen. Dad doesn't get it that washing up can't be given "help" later. Being helpful is a skill of the here and now. 'After all, how often do we watch TV together? Jasper!' He calls Jasper who seems to be drawing on the iPad already. 'Help Auntie Stella, please! Go!'

'I'm drawing, Gung Gung,' he whines.

'Draw later,' my dad says. 'Just help for 5 minutes so your mummy and I can watch TV. You know I don't watch alone, right?' My father explains patiently. 'Five minutes and it's all done. Now, put that thing down and go!'

'Grrr,' Jasper groans and puts down the Apple Pencil. He drags himself into the kitchen. Like me, he knows washing up is not five minutes' work unless it's just a mug and a spoon.

'Come, come,' he pats the seat next to him on the sofa. Reluctantly, I sit down and before the opening credits finish, I blurt out my good-bad news that I have a restaurant trial tomorrow night, but I need babysitting for about 4 hours which covers the travel time there and back too. 'Oh, he says, sure! No need to hire anyone. Stella will do it.'

He may have volunteered her, but she may still refute it. I add, 'If she can't, I can ask—,'

'Don't be ridiculous. Of course she will, she's like family.'

Uh-oh, oops. But now is not the time to disagree with him. The show has started.

42
STELLA

I do *not* want Jean-Viv to help me any more. I'm relieved she's watching TV with Richard. I don't enjoy watching TV as it's the time when I sit down on the sofa and want to fall asleep from exhaustion. She'll be encroaching into my space. If she starts doing chores, what will *I* do? She is trying to make *me* redundant. At my age it's not going to be easy to get another job. She already has seen for herself how tough and ageist the job market is. Every night I put up with it while she tries to help. I give Jasper tasks, and teach him a little rhyme: 'What's on the rack? Put dry things back!' Is this how it would have been to bring up a child? Something I have missed, or rather, missed out on.

When Richard tells me later during his massage, 'Oh, by the way,' I know what's coming.

When he says *by the way*, what he means is, *I have a favour to ask you, and you must say yes.*

'We're babysitting Jasper tomorrow night.'

'What? Why?'

'That's not the right answer. How about *I'd love to*?'

I smile decorously but how can I say that I'm not Jasper's babysitter? I already have a big responsibility for which I'm paid. I am his caregiver and housekeeper. And this is a huge house to keep. I work from dawn to midnight with a day and a half off per week. I can't take on looking after his grandchild too. An inch becomes a yard. Soon I will be his afterschool nanny, the moment *she* starts working day and night.

'No, as much as I love Ah Boy, and I'm truly honoured that you would ask me,' I am quite likely lying. 'But this is too much.'

'Do you want paying?' He asks. 'What's the going rate for babysitting?'

'It's not that, Richard. What if something happens to you while you're in my charge, or to him? My attention will constantly be divided.'

'Well, I don't know,' he weighs up the consequences. 'What could possibly happen in a few hours?'

'Many things. He's a child. No one can do two jobs, simultaneously. I am a professional. A nurse—,'

'I know, I know. You don't have to remind me. We must help Jean-Viv to get her life back on track. She is going crazy. I can give her an allowance, sure, but for long? What will she do at home all day?'

She's the kind of woman who values independence, like me. Of course she wants my job. That is why she's come back. But I hope she's seen that no one does my job better than I. There is no way a spoilt entrepreneurial wine brat like her could polish windows and glasses and cook nutritious meals 6 days a week. She might keep track of all his medications and appointments, but that's it. She will feed her father like her son: the instant processed junk from supermarkets. She will hire a cleaner to save time.

'While I don't need your attention,' says Richard, 'I promise I will be a good boy and sit in my chair or lie in bed with the monitor on.'

I make an involuntary face, like a muscle gone wrong and has distorted my expression. There goes the £249-for-three-areas dermal filler from 3 months ago. Botox has taught me anger management. For a smooth forehead, you shouldn't and couldn't get mad. No one can tell my expressions apart. I still manage a huge smile when it is due. In fact, that is all I can manage. All other expressions have been wiped away with the creases and lines.

'Richard,' I exhale. 'I am going to babysit Jasper on one condition.'

He waits.

'When Jean-Viv gets a full-time position, I would like her to move out. With Jasper. I have been very tolerant and responsible, caring, washing and cooking for everyone since she arrived, thinking she is a guest, but now she is here permanently.'

He listens, blinking. He looks at me straight. It is my turn now to not understand his expression. He is a fair employer, surely he can see that I am paid to care for him, not two more people?

'For a minute, I thought you were someone else. Someone from back home.'

I ignore him. Old people have a tendency to think you are someone. My own mother forgot who I was, off and on. I add, 'Of course I will babysit, ad hoc, whenever she needs it but once she has a job she will be able to hire a nanny in her new home.' I work on his neck and shoulders, an area I know he has problems with due to his slight hunch from being tall.

'Deal,' he says. His eyes are stony as he immediately turns away.

43
GENEVIEVE

Thursday 5th January

'Trudie?' My dad gasps, white as a wall, when he sees me in the Michael Kors shirt.

'Oh, Trudie, forgive me, please,' my father mutters, his eyes squinting. I rush over and grab him by the shoulders. He looks fragile and his misty eyes stare into a faraway spot beyond the front door.

'It's me, Daddy. I am on my way out. Thank you for looking after Jasper,' I put both my hands on his shoulder, to make sure he understands what I have just said. *One day at a time,* I calm myself. I am ready to tackle the restaurant trial and interview.

Jasper creeps out to the entrance hall. 'Mummy? Where are you going?'

'I told you already, Jaspberry Raspberry,' I stoop down

and hug him. 'I'm working. I will be back in about 4 hours. I'm only going to Mayfair, not far from here.'

Stella is nowhere to be seen. She must be very busy and I will not interrupt her. I won't say goodbye to her as she already knows my schedule.

Time to focus on the job and not think about them.

The moment the door shuts behind me, a heaviness lifts. I descend the steps with a jauntiness in my step I had not felt since I was a little girl.

Someone across the road is staring at the house. It's now dark and the shadows cast by the streetlights offer not much visibility on someone so far away. A figure is standing under the oak tree. It makes me stop and blink. I look at my watch but feel a chill. I have no time to go back in and warn my dad or I will be late. When I look up, the figure seems to have gone. My eyes search the distant darkness of the park with its enormous old sycamore and oak trees. I can't see him. I don't know if I have imagined him for those 1 or 2 seconds.

It's time to get going. I want to make a good impression as it's my first time. My mother's clothes have given me new life. I am like her ghost. No wonder I frighten my father. I even feel hair-confident, which is rare these days as someone who wears a rat nest fastened by a claw clip, a crop top hoodie and Mom jeans day in and day out. My glasses are Dior and make me look professional and learned. Chances of being hired are higher for those who wear glasses according to some job search article on LinkedIn.

I have worked out the journey time and my heart thumps with every beat my foot pounds on the pavement. I do my breathing exercises like I am about to go to the moon. My nervousness will knock me down and I won't let it.

· · ·

The restaurant is stunning, intimate and it stinks of old money. The diners are tanned and it's January. I am going to oversee wine pairing and chat with the customers. This is my forte. Thank God this evening has arrived. It's like I am a magician on stage and I will now wow them.

Being a sommelier requires routine and accuracy, almost an OCD. You have to really get lost in your own world (and not mind it) reading the Wine List in silence and checking facts and figures. Each number means something. It's probably not for those who enjoy drinking to excess or losing control. In fact, it involves almost no degree of excess in eating or drinking to keep the senses raw and the wit sharp. The lifestyle is what got me into it. Since I was 16, I had been reading the leather-bound lists at The Peony and became fascinated by vineyards and climate.

At The Peony's reception bar during my Uni days, I had often spent lunch and dinner times polishing glasses, uncorking, enjoying the chat with hotel guests and sharing my knowledgable schpiel about aromas and countries of origins of each bottle. I made my father so proud. Without intending to, I had joined the hospitality industry. Do I still make him proud?

The manager is a tall camp bloke called Jared, with glowing K-skin and dark hair. His eyebrows have been "done" and they look like a devil's wings about to take off. He sounds like he has been in hospitality all his life, like me. I get a whiff of his strong leathery scent. Hermes.

If I don't get an offer, it will be another setback. He has said that they must trial and interview another 9 candidates, so my hopes are not up.

The evening disappears, like stardust. At home, time creaks on while Stella and I exchange sullen glances. But here in *Republique*, the ambience and the buzz fill me with inspiration and the hours fly by. Five out of five for perfectly chic setting with impeccable staff and service, I picture myself writing a one-liner review for The Fork.

I am allowed a 20 minute break when I wolf down whatever they give me. Chorizo with kidney bean stew and a hunk of sourdough. Oh my god, I am starving and I have really missed rich greasy meals. Although I don't really want to drink a drop, Jared does offer me a 125ml glass of my own pairing: the inexpensive Ribera del Duero, where I have matched the wine to the sauce not the protein. This is just what I have craved and needed. I nearly fall onto my knees. I shut my eyes and enjoy the wonder of the moment. I have so little of these precious moments now. I am drunk on my own happiness.

At 9pm, the end of my trial, Jared calls me into his cramped office filled with IKEA Callax units and Micke desks. He shuts the door and I dread every word that he will be saying.

'How do you think it went, Genevieve?' He says, picking up a pen and a branded notepad with the restaurant's leaf logo, poised like he's about to write a letter.

The suspense drips from every consonant. He looks very grim: not a good indicator of my trial evening.

'I— I think— I did OK. The customers enjoyed the wine I paired with their meals; umm, they gave their feedback—,'

'Genevieve, you did great,' he says, still serious. 'The customers enjoyed chatting to you about California, New Zealand, South Africa— I mean— you know your stuff!'

I stare at him. 'I just— I— well, thank you so much, Jared; I can't believe it,' I really can't since it is the eighth position I have applied for and the first I have been asked to come in for a trial. 'I have been to all those wine regions and taken people on tour—,' I start to reminisce, my spirits soaring as I think back to the good times before the pandemic.

But he cuts me short.

'We will only be offering a full-time position to the applicants. You are a single mother, I believe?'

'Yes,' I nod vigorously like I am a single mother with bells on.

'What will you do about the all-important question?' He leans forward, lowering his chin, his eyes piercing me. 'Childcare.'

44
GENEVIEVE

Friday 6th January

It is Jasper's first week in Year 2. He has been glum and eats what's left in the packet of Sainsbury's chocolate brioches. He is unusually quiet and my heart twists in pain. I go with him, holding hands and we both don't want to say goodbye. In the cold damp air, we trudge the 8 minute walk which we have timed on day one when we walked around Fulham and Parsons Green. It seems like months ago but it has only been more than a week. We pass brightly and colourfully lit newsagents, Bayley & Sage, a gourmet super-market, an expensive gift shop called Lark, a Smile dental clinic with fairy lights. Everyone is still hanging onto Christ-mas. They are hanging on with both hands. Everything here is geared for the larger and more comfortable wallet.

I haven't heard back from Jared at Republique. I keep replaying the trial I did, and I so believe that it went well. Who can say who my 9 competitors are? It may have gone better for them. Some would drop out of course, and there may be fewer, say 5 competitors. At least I've been paid £150 for the 2 hour trial. Temporarily, I am buoyed.

A few dog walkers in hooded puffer jackets stroll on Parsons Green in front of the White Horse pub with their labradoodles, King Charles cavalier spaniels and grey-hounds. The streets are busy with commuters catching their tubes or buses, and school children in groups of 2 or 3 with their childminders or parents. We pause briefly outside Nomad Books while he gazes at his solemn reflection in the window glass decorated with giraffe, koala and gum tree illustrations and murals. Today there is hardly daylight. At almost half past eight in the morning, it looks like it's evening.

I'm relieved when he doesn't toss a glance back once we get to the classroom and he is distracted with the colourful displays and educational toys. I have not made him a packed lunch as I want him to acclimatise to the infamous state school lunch. He needs to. It will be good for settling in.

When I come back, it's the NHS carer who answers the door.

'Yes, it's Stella's day off,' he reminds me. 'I am here to cover her.'

'Do you wanna cuppa tea or anything?' He asks as I stride into the kitchen, looking for my father.

'No, thanks,' I answer. I wander to the kitchen through the hall, living room, dining room. 'My father's not downstairs.'

'I think he's in his office, Genevieve,' he says, following me.

'OK, fine. Thanks. Remind me your name?'

'Qamal.'

'Great,' I say without looking at him, as I ascend the stairs. He doesn't follow me this time.

I knock on my dad's slightly ajar door and listen.

'Just a minute! I'm checking emails and the news. Qamal? Stella?' My father calls out. 'Is that you?'

'No, it's me,' I reply, swinging the door open and I immediately shut it behind me.

'Ahhh, who?' He appears confused. He swivels around in his office chair to face me, taking his reading glasses off. He puts them on his knee and they slide off, falling to the floor. He completely forgets where he is and who I am. It throws me, as it does not happen often.

'Daddy, it's me, Gen.' I pick up his glasses and return them to him.

'Gen, hi, yes!' He takes the glasses from my hand. Then his expression clouds over when he sees mine.

'Can I talk to you quickly, Daddy?'

He looks stern, like he did when I was a child and had done something wrong.

'I— I can do Stella's job. You don't need to waste a ton of mon—,'

'Whoa, whoa, whoa. Stop right there. You can't just come home and kick her out. I hired her months ago. Anyway, I doubt anyone can do the job she does. You're not a nurse.'

'I don't have to be. I've looked into this,' I am winging it, but it sounds plausible. 'Carers just help you with day to day stuff.'

'Just? *Just*?' He repeats incredulously. 'You might like to give her more due respect.'

I feel like a child again, asking for a new game or fancy trainers.

'If it's money you need I can give you some to get going. But I'm not letting go of Stella. Thing is, she makes me *so* happy. You don't even care.'

My heart sinks. He says *so* with such longing, his hands are balled into fists. I protest. 'I do care! That's why I'm here!'

'You don't,' my dad shakes his head slowly, not looking at me. 'You're here because you have no roof over your head.'

What? How is he saying this?

'C'mon, Gen. I see the 9 pieces of luggage you've brought with you. I wasn't born yesterday. Stella has put them in the basement.'

'No!'

'Yes! You can't leave them lying around, Gen. Can you not see your stuff which has landed from nowhere is just unfair on me and her?'

I watch him and what he is trying to say.

'She is meticulously tidy and an enormous amount of effort goes into keeping this house in this condition,' he explains slowly like I'm a guest in my own home. 'It was completely run down in the last 4 years; no one cared! None of my children, Auntie Evie, Przemek or the cleaning agency. They just come and go. No one can help. Stella has changed all that. She's saved me, and this house. I feel *alive*. I am twenty years younger since she arrived.'

He languishes in the long vowel of *alive* like he's sighing. These are the sickening cliches the lovestruck come up with, but I cannot shut my ears. I want to bring up my breakfast. 'I appreciate it all. Daddy, I do,' I put my hand on my neck to stop the nausea. 'I know what she does for you. But you give her your bank details and your cards.'

'Gen, she books all my appointments. She controls all the food and finances.'

'But how do you know you have anything left?' My voice is shrill and strange. Not only my throat but my entire face constricting and burning bright.

'Just listen to yourself, Gen. If I cannot trust someone who lives in my house, then who can I trust?'

'You can trust me; I am your family. She isn't.' Surely my father can see this. Can't he?

'So what? You can't do this job. Can you even cook?' he repeats in a pitiful tone. 'Gen, I see her as part of our history, our family. She is someone from back home. How many times have I said this? She is one of us. Kaki lang, as the Hokkiens call it. *Our own people*. You're a professional woman, an entrepreneur, a smartarse. Why would you want to help me dress and go to the toilet? Do you not want me to age with dignity?'

'And you think she cares about you, Daddy? This is her job! She's spending your money freely. Look at your clothes, her clothes, the interiors of this house. She does *not* care about you!'

'Gen, I will politely ask you to back off. You think you have a right to barge in, and deny your father of such petty pleasures? Nice clothes? New curtains? TV subs? I should have NO luxury, is that it? I'm in my last days!'

Oh, Jesus. 'I can't believe I am hearing this, Daddy. Are you out of your mind?'

'Don't call me crazy. I'm old. Maybe forgetful. Confused. Useless. But I'm not bloody out of my mind,' my father is ranting. I don't think he's ever shouted at me before. At my mum, yes. All the time. I thought it was normal for couples. But this is one symptom of the senile condition: uninhibited rage. 'You are back here only because you have no choice. I have never asked you what's happened to your husband or your wine merchandising, tours, sales fairs, god knows what else,' he gesticulates sardonically with alternating hands to describe the peripathetic nature of the multiple income streams. 'That's your business. My grandson is attending a local authority school when he used to go to United World College with eye-watering fees. You never wanted to come back. Don't kid yourself. You did not care about your mum when she was sick and you don't care about me now, and I'm not sick.'

I start to protest as this is all wrong. I reach out to touch my father's shoulder but he retreats, sliding back on the office chair wheels to avoid me. I resist the tears pricking my eyes, but instead they pour out and fall on my dirty 3-day old UCL hoodie. I squeeze my eyes shut. I don't want to listen to his accusations but I am standing here in his office like an employee being dismissed. How could I have been caring for my mum when that time had been the best years of the business I built with my husband before it went wrong? And those were the years of my IVF treatment which I have kept away from my parents.

'Now, I do welcome you and my grandson but you need to keep yourself occupied,' he continues his rant. 'Don't meddle in my life. Get a fucking job, like everyone else. Get out!'

'Is everything... OK...?' Qamal's soft and fearful voice comes from the corridor. He taps the door lightly. Oh damn, he must have heard everything. Shit. I just want him to go.

'Are we ready for your walk? Mr Ho?' He calls out again.

'Sure!' My father answers in a fake-loud voice. He is quivering; a damp sheen on his forehead and the colour of his cheeks do not look good. He shuts his eyes, inhaling to steady himself. He uncurls his fists and lays them on the armrests of his office chair to push himself to standing. I feel bad. I caused my father's anger. He looks old when he is angry. Either he has changed (because of *her*) OR I do not know my father well enough. Why did I come in to talk to him? I am probably in his bad books now. Things had been going well when we were in Paris, had they not?

I hear their voices down the corridor and then the whirr of the stairlift taking Daddy downstairs. I imagine him being helped into his coat and Qamal getting the wheelchair and the stick, some bread for the ducks in the pond at the park. Everything is back to calm and order. The front door slams and I hold my face in my palms for 17 seconds for my silent scream.

45
NAFISAH

Monday 9th January

Nafisah folds the curtains as tightly as she could into two large bright red TK Maxx bags. She pays for store bags but she keeps them for occasions like these: packing and transporting her work. The TK Maxx ones are very tough plastic.

She has had to wait for the rain to stop. The children in school, and her husband at work, it is her opportunity to deliver the new gold jacquard, triple-lined goblet pleat blackout curtains for an old client. They are hotel grade and a good earner at £1200 for two pairs. They took three days and the customer bought all the fabric and trims.

The customer previously had alterations made for "show" clothes or costumes to be lined and made more wearable for every day use. For example, she removed the ripped and stained original lining and re-lined the pin-striped Victorian jacket with a more durable satin polyester mix in a contrast fabric, and added piping to the torn lapels to toughen them up and to hide the frayed edges. Nafisah was born in East London, but she comes from a long line of seamstresses and tailors in Dhaka. Fixing stuff is their pride and expertise. Anything that could be mended was mended and those which couldn't were upcycled into something else.

She enjoys challenges, and does not mind fixing up old clothes for her customers. Like them, she values quality and workmanship in vintage or antique clothes. That's why they have lasted decades or even a century. *They did not live in a throwaway culture, like we do*, she has said to her customers.

She hurries to Whitechapel station to take a tube stop's ride to Bethnal Green. She walks the not-quite-short walk to the tree-lined avenue of smart Victorian mansion blocks in yellow brick on Corfield Street with their mint-painted facades and grand bay windows fitted with Californian louvred shutters. She senses that something is not right.

An ambulance has pulled up outside the block and the front door has been propped open with a bin. She could hear the splutter of walkie-talkies and the paramedics in their dark green outfits and suitcases of equipment heading out of the building. As she gets into the stairwell and climbs to the top floor, her heart pounds, not just from the weighted cardio, carrying bulky curtains, but the dizzying sensation that it is Angela's flat door that has been propped open.

'Can I help you?' Announces a ginger bearded paramedic, in an Irish accent.

'Well, I — I'm her — seamstress?' Bewildered, Nafisah can hardly believe what she's saying so it comes out sounding like a question, or that she has no idea who she is.

Angela is also like a friend to me, she thinks wildly, but doesn't dare say it. 'What's happened to her?' She asks abruptly instead.

'We need to know why are you here,' The paramedic repeats.

'I am delivering curtains she's ordered. Oh. And a jacket I altered for her,' Nafisah blubbers. She can't breathe, her voice so nervous that 'jacket' comes out as *gackack*.

'What's your name?'

Her mind goes blank for a second. 'Nafisah,' she stutters, her own name sounding alien.

He makes a note with his blue surgical-gloved hand on his iPad. He looks tired and touches his eyebrow with the back of his palm. 'Nafisah—,'

'Ahmad. Call me Naf. Please.'

She glances at the paramedic's name on the lanyard. The instant she has read it, she's forgotten it. Her mind is shot.

'We may need you later, Naf. But you have to go, I'm afraid. We'll have to take her to hospital now.'

'Why? What's happened to her?'

'Angela seems to have had an accident. Her cleaning lady found her this morning and called an ambulance.'

'No!' Nafisah gasps, but it comes out as a shout. 'What happened?'

'We don't know yet. Naf, when did you last see Angela?'

'Er...only... um... four days ago! I had almost finished the curtains but she called me to come and do a fitting for the jacket. She says she is "bloody chuffed" she has lost weight and needed this— this favourite— jacket — ,' Nafisah starts to cry when she recalls Angela's irritation at her weight gain and then utter delight at the weight loss. She had told

Nafisah that she used to be slim. She had been a dancer, amongst other jobs, when she was young.

'Angela was the kindest, most helpful customer,' she suddenly offers to the paramedic. Her breath is short and her hands are freezing and numb from clutching those TK Maxx plastic bags. The weight of the curtains have caused the handles to cut into her fingers. 'She used to buy me gifts, treats and clothes for the children.'

'Do you know if she is ill or has been ill?'

'She always talks about her meds, changing meds, watching her diet, appointments. That's all I know. We used to chat when I came to take measurements. I made her sofa covers, cushions, curtains... her clothes. She made me cups of tea, cake, cookies. I just— I can't believe it—is she — is she dead?'

'I'm afraid so. Really sorry about this. It's just so awful. I know.' He shakes his head sympathetically, laying his blue gloved hand on her shoulders. Nafisah squirms, embarrassed by the cold sweat seeping through her hijab to her forehead and temples. 'We will need you to fill in your contact details here, please.' He jabs at the iPad to bring up a form and rotates it to face her.

'What should I do with these now?' Nafisah lifts the bags, realising with shame and guilt that she will *not* be paid the balance of £1000. Angela has only paid £200 deposit! To afford anything, she and her husband have to work non-stop. Finances have always been tight in her household. Nafisah used to work in retail and the pay was so poor that it wasn't hard to give it up to be a stay-at-home mum and carry out these freelance sewing and cooking jobs. Angela, in all her experience and compassion as a customer and a friend, would understand why the thought of not getting paid has popped into Nafisah's head. She would, wouldn't she? It's too late now. She's dead.

'Would you not be able to leave them in her flat? They are hers anyway?'

'I'll— I'll take them back with me,' Nafisah counters him.

'Up to you, Naf.' The man shrugs. He is busy, looking away from her and moving onto doing his job now. 'Hang onto them. If her lawyer contacts you once they've checked what happens to Angela's estate, you'll know what to do with them.'

She can't sell them on Vinted or eBay yet, to recoup the hours she has spent on them and her loss. She feels terrible, but Angela certainly will not need them anymore where she is now. Nafisah does not need them either. She starts her descent on the three flights of stairs and leaves the ambulance workers to do their tasks and tests.

Inna Lillahi wa inna ilayhi raji'un. RIP in Arabic. Nafisah wipes her tears with the back of her sleeves. Each downward step her wobbly feet makes is like a mini waterfall. Going down is worse than going upstairs. The bags of curtains feel ponderous, crushing, like bags of cement. She puts them down for a few seconds to remove her charity shop fake Michael Kors tote bag, and retrieve tissues from the outer zip pocket. Her hands are shaking, her tears falling. She dabs the sweat from her forehead and neck. She presses the tissues into her eye sockets and blows her nose noisily.

This is probably the last time she comes to the genteel and tree-lined Corfield Street with its elegant Victorian brick facades. She casts a final glance at the building. Poor Angela. Just awful. Rahimaha Allah — may God have mercy on her soul.

46
ELIJAH

Elijah's replacement bank card arrives by post in an unremarkable handwritten envelope. Blimey. That only took 7 days, quicker than he thought. He is days away from his rental being due. He tears it open in a hurry. It is almost evening and he's starving. He needs to get out and get food.

He puts on his old, ripped £5.89 trainers from Temu since he has lost his current shoes during the attack. Near his front door, Elijah stuffs the huge black Hanwags into his black Primark backpack. Dealer Dave whom he knows at Spitalfields market buys used items for his secondhand designer clothes kiosk called Posh Stuff.

Elijah practically runs to the High Street Lloyds ATM and checks the balance. His father has given him £100 more than usual. *That's a miracle*, he hears his mother's voice again, with a little chuckle. *Not enough for a phone, mum*, he thinks in reply. He can't return the borrowed phone to Nafisah yet. He'd better hang onto it first. If he buys a phone, he'd be left with nearly nothing.

. . .

When he leaves Spitalfields market, he is £80 richer. He knows he should get at least £110 from Posh Stuff for the Hanwags. But Dave explains that you can't shift shoes. You need that one person who wants it who's the exact size. Dave will transfer the money onto Elijah's card immediately. The chances of selling shoes are low, Dave prattles on, in his post-sales reassuring monotone. He has boots in his kiosk which have been there a year already. And the Hanwags are not exactly brand new.

The haggling does not go well when Elijah already has a mild headache. Elijah settles for thirty pounds less than expected. Oh fuck it. He has no choice, he does not want the boots and he needs the money.

He walks out, no, strides, like he owns the street. Taking a deep breath of the damp evening air mixed with diesel fumes, chorizo smoking from a stall and the whiff of expensive organic handmade perfume from the apothecary boutiques, he steps into Brushfield Street. OK, he is richer, but he is not wasting his hard-earned cash on the overpriced gourmet food at the market. He'd be better off heading towards Liverpool Street station for cheaper, commercial fast food chain alternatives catering to commuters on their way home to Essex, Kent or wherever they leave the city for.

He turns left and passes COS, Anthropologie and T4 Bubble Tea. The East London that he's grown up in has changed so much it is unrecognisable now. He doesn't dare enter any of these shops. He may as well be abroad and staring at foreign signs. Actually, they *are* foreign names. He has no idea what they sell or at what prices, and yet this is his area. He's a local.

At Pizza Express, he turns left again onto Bishopsgate. He is tempted by Slim Chickens. The aroma of fried battered food is driving him insane. He is so hungry he will eat the first chicken he sees, dead or alive. But no. He should hang on until he gets to KFC. The familiarity warms him like a hug. He crosses Artillery Lane, and passes Boots, then Five Guys before finally arriving at KFC. The joint is jumpin'. You'd think it is the most popular destination here. Just as he picks up his order and leaves, he almost runs into someone he recognises.

Clutching his warm paper bag of Mighty Bucket for One closer to himself, as though anyone "mighty want it", Elijah screws up his eyes for a better look. He creeps up to the glass window and watches like a bird.

He laughs. It's the Hairy Potter, innit. The hirsute flat-mate toy boy of his landlord, who's just crossed Victoria Avenue and about to head across Bishopsgate for Liverpool Street Station. He is dressed all smart, like an old gent'mun, in his standard London black coat and shiny shoes.

Wonda where'e's goin'? Elijah decides to follow him, crossing at the zebra outside SushiDog, onto the concourse, down the escalators and jumping onto the Central line. At this time of evening, the carriage is an oven and packed like sardines. It is a hard job threading through the commuters with a KFC Mighty Bucket, yet easy as he won't stand out. There is always someone to stand behind or beside. He wishes he does not have a takeaway with him or that he could eat it immediately to avoid carrying it around anymore. There is no chance to even hold anything in front of you as personal space has shrunk to a six inch radius only. Any closer and someone would indeed be touching either him or his Mighty Bucket for One.

The Hairy Potter gets out at Bond Street.

47
SAHIL

6:25 pm

Sahil pushes the menu around back and forth, side to side like it is a boat he's sailing on the broad expanse of the white table cloth. A menu is only a glorified spreadsheet; his eyes being trained to read the right hand side price column first before he glances at the left hand side description in which he had no interest. Anything is bound to be achingly good at these prices. He looks into his phone's glass screen. His hair is greasy and unwashed. He is gaunt and unshaven. His reflection looks like a skull wearing a mop. He can barely eat or function, yet he is sitting in a posh restaurant.

It is Anjali's birthday and he's booked her choice, which is Hakkasan in Mayfair. She's keen on Cantonese food and she's acquired the taste from previous Hong Kong flatmates she had. They obviously also have quite refined tastes. When middle-class Indians eat out for special occasions, they always choose Chinese. Choosing an Indian restaurant would be like eating at home, but worse. No one could cook like your mum or your mum's cook.

Everywhere he looks there seems to be a huge figure with a crewcut, or a hoodie with jackboots, or the shadowy suggestion of the monster plaguing him.

He looks at his watch and calls the waiter. When his Southern Comfort is brought to him, he throws it back in his throat. His eyes bulge from the fire in his throat and the dimly-lit decor swam in amber hues.

Anjali has arrived expecting cocktails or at least a glass of bubbly. Her grin is infectious and Sahil returns it, unable to help himself. She always manages to cheer him and anyone up on a bad day. The waiter takes her coat, which he remembers buying with her in Zara on the Kings Road. She is wearing the most amazing shimmery bronze outfit but she sits down too soon so he does not get a proper look.

The outfit perturbs him into thinking that she wants a proper night out. He hopes that her friends and their cohorts would take care of *all that* on his behalf. In his current state, he would keel over if he has to do more than dinner. Already he has much less sleep than a vampire and each night is haunted by visions of blood, the van, the thug's thumping pig head with its crew cut.

He's bought her a bracelet from Pandora, which has set him back £70 for not exactly the Rolls Royce of high street luxury jewellery, but a basic entry model. He slides the box across the table and wishes her, 'Happy Birthday!'

She opens it quickly, like a child, and he helps her put it on. 'It's so pretty. I love it; thank you so much,' Anjali leans over the table and kisses him. He inhales her apple-scented hair when it tumbles forward.

Life should ideally be a haircare ad in good, clear sunshine, instead of being seriously wrecked since the night of the incident ten days ago. He didn't even have a perfect life before, but now it is considerably worse. His eyes sag with fear. He looks at her with a hunted, drawn stare.

They order all her favourite items and the waiter goes away. She talks about her day but he is not listening. She talks about Classmate X or her mother's trip to Hong Kong or her brother going to Mumbai for an interview. His mind drifts.

Whenever Anjali or Classmate X ask 'what's wrong?', he always blames it on exam pressure, even though there are no exams right then. It is only January and he is supposed to be writing his dissertation and doing a bit of work experience. He is not sure about the work part, but the experience sure has been hell.

He has conveniently forgotten about Classmate X, careful not to mention to Anjali that Classmate X is actually a very distant relative and should therefore be referred to as Cousin X. She is probably a spy for back home and therefore he has kept her from any news about three things: him, Anjali, money. She would be the first to report any tidbit, no matter how trivial, to his family.

Sahil keeps looking around, thinking that surely the thug, the thug's gang, the cops, immigration, any number of members of authority or organised crime would be back for him, not Marcus. Marcus not defending himself had left Sahil to do the wrong thing. Pain and suffering are always inevitable for a large intelligence and a deep heart, said Dostoyevsky. Sahil is soothing his own burns with thoughts of his own kindness. How little they help now while he sat like a crash test dummy at this candle-lit table.

Anjali eats and he picks at the delicious meal. He can't stomach much.

'What's wrong, Sahil? Lately, you have not been yourself.' She stares into his sunken eyes.

'No, I haven't. I'm sorry! Let's get us some drinks.' He looks at the waiter.

'Have you noticed something?' She asks.

'If it's the dress, I think is really cute.'

'It's not a dress, it's a jumpsuit. See how it starts like a dress but it has trousers, not a skirt?'

She stands up to illustrate her point, half-twirling to the left and to the right.

Now he could see. It is like a bronze-coloured boiler suit. If there was anyone who could make a uniform sexy, it would be Anjali.

'I have great news. A surprise.'

'Oh, yes?

'Please let it be good,' he breaks into a smile, and puts his hands together into a namaste. He has had enough of bad news.

'Are you not going to ask me why I am late?'

Sahil grins like a mask. He has no patience for this game.

'Well,' Anjali continues not waiting for him to ask. 'You know how I told you about half a year ago that my dad has been looking to buy a flat in London?'

'Yes?' His eyes briefly light up as though he knows what she's talking about. He might have known her then but they had not been dating.

'Well, we completed tonight!'

'Completed?'

'I went to get the keys. We got the flat! That is why I was a little late.'

She says *we* like it is him and her but of course she means her family.

'But will you be...,'

'I will not be able to live in it of course; it needs renovating first. Nothing much. Just changing the tiles and moving walls around, repainting, a new kitchen and bathroom, new wardrobes. It's only a small flat.'

'That sounds like a lot of work for a small flat.'

She nods the Indian way, side to side, rather than up and down.

'You'll want to see it with me. Sahil, I'm so excited.'

Does she think he'll be living there? They would have to get married first. Fat chance. She shouldn't be in the nightmare that he is living. At the same time, he wants so much to escape the nightmare. He would if he left the flat he shares with Marcus. They'd never be able to find him. He'd disappear as immigrants do, into new postcodes, local authorities, jobs. He wouldn't be working with Marcus. The thug doesn't even know his name. Surely he's fearful for no reason. He is only an overseas student. Their sole purpose is to pay fees through their noses, gain their credentials and leave. They have no other objective.

They have no roots here, no groundwork, no Thames Water account.

Temporarily happy with his rationalisation, he grins and returns her side-side nod with his own.

'That's the surprise,' she confirms.

'Really great news,' he gives her two thumbs-up. 'Thanks for sharing it with me.'

'You sound like a social media post. *Thanks for sharing it with me,*' she mimicked him. 'Hashtag: news update.'

'Wha..? I'm truly excited for you.'

'Are you not going to ask me where it is?'

'No, you must surprise me, right?'

'Tomorrow I'll meet you at the tube station and take you there. You have any classes on?'

'No,' he says in a perfunctory way.

'Maybe you can get another job in a reputable firm in the city that pays better.'

'I've been on LinkedIn. Going to get a new job soon. All the hours count in the worksheet.'

'I just think we can spend more time together now. It's the last hurrah. Right?'

'The last hurrah,' he repeated, in a trance.

'Are you OK?'

He is quite sick of being asked if he's OK. Sahil's thoughts have drifted to Marcus. A blade of disloyalty slices at him. He wants to leave Marcus but he also sees him as a friend, someone he would lay his life down for. Marcus has helped him so much. When Sahil's uncle was ill for 6 months and Sahil received no money, Marcus accepted half the rent. When Sahil's cousin needed funding for a new patent, Sahil never thought about asking Marcus for help, but Marcus immediately asked *how much* and transferred his contribution. The pound goes a long way in India. Ten times, in fact. Sahil knows he has Marcus's unquestioning trust.

'Are you listening? Sahil? What are you thinking about? Sahil?'

He snaps out of his thoughts and blinks rapidly. *Was this what it was like being married?* He has heard his mother talk this way so many times to his father, *are you listening?* being her punctuation.

'What... what did you say?'

'I said I will see you at 10 at Aldgate East. OK?'

Sahil calls for the bill. The waiter, a young Chinese guy with a moon face and a black Mao top, catches his eye. He brings it over, gently placing it on his side of the table.

His Visa card in hand, he picks up the small white print-out. He looks at it, then at the waiter. 'Umm...,' he says, 'The drinks... is that— are they— on a separate bill?'

'No. I'm pleased to say they have been bought for you on account of the young lady's special occasion,' says the waiter, breaking into a big smile, a crescent on his round face. He then looks at Anjali and wishes her, 'Happy Birthday!'

'Thanks so much,' Anjali grins, her relaxed arms folded on the table.

'But... by who?' Sahil looks at him, bewildered. 'Who paid?'

'He says he is a good friend. Barry O'Keefe.'

Blood drains from Sahil's face. He's struck dumb. He stares in horror at the bill laid open in the upholstered leatherette folder, and then the restaurant around him, the diners, business types, smart middle-aged groups of women, the carved screens and the ambient lantern lighting. The room spins.

'Sahil? What's wrong?' Anjali's voice is low but burns with alarm. Her head tilts from side to side uncertainly, her eyes widening while studying him.

'Is everything all right?' Asks the waiter. His smile disappears.

Sahil throws his card down and pays.

48

MARCUS

When Sahil gets in early from a special night out, Marcus knows something is up. 'So?' Prompts Marcus. 'Are you going to tell me?'

They sit on the sagging sofa, saggier with the weight of Sahil's silence. Sahil's pupils have dilated and he is in a daze. He does not speak for a minute or two, but his mouth opens and shuts like he is about to say something.

'It's OK, let me get you something. A coffee? Or chai, maybe,' Marcus offers.

Sahil turns and faces him with gratitude.

Marcus comes back in from the kitchen with two mugs. He hands Sahil one.

Sahil exhales with his mouth. 'You won't believe it, the bastard. He... he bought a round of birthday drinks.'

'Who or what are you talking about?'

'Marcus. I'm serious. He knows.'

'Who?'

'Marcus, oh fuck! He *knows* who I am. He's been following me. He was there at the bloody restaurant,' He whips off his glasses, clutches at his mass of black curly hair and leans over in an emergency position, head between his knees.

The bravado overwhelms and perturbs Marcus. It doesn't feel like it's him. He folds his arms and leans back. 'How do you know it's him?'

'The waiter said. Someone called Barry O'Keefe paid.'

Marcus doesn't answer. He stops sipping, and puts the mug down. A screw somewhere has tightened a round.

'Say something!' Snaps Sahil.

'What can I say? There's nothing we can do. We don't even know if this guy who paid the bill is the same guy!'

They are having a shouting match again, like some ancient married couple. If Bloody Angela was listening outside... he can't bear the thought.

'He knows where we live!' Bleats Sahil.

'He knew it anyway,' Marcus throws his hands in the air. 'The attack was very near here. He had already been following us.'

'Then why is he not here? Why is he not back?'

'Oh, God. I don't fucking know.'

'Why don't you know? Don't you know everything?'

'Sahil, please. Just shut up. How is this helping?'

Sahil gets up and goes to his room. He *doesn't* slam the door.

The thug may have done Marcus a favour. The Hanwags did make him feel like an impostor builder. They cloaked him with a faux-machismo like his stupid patchy moustache. But now he has new glasses and a new watch. He got rid of the moustache which had only made him look like Fu Manchu.

His replacement glasses are the enormous black framed

futtpod (fashionably ugly to the point of designery) kind that wealthy Chinese fine art students would strut around in, incognito and ironic.

His appearance is now his ammunition. Marcus has shaved the bottom half of his head and coloured the longer top half amber. He got the DIY dye from Superdrug and he watched TikTok to learn how to do it in 15 minutes. Short-sighted and slight, Marcus has always been a prematurely-aged family man, developing a stoop from being dragged through life's burdens. Now he is a rejuvenated hipster.

Marcus was dressing out of fear, not confidence, unlike wealthy students from China. If the thug came back, this would unnerve him. He imagines the thug's what's-going-on curious stare, which would buy Marcus more time to escape. A crude desperate tactic, Marcus hopes it will outwit the thug, because he sure would not win any physical alter-cation and this time there might not be a Sahil to get him out of it.

49
NAFISAH

Tuesday 10th January

Nafisah hears the doorbell. The sewing machine's motor is loud: when she is working at high speed she sometimes she can't hear the door. Her right foot stops depressing the pedal. She gets up and focuses her left, and better eye, through the peephole.

Two police officers in uniform.

She unhooks the chain and opens the door to the width of her face. 'Ms Nafisah Ahmad?'

'Yes?'

'Thanks for leaving your name and contact details with the ambulance staff yesterday. I'm DI Marc Beauchêne-Gill and this is DC Jenny Holden.'

Her brow knits in incomprehension. He repeats his name Although Nafisah doesn't expect him to, he elaborates, almost apologetically, 'French Creole. My mother's family was from Martinique. My father is Indian. From Punjab.'

She has a feeling he has to say or spell his name several times a day and softens when both officers smile. Though he has bags under his eyes and a tired complexion, he has kind amber eyes and grey Afro hair cut close.

They flash their ID in tandem and Nafisah glances at the small photographs and shiny badges. She might as well have not looked at them. She cups her hand over the back of her neck wondering what the hell is coming next.

'We are here about Miss Angela Mae Fort,' says DC Holden, cutting the DI's pleasantries short.

Nafisah bites her lower lip.

'May we come in?' The DC adds.

'Of course,' she replies. Nafisah opens the door fully. They don't sit down or ask to. Instead they stand at the shoe cupboard, near the entrance door. They must be in a hurry and don't remove their shoes.

'Would you say Miss Fort was forgetful?' DI Gill begins.

'Maybe not more than people her age. She would forget to make a cup of tea but that's totally normal to me.'

'Sure. When you say people her age, what do you mean?'

'People in their 50s or 60s?' Nafisah makes a guess.

'Miss Fort was 47.'

This comes as a surprise, yet not really. All the expensive treatments, creams and serums don't work as strong as genetics.

'How... how did she die?'

'She... sustained multiple traumatic injuries consistent with a heavy object falling on her, which was the bookcase,' he pauses and takes out his phone. He reads in silence from the email. Then he continues aloud, 'Just reading out from the autopsy report. *The primary cause of death is attributed to blunt force trauma to the chest and abdomen, resulting in multiple fractures of the ribs on the left side, leading to a flail chest condition,*' the DI pauses, his eyes scan side to side before he reads on. 'Ah yes. *She had pulmonary contusion, significant bruising and injury to the lung tissue, causing respiratory distress and impaired oxygen exchange and haemothorax an accumulation of blood in the pleural cavity from lacerations and internal organ damage, contributing to respiratory compromise.* She went into shock and never recovered.'

Nafisah shudders. Angela was crushed like a doll by the huge bookcase. Nafisah had once noticed the antiquarian books and enormous ceramic midcentury vases that Angela collected.

'Did she seem well when you went over last Thursday?'

'Of course. She always makes an effort and appears fine. She loves the company.'

'She has friends in the area?'

'I don't know but she says she needs the outfit in case she is going out somewhere nice with an old friend. That's all I know and I'm afraid I didn't ask who it was and where they were going and so on—,'

'What were you doing there?'

'I was picking up a Christian Lacroix jacket she wanted altered so I had to take her latest measurements.'

DC Holden makes notes in her little notepad which Nafisah can't read as the handwriting is small and tight.

'And when I had completed the alterations along with the curtains I had already made, I packed them all and were delivering them to her yesterday. But I saw the ambulance... and... I—,'

'Yes, go on.'

'I still went to her flat which was on the top floor. I just couldn't believe it.'

'How long have you known her?'

'About 3 years ago.'

'How did you come to know her?'

'I answered one of those posts on the Next Door app where she was asking for recommendations for someone to do alterations.'

'Do you know if she's been ill?'

'She has more than one ailment, yes, but I'm sorry, I don't know what they are. She's always talking about her medications and what she has to take for which condition. Wait. One of them is Type II diabetes. I only know that because she says one of the side effects of her medication is losing tummy fat. She was so thrilled and she couldn't wait to go down a clothes size.'

'Do you know what she does all day?'

'She enjoys life,' chuckles Nafisah. 'TV, theatre, books, restaurants, London. Look at her kitchen cupboards. Everything is from Waitrose or Marks and Spencer Food Hall. Nothing cheap. She does not have to stinge or scrape or save. She told me she hires someone to help with everything. She has a handyman, who lives downstairs on the ground floor, a cleaner who comes once a week... me, of course to sew and mend her clothes and soft furnishings. Angela can't even sew a button on.'

'It's not cheap, right? Cleaners. How much is it now?'

'I don't hire one. I can't afford it. I charge £20 an hour for sewing, and cleaning costs £15 an hour. That's £180 a month straightaway. I couldn't do that. Cleaning is better paid than any office, retail or service industry job. Angela has a Romanian girl who comes weekly for 3 hours. Like she needs it! She has no kids or pets that make any mess. But someone needs to polish her white marble kitchen worktops. The most impractical surface, if you ask me. Her flat is always in pristine condition, beautifully decorated.'

At the word beautifully, Nafisah gesticulates with her hands spread as though on a luxury blanket. She is on a roll; she can't stop. A film of sadness flecked with candour spreads across her memories of Angela.

'Yes, we've had a word with the Romanian cleaner who found her. Ileana was understandably very distraught. She said the bookcase was unstable due to a missing support at the back. She mentioned this to Angela and the handyman was supposed to fix it.'

'Her clothes are all vintage or designer or both,' Nafisah continues, 'And that's why she would rather alter them than buy new clothes.'

'What work was she in?'

'She is one of those women who seemed to have done a bit of everything. Office work. Dancing. West End theatre administration. Healthcare.'

'Does she mention what she works as now?'

'No. I don't know if she's still working. She may have a private income, though I'm just speculating. She has to step down her taste and get her fabric from Dalston Mill Fabrics rather than John Lewis. I think Angela once hinted that some bloke pays for her flat and her expenses. He doesn't give her much more, she says. Just enough to keep her going. That's why she has to reduce her decorating budget drastically.'

It would not be hard to find out from her bank records, Nafisah thinks. When the officers had left, she feels emptied of her momentum.

She had once met Angela's gentleman friend. Once. She

replaced the zips on two pairs of his suit trousers. They were Zegna, not Zara. He was tall, though not very attractive, bulky in appearance, probably rich. He was distinguished-looking. Anybody using her for alterations obviously had money spare. People who bought trousers from Primark would not pay for work done when they can simply buy another pair.

She sits at the machine for a long time, unable to sew. She finds it hard to control her imagination once triggered. She kneads her fingers together.

With her eyes shut, she can almost touch the rough frothy texture of the tutu skirts that Angela would have worn. Nine to twelve layers of stiffness and tradition. Angela would have been thrilled and so proud to show them off, with stories of her backstage, at rehearsals all backed by crass but humorous anecdotal evidence. She was a storyteller.

Nafisah never got to see them.

50

MARCUS

0:47 am

1   Marcus gets to the property after picking up the keys from the agency . He has never met the client before. He works through the agency for new clients. Crossing from east to west is like going to another country. He watches the halal butchers and household shops selling mops and brooms turn into wine merchants, pet grooming salons and charcuteries. He can remember this area well, though it has changed a lot, as all places do in the process of gentrification.

Much has to be said for the housing boom. From despicable to desirable through market forces. Marcus moves the piles of letters and clears a path in the corridor. He takes out his phone and types in his Notes app. The carpet is from the Natural Flooring Company; he recognises the weave. The kitchen is old, just basic white matt melamine units from Wickes or B&Q.

Now that Sahil has declined to come in with him, he has no choice but to take notes since Sahil is the one who usually enjoys looking at defects, if *enjoys* is the right word. He has an inquisitive mind; he's good at identifying the sources of cracks, damp patches or damaged plaster, ceilings, walls and floors. Sahil has learned a lot through his family's construction business. Although with Marcus's experience he could tell too, and it is handy to have an assistant with young eyes.

When the door bell rang, it interrupts his thoughts and he hears a couple. Their voices are outside. He starts to go from the back door to the front, making his way past the two bedroom doors and the living room door into the corridor. They have keys too. He hears the unlocking and they enter.

'Oh, hi, you must be Marcus? I'm Anjali, the owner. The agent said you might be early.'

Marcus could not hide his shock.

'Allow me to introduce you,' says Anjali, smiling. 'This is Marcus,' she says to her partner. 'We talked on the phone?' She prompts Marcus.

'Yes. I...,'

'Yes,' she nods, as if affirming her identity. 'I just got the keys yesterday and it was my birthday! Such perfect timing. I'm so glad you can make it.'

'OK. Great.' He says as he follows her around while she explains what she wants to do, which is to reinstate the knocked-through kitchen and living room into two separate rooms. 'I'm glad you're Asian; you understand, don't you? Asians don't like open plan because of the cooking smells. Also, the help has to go somewhere while we're trying to relax and watch TV for example,' she giggles with honest amusement as she genuinely finds it a practical and reasonable reason. *The help*. That sounds very Asian already.

Asians laugh out of honesty and also embarrassment

while explaining something, and it doesn't even have to be funny; the laugh is also a kind of punctuation.

'I want to change the kitchen layout,' she says. 'I'd appreciate if you could direct me at some shops or online kitchen design showrooms where I could shortlist a selection.'

The way she says *shortlist* makes it sound like an international prize everyone had been waiting to hear about.

'I have a trade account at both Benchmarx and Howdens if you're interested in a trade kitchen?' He mentions. 'I can send you the links.'

'Oh sure, but I'm more interested in bespoke? I don't want anything ready made. This is a small flat. I want it to all fit and be made-to-measure. We want good quality. I'm sure you know what I mean as the agency told me you work for luxury investment property owned by the Chinese. We want *that* kind of quality.'

'Sure,' Marcus replies. This is going to be a tough client. He has met the type before, in his previous job handling multimillion projects, which ironically is easier than handling the small bijoux flat owner who obsesses about every light switch or door handle.

'Would this be for tenants or would you be living here?'

'I might be. I might not be,' she says with a grin. 'If we get a job abroad, then we won't be, but if we...,'

'*We?*'

'I'm sorry, how rude of me. This is my fiancé Sahil.'

51
NAFISAH

Wednesday 11th January

After the school run, Nafisah drags out the IKEA Trofast white plastic trough of her current mending jobs.

She picks up the trousers from the top of the pile. She ought to mention to the cops about them. She pulls out from under her sewing machine the card that the officers had given her the day before.

She makes her way to Victoria Park Square to the nearest police station, and asks for DI Marc Beauchêne-Gill or DC Jenny Holden. They're both not around but she doesn't want to leave any messages.

'Just let them know that I came by, and if they could please contact me,' she tells the lady at the help desk.

'What's your name?'

'Nafisah Ahmad,' she says.

As she leaves, a female voice calls her. 'Nafisah?'

It's DC Holden, propping a self-closing door open and beckoning to her. 'Sorry, I've been in a meeting. Please come in.'

Nafisah heads into the corridor that DC Holden is standing in, and the fire door swings shut on its closers.

DC Jenny Holden points her to an interview room which is greige — grey and beige. It's boring but usable. The chairs, window frames and any other features are blue in line with the cop branding.

'Thanks for coming,' says DC Holden. 'What can I do for you?'

'It's these.'

'What are they?'

'It's two suits I h'd already altered for that man, the friend of Angela's.'

'Is it just the trousers?'

'There's the suit jacket too, here, but nothing is being changed. I am just keeping them together, as one should.'

When she says *as one should*, a twinge of self-right-eousness pinches her.

'What should we do with them?' asks DC Jenny Holden.

'Maybe you can return them to him. I have no idea how to contact him as I was only doing the job for Angela so it's come from her. I'm sure his contact details are on Angela's phone.'

'That's great; thank you for this. Do you know who he is? Is he her special friend?'

'I think so,' Nafisah replies, turning red. 'He must be.'

When she says nothing more, DC Holden says, 'Let me show you the CCTV footage which we have from the building management.' She turns on her iPad and scrolls through videos until she finds the one. Nafisah can only tell by the gait since it's such a fuzzy poor quality video. He has a large weekend type bag, which has wheels and a pull-up handle.

'Is that his bag?'

'I don't know as I've never seen it. But I think it's him. Is it possible to zoom in anymore?'

'It's already zoomed in.'

'He must have stayed the night as I took his measurements for his fitting the day after this video.'

'He did. He left the next day according to this other video. She points to it, and the man was in a different outfit but pulling the same bag along.'

'She— she—,'

'Yes?' Prompted DC Holden. The police constable Mona Lisa smiles.

'She told me that she has seen her ideal wedding dress, which she wanted me to sew,' Nafisah recalls. 'She knows what she wants and I can sew anything.'

Nafisah starts to hyperventilate when conjuring the image of the simple and structured midnight blue short dress with a matching bolero jacket in Duchess satin that Angela showed her on her phone. Nafisah hangs her head, her hands falling onto her lap.

'Go on.'

'She's been with him a long time,' Nafisah speaks in a monotone. DC Holden does not take notes. She listens. This gives Nafisah the confidence to continue. There is nothing like the distracting scratching of a blue ballpoint pen to make her stop talking. 'She told me that he left his wife for her. Decades ago. Angela still dreams that he would propose. But he never did. Yet she's been on holiday with him. France. Portugal. Posh hotels. She's shown me pictures.'

Nafisah could only dream of places like those that Angela had been to with... with...

'I can't remember his name,' she suddenly looks up and tells DC Holden. 'I've only met him twice and I was too focused on the details of the alterations I was making. He had two concealed zips replaced the first time, and they were not quick easy jobs.'

'But when she used to talk about their holidays and about him?'

'When Angela talks about him, it's always secretive and discreet, she never refers to him by name. She just uses the pronouns, he, his, him.'

That sounds strange, the way Nafisah explains it, but DC Holden seems to understand.

'Thanks for leaving the suits here, says DC Holden. When she digs her fingers into each pocket, she finds two tickets in the inside pocket of the jacket. 'Looks like it is the last time he wore this,' she says to Nafisah.

'I haven't looked in the suit jacket as there were no changes to be made. It was only to keep it together with the trousers as a set.'

'That's strange,' says DC Holden. 'It's from the Novello theatre and dated third January. Mamma Mia.'

'Why strange?'

DC Holden pauses. 'A wallet found in the theatre was handed in on that night. Never mind. It may be nothing to do with Angela. Thank you Nafisah, I really appreciate your time. If you think of anything else, you know where I am.'

52
MARCUS

When he sees the blue and white car on Corfield Street, he knows he will be late on site. He swears under his breath. Is this about the thug? It can't be about his wallet. He's got it back now.

'Good morning,' DI Beauchêne-Gill says as he climbs out. 'Marcus, do you have a few minutes?' he adds.

'What's this about? I've got my wallet back, thanks to you, and I am fine,' Marcus stutters mechanically with a frown, 'I am about to head off to a new project,' Marcus bristles, breaking into a false smile as an afterthought.

'It will only take a few minutes,' says the DI.

'I'm sorry. I really can't and I have to get to my job now.'

The DI does not return his smile. 'Then we will have to hold you on suspicion for the murder of Miss Angela Fort.'

Marcus blinks. 'Pardon?' He mumbles.

'Miss. Angela. Mae. Fort. She used to live on the third floor of your building?'

'I know who you mean,' says Marcus.

'Did you see her last Friday?'

What is this DI talking about? 'Yes. Yes I believe I was working on her flat—,'

'Miss Fort passed away that day.'

'What? No!'

'Yes. Now according to other residents, you have been heard to call her Bloody Angela. Is this true?'

'No, I mean, yes, but come on. That's just a nickname.'

'*Just a nickname*,' the DI repeats, stressing each syllable.

'Oh, please. It's not meant to be harmful. We chat all the time. We were friendly. We banter,' Marcus is winging it now. He has barely exchanged a few words with Angela in all these years, just grunts and demands of money while she in turn extracts gossip out of him.

'Really? That nickname doesn't sound friendly.'

'We were! She always asks how I am. I mean no harm. I can say bloody about anyone else.'

'Oh? Who?'

'Like, the bloody council. Or another bloody leak,' Marcus tries to think of examples of *bloody* but it's getting to be a joke. He can't ad lib like this. 'It's really no big deal.'

'So you would say she gets on with you. You don't harbour any negative feelings.'

'No!' Marcus continues shaking his head vigorously.

'But how are you at handling the fact that she owes you thousands of pounds? Does it not bother you?'

'It's only a couple of thousand. You're not saying I killed her? For two thousand pounds?' Marcus pictures his own clownish grin at the ludicrous implication. It was closer to three thousand now, but he plays it down.

'Not at all. But neighbours have heard you arguing.'

'Arguing? We have heated discussions, yes. She's a terrible client, always changing her mind, makes me absorb the costs of adding works, starts a job and stops it for a week while she goes on holiday. Late at paying. Just awful.'

'I understand. How frustrating,' the DI says, though Marcus doubts he means any of it. 'Do you know if she has any friends or visitors?'

'I wouldn't know,' Marcus pinches the bridge of his nose. His eyes want to shut but he forces them open. 'I— I work from morning to night.'

'Is it true that you have the CCTV footage for this building?'

'Yes.'

'We need last week's recordings, please.'

'Wait. Why?'

'I'm just letting you know that if you withhold any information, it will delay our investigation and put you under suspicion.'

Marcus listens, not knowing if he should be relieved or panicking. Firstly, this is not about the thug. Secondly, he can't figure it out. What did Angela say about all those jobs she did? One of them was working in the government. It must be a leak. Someone knows that she knows something. Marcus's speculation makes him feverish and he stands staring at the floor.

DI Beauchêne-Gill silently scribbles in his notebook. They look like they are at a bus stop, passengers each lost in his own thoughts. The DI snaps the notebook shut.'Will you drop it off to us today on a data key? At the same time we can get your prints from it.'

Something is not right about Angela's death. Surely it can't be linked to him!

53
ELIJAH

Thursday 12th January

Elijah takes the district line to Parsons Green, to the address on all her letters. Although he's never been there, he's seen it enough times to have memorised it.

He follows a large person in the wider "family, disabled and luggage" gate at Whitechapel station. He's not wasting a tenner on travel costs.

The underground system has been increasingly automated and this is a good thing for him. *Rejoice, Elijah!* His mum would cheer. Reduce the staff and increase the fares.

He waits opposite the big house near a tree, unsure when she'd come out of the big house as he doesn't know her routine. He did try to call once, but never again as it was like being gagged.

The cold starts to bite at his hands and he digs them into his pocket. He's almost trying to spot a member of the royal family coming out of the Palace. He watches passersby, but pretends to study his phone so as not to look suspicious. He stares at the roadsweepers with their blinking machines. The clouds thicken as it gets darker in the bleak winter light, threatening to rain.

His *new* mother, he reminds himself because she isn't really. Since he received the letter and has been told he was adopted he'd got very confused. His grandmother is in a care home in Singapore, and had been writing to his mum Irene, who'd sent her his photos. She has more to show him, she writes.

At last, after an hour, a tall Chinese woman in an apron opens the door and comes out to polish it, first the brass ironmongery, the lion's face knocker and the octagonal pull knob and then each of the door panels to make the olive paintwork shine.

Elijah crosses the road and mounts the stone steps.

'Stella?' He calls out.

The woman turns around. Her rag drops to the floor.

54
STELLA

He is standing on my doorstep, only a metre from me. I swallow. He has my height and disarming staring eyes. I am just about to burst into a big grin and hug him, but I hold myself back. He makes no attempt to smile; he looks surly, like he is on a callout to do a job.

Boy and Richard are safe in front of the electronic babysitter — the TV. I complete what I started in the morning, sweeping the front steps, cleaning the sills and polishing the front door.

'Stella, hi, I'm Elijah,' he announces, then as an afterthought, he adds, 'Pleased to meet you.'

At this time of night-day, footsteps on the pavement are usually local runners, mums, dog walkers and commuters on their way home. Sometimes we get chuggers — charity muggers — those who collect money door-to-door for various charities, real and fake. They always arrive in the early evenings to disturb your peace. I never give them anything. I just don't have money, time to sign up for shit or to listen to their sob story pitch. Charity begins at home.

I have never laid eyes on him but I know it's him as sure as a mother knows her son.

'You... you must call me Mummy. Elijah, I am your mum,' my voice quakes. 'Your *real* mum.'

His mouth twitches. A frown builds on his forehead and he narrows his eyes, studying me. He does not answer. His hollow gaunt eyes shift down to his dirty, torn old trainers. With his uneven crew cut, he looks unemployed, rough and ill. He is just unwell, I tell myself. My boy. I hug myself since I can't hug him, and think of what to say. It's bitingly cold, and I am starting to shiver. He has never replied to my letters, texted or called me. It has all been a one-sided conversation.

'You said if I need anything I could come to you,' he finally speaks.

'Umm... I... I did. But I am working right now,' I shudder. 'My day off is tomorrow. Why don't we meet somewhere then?'

'I haven't got time!' Each word comes out hard and punchy. 'I need to talk to you right now.' His voice disarms me. It's deep, with a growl.

I hesitate, and blink at him. 'Ohhh, OK, please come in.'

When I wrote to him I mentioned that he must not come here unannounced. He just has. But he seems rather desperate. Jean-Viv must not find out. Luckily she is out buying clothes for Jasper from the Fulham Road charity shops, so I can introduce Elijah to Richard without her meddling presence. She makes it very hard for me to do my job.

I stuff my rag into my apron and beckon to him. 'Come

in,' I repeat, as I have nothing else to say. He strides lazily in like a teenager. I could visualise him as a toddler or even Jasper's age. I would have found him adorable with his hooded eyes, brooding, irritable. I've always found children as grumpy as the elderly, and just as unpredictable.

'The plumber's here,' I am about to lie to Richard but he seems preoccupied and hasn't noticed or heard Elijah and I coming in. Richard is lost in a world of Lego pieces with Jasper. They are building something on the coffee table. I hear the crunchy plastic rattling of pieces being found and clicked.

'I need a red, with 8 dots,' says the boy, thoughtfully, not looking up.

'The tall or flat one?' Richard asks.

'The flat one, Gung Gung.'

They are deep in conversation.

'Would you like a cup of tea?'

'Go on then.' He follows me into the kitchen.

I put the kettle on while he stands. My spine prickles with the sensation of being watched. 'White?' I call over my shoulder.

'White. Two sugars.'

He won't call me mum. Not yet, maybe. I place the mug in front of him on the kitchen table. 'Sit down,' I say. My voice is shaky.

He sips. At any moment now, Richard will be coming into the kitchen. I have to think of what to say.

'You said I could contact you.'

'You can,' I agree, but I am not sure of what I mean now. What does he think I can do for him?

'I owe three months' rent. I... I can't find work. I'll pay ya back as soon as I get a new job. Not being funny, but times are hard,' he slurps from the mug. 'Haven't you heard? Cuts. Inflation. Cost of living crisis and all that?'

I swallow. I am guilty of living in this marble castle, unaware of his predicament and that of many young people in the UK.

I put my head through the dining room opening into the living room. Richard has fallen asleep in his chair in front of the TV where Jasper is transfixed by a children's programme. There is a rustle of papers dropping to the floor. I clear my throat. 'We can't talk here,' I say. 'Bring your tea with you. Upstairs. Quickly.'

He leaves the tea on the table, half drunk. I don't blame him. It's the worst cup of tea I'd ever made.

Outside my room door, I stop. 'What is it that you need?' Might as well be direct.

'I. Need. Rent. Money. Loadsavit.'

'Pardon?' I blink. My ears are straining. He has a strong Cockney accent that I'm not used to. It takes me a second to understand him.

'Look. Don't mean no harm. I am being evicted.' He says *lock, down me now arm*.

'Sorry to hear that.'

'I need £3,300. Make it three-and-a-half, will you? My rent is due in two days. I haven't given you much notice. I know that. I know. And I'm very sorry.'

I stare. Either he has no social skills or he is not sorry at all. My heart skips a beat. After all the trouble I have been through to find and connect with him, this is not how I visualised the first meeting with my son.

We head to the en suite bathroom or what used to be Richard's wife's bathroom. Such a beautiful double basin (his and hers) bathroom with black and white marble tiled floor wasted on her. Even a double-ended bath for them to sit together. She could not have spent more than 20 seconds in here every day. She was plain as a plate. She had an expensive layered hair cut even when she was ill, but it just looked like a grey rag on her head. I know what Richard saw in her. Her bank account. Without her, he could never have had The Peony, his first and only business. He was only a piano-player with some experience as hotel staff. Of course, without his business sense the enterprise would have collapsed. He had the sharpest style. Some people just have it. He is one of them.

Elijah stands with his hands dug deep in his hoodie pockets, pouting, not looking at me. A deep reticence shows in his sidelong glance. He doesn't want to be here. His being here is endearing and profound at the same time. Tears come to my eyes. I want to say something but I can't. There is nothing to say.

I reach into the vanity cabinet that Richard shared with his late wife. I wouldn't even mention her name. How cruel she had been, cold, just like her daughter. They don't remember but I do. I get a key that his late wife hid in the basket of toilet tissue, unlock and pull open the first drawer. The Rolex in its velvet box. He never wears it. What use has he for this white elephant?

'You don't have to,' I blurt to Elijah, 'But take this.' I must give him something else. From my uniform's apron pocket, I grab my purse. I pull out all I have which is £50. I have to carry cash when I take Richard out, just in case, for emergency treats, a taxi or a drink. I also have a card to use, but it is Richard's so that is of no use to Elijah.

'This is all I have,' I thrust him the wad of plastic money and it springs open like fake flowers. Plastic cannot be rolled or folded. It has a mind of its own which flings it open.

'Thank you,' he replies gruffly and turns to leave. Not a word more. No conversation. Which is just as well as Richard would be waking and wondering where I am.

'We'll talk more tomorrow, yes?' I ask in a hopeful and light tone. I manage a small uncertain smile.

'We will. I need the rest of the money.'

'Why?'

'Why?' He repeats, blinking. He shakes his head slowly; he looks faint. His chin rolls back and he shuts his eyes. 'I am being evicted.'

I shut the vanity cabinet drawer and re-lock it, chucking the key back into the basket. I have seen all the other items in there. Richard has given me luxury gifts. A Chow Tai Fook gold bangle here, a Tiffany diamond pendant there. All of which fill me with a creepy aftertaste. It's not like he bought them *for me*. Ugh.

I declined them, which Richard interpreted as a good sign. That I am decent and honest and could not possibly accept expensive gifts from my employer. Now I regret it. I would take any old luxury designer gifts for my son. Everything has a value.

My mother's jade earrings from San Francisco have been

the source of non-stop guilt trips. I still have them. The guilt *and* the earrings.

Elijah trudges down the stairs. I follow him like a mannequin.

My heart is ripped seeing him leave. 'Where shall I see you tomorrow? Where?'

'You can come to the flat. You know the address. You've been writing to me long enough.'

'Elijah.'

He looks up, with his hooded eyes.

'I...if you... I want you to call me Mummy.'

He screws his eyes up again, before he turns away and descends the grand mahogany staircase which I have polished to death. The handrails gleam like mirrors; the stair wall panelling dust-free as a new book. He just needs time. I will give him time. After he sleeps over it, he will realise there is no one who will hand over money to him like I have. I am his one true mother. Tomorrow, he will accept me and call me Mum.

'Oh Stella, Stella? Where are you, Stella? Are you there? Stella? Are you upstairs?' Richard pipes in his shaky voice from the living room "Lego table", as it is now known.

Oh, for crying out loud. Does he have to call my name four times?

'Boy is hungry,' he says towards the staircase from the living room. 'Have you started making dinner? Stella?'

'I'm coming, Richard. Are you OK?'

I sound patient and sweet. I've learned that the high pitch voice works well, from when I was at Dover Heights. The elderly could not hear low registers very well and the high pitch is the sound of youth so they are automatically tuned in. If it could get my mother's attention, it could get anyone's.

He has staggered to the tiled entrance hall now, and his sheepskin slippers shuffle noisily without the insulation of carpet and rugs. 'Oh!' He exclaims. His face has gone white and his hands fall to his sides. His eyes meet my son. He's astonished, as he should be.

'Richard, I would like you to meet Elijah.' I announce quietly.

His eyes widen, as if he had seen a ghost. His jaw hangs open and he squints. He holds the banister to steady himself. But Elijah is tall, and is still on the third step down. Richard is looking up at Elijah like he is in front of a giant marble statue at the V&A.

'You remember him, don't you?' I say.

'No, I don't, sorry,' Richard says, his voice trembling. 'Stella m-mentioned— a— someone coming—, y-you— you're—,' he starts to cough.

'*I'm* Stella, Richard,' I correct him. He's got me mixed up with Jean-Viv.

'Owju do?' Elijah growls, not putting his hand out for a handshake. He keeps them tightly tucked in the pockets of his ripped tracksuit bottoms. The Rolex is in there. 'Just need to pop to the toilet, if ya don't mind.'

'No, it's the door on the right under the staircase,' I tell him.

'He's just leaving,' I say to Richard, who stares at me. His eyes are full of questions, but his lips utter nothing.

I show Elijah the door and he marches out without a word. I shut the door quickly to keep the wintry air out.

'Well, bye?' Richard says in a strange high-pitched voice. 'Good of you... to... come... by,' he adds wistfully.

When I clean the toilet downstairs that night after dinner, I see that Elijah has taken all the little pieces of soap, towels and scented candles. Diptyque. He has assumed that either no one will notice or care.

55
SAHIL

Marcus usually celebrates every new job with a pub night and has invited Sahil along to their local on Globe Road, a leafy street behind the V&A's Museum of Childhood. No gastro-grub, DJs or pretentious wine lists here. The Camel is a cute, well-loved indie gem in edgy east London, saved from the horrors of corporate "brand identity" gentrification. Marcus and Sahil love their neighbourhood's restored Victorian tiled and floral wallpapered boozer with 1960s bronze pendant lights. There is not a table empty. That's inner city London for you. In the winter it's cosy and warm. In the summer, with the sun-baked picnic tables, dogs, families and buntings outside, it takes on a modern hipster village atmosphere.

Tonight is not a crazy drunk night for the mismatched pair, but just dinner and one or two drinks to talk through the project. Sahil knows that this has to be the smallest yet most expensive odd job that Marcus would be doing, yet they are still celebrating as per tradition.

'What will it be? Wandle or Freedom Four?' Marcus quizzes.

Sahil picks the former.

Marcus goes to the bar to get the menu and to order the drinks. Sahil watches, not able to relax. Marcus has recently transformed into someone else. When he'd been cooking for them at home, Marcus would slam the wok and it would clash like cymbals. His temper now flares unannounced. And no new designer glasses or dyed hair could tamp down his rage.

'Your fiancé? Why didn't you tell me?' Marcus blurts out, pressing the pint of Sambrook's Wandle into Sahil's hand, not looking at him. He drops the menus on the table like they're scorching.

Sahil grabs the cold pint glass to raise a toast to Marcus, but instead his shoulders rise in despair. He's *not* used to this. The confrontation is unlike Marcus. He is the most chilled, easy-going landlord and... friend.

'Look, I can explain to you,' says Sahil, putting the glass down without taking a sip. 'Firstly, I haven't proposed to her. But *she* thinks we're getting married! Secondly, she did *not* tell me she was hiring you.'

'Of course she knew who you worked with. You must have told her at some point.'

'I might have and so?'

'She wanted to surprise you; that's what I think,' Marcus quickly replies before gulping from his glass, looking up at the pendant lighting. Marcus seems to be avoiding eye contact, but Sahil knows it won't be for long. They are in too deep. 'That means you would be moving out, does it not?' Marcus asks.

Ah. So that's what concerns Marcus. 'I'd never agree,'

Sahil says. 'She never even asked me to move out. She makes all these assumptions, and it's like I'm on a train I can't get off.'

Sahil is caught in the middle. He doesn't like it but has nothing left in him to fight it. He glances at the menu absent-mindedly.

'I usually have the same thing,' Marcus says without looking at the menu. 'The Pieminster beef steak and ale pie with mash, minted mushy peas and red wine gravy.'

'I'll have the chicken and ham hock with leek and thyme,' Sahil reads out like a child. 'Please. With all the trimmings. Vegetables, sauce, whatever.'

'Mash or chips?'

'Mash,' he replies, and Marcus goes back to the bar to order.

Mashed is how Sahil feels now. Earlier in the evening Sahil had walked out of the flat to get his kebab dinner at some middle-eastern takeaway but his plans were waylaid by Marcus and he didn't want to say no. He didn't want to say yes either. There was no escape from "celebrating" the new job which ironically is Anjali's flat.

These days are short and the nights long. It isn't because it's winter. He couldn't and doesn't want to live with Marcus any longer than he has to. But while he's saving money, Anjali is getting ready for life with him. Sahil has no money to buy a flat let alone do it up all "bespoke". She is elegantly swanning in her world, and he's like Daffy Duck dragged in with reluctance. Although he has never disapproved of her or her lifestyle, he also very much wants to be left alone by both of them. Cousin X is probably jealous. He bursts out laughing from the tragicomedy that's now him.

'What's so funny?' Marcus jerks his head around, looking at him directly for the first time tonight.

Sahil lowers his chin, putting his hand over his face and shaking his head.

56
ELIJAH

:

Back on the Central line, Elijah gets off at Bethnal Green rather than changing to the District Line to get back to Whitechapel. Time to celebrate. He's starving and it's freezing. A heavy mist has descended on the street, casting a shadowy whiteness on the night. The winter never ends.

That has been a pain. The visit, the old man, the woman. He's only got £50 out of her and a stupid watch. He hasn't enjoyed barging in to the big house, but he has no choice. He hates her guts. Her doll-like face, the dyed hair, those red lips and most of all the house. She has no idea the hell he is in.

He staggers to the corner of Sugar Loaf Walk and Globe Road. There is a biting chill to the evening now. The temperature has dropped to under 5, and he longs for 3 square meals, not per day, but all at the same time right then. His nickname is Python. He could eat that much and last *that* long. He has had one meal at Nafisah's since his escape from the hospital but that was vegetarian so didn't count. Then he'd had the Mighty Bucket but that was no sit-down meal. He certainly can't afford heating at home so he needs to sit somewhere centrally-heated and eat a proper dinner for once. No one has been searching for him. They are clearly too busy. *That's the NHS for ya. See?* He lowers his chin, as if he is talking to his mum. *You were right, mum, you were.*

He picks 2 dishes from the menu, two pies, the steak and kidney and the chicken and bacon. One with mash and one with chips. Vegetables. That's all yer fifty quid can buy these days: 2 dinners, 2 drinks. Times are hard and the inflation is at an all-time high. Out comes the blue Barclays Bank card in the name of Barry O'Keefe. There was a time when he was at the pub at least twice a week, and now he could afford it once a month.

He stares at the diamonds on his watch, glinting ominously and he is inclined to take it off. He might get mugged. On second thought, *Naaah*. No one mugs Elijah. *He* does the mugging. Could a watch feed him for a year? Only if it sells, innit. He would look at the resale value in the morning. He knows a dealer of expensive shit like that. Dave's useless for this. He needs a pawn shop. That's more like it. A shop that has TVs, sound systems, games, jewellery, computers, watches.

He might recoup enough money for the next few months or even years' rental.

After his meals, he gets up to go to the toilets. It is getting late now and he looks forward to the heavy meals turning into concrete inside him and him into a dead-to-the-world slumber like Sleeping Beauty. He emits a huge belch as he comes back from the washrooms, and he glances in the extensive mirrored wall in the main room of the pub next to the heavily-patterned wallpaper, as if he needs to check his appearance. His current state is not exactly his best right now. Very bruised and lopsided, his jaw is at an odd angle. The bastards.

At the Hakkasan restaurant in Mayfair, Elijah was amused that he passed as security. He told the concierge he was the girl's bodyguard, hired by her uncle, Barry O'Keefe. That is how he got to pay for the drinks for the toy boy's dear girl. His father's card has come in handy. His heart bled when he has to use his own allowance on drinks he would never have had spent on himself or his poor mum. But the face on the toy boy made it worth it. He went completely pale as a corpse, didn't he? Elijah enjoyed the evening as much as he could carrying a bag of KFC which he ate outside on a bench on Conduit Street.

Suddenly he spots two faces in the crowded room. The first being the hairy one with glasses. Hairy Potter.

It's *them*, innit! The bastards who did this to him. Are they having a laugh? Out enjoying themselves? He couldn't Adam and Eve it. What the actual...

He rotates his huge neck around to look at the room. It feels like he's turning a motorcycle. At the backlit bar, tiered bottles of Jim Beam, Bombay Sapphire, Campari, rums glitter like a Victorian crystal mountain. His eyes dart from side to side, up and down. In that second he turns, he can't see their faces anymore. Are they in the room? Which side of the room were they when he saw them in the mirror?

His neck aches and creaks. Nothing has been the same after the incident. They were going to throw him away! He was in their van bundled up. Course he remembers. He just wasn't going to tell the NHS. He wasn't that stupid. He'd have to spend a day in the cop shop giving his exact details, name and address and he was in no position to do that.

As he gets up, he sees through the little cottage windows the vehicles parked outside in the pub's forecourt. It's the van! He is sure of it. Grey with a dent on the side. There *are* lot of these vans with dings but there is only one with a flower sticker on the windscreen mirror. Now. What flower is it? It does look familiar, but Elijah is not good with exotic plants or animals. He just knows it's a logo.

A sharp pain splits his head but it goes in an instant. He grips his temples with his thumb and ring finger, his span large enough to form a kind of helmet shape over the dome of his shaved head.

His assailant is here somewhere. The hairy guy with glasses. In this bloody room. His eyes float and search, but the lighting, all cosy and twee, isn't great.

Then a gust of wind indicates the entrance door opening. They are trying to "slip out", as if they have not seen him! Course they bloody did. He spots the back of the coat. That smart black coat. They have jobs, money, clean clothes. He has nothing. They have their winter beanies on, both West Ham. The short guy leaves right behind the Hairy Potter. It's Elijah's landlord, Marcus.

'Hey!' Elijah shouts and bolts after them but they try to pull the door shut. He stops the door with his foot. Elijah instantly grabs Marcus's wrist. 'Got ya! Yew wanker! Slum landlord. That's wot yew ah.'

'I'm NOT your landlord!' Shouts Marcus, his voice rising. Elijah is surprised by the volume.

'Yes, yew ah. Can't fool me.' Elijah enjoys intimidating him; he is a little non-white guy. Easy.

'No! I am not!' Marcus frowns, gritting his teeth inches from the thug's face. 'It's a horrible mistake. I have no idea who you are!' Marcus shakes his head. 'Let go of me,' he hisses. 'Who are you? What do you want?'

'We know you're Barry,' Sahil says. 'Barry O'Keefe.' Sahil shoves Elijah to get him to stand back but Elijah's ambidextrous, not that anyone would care. Elijah tosses his head back and a long bark of toddler laughter erupts. His left hand strikes Sahil's face and the force throws Sahil backwards. Marcus shoots a glance at Sahil, who tumbles into the street.

'Yew sort out my lease. I got your eviction notice. Been chattin' with the agency. Yew are definitely my landlord,' Elijah pauses. He has practised saying this line so many times, he can say it asleep. 'I am NOT moving out. My mother and I have lived there since I was born,' Elijah is as surprised as Marcus. The thought of how long he has been living in Bullen House, in the damned flat makes him red in the face. 'I ain't going nowhere!' He growls.

Elijah has made heads turn. He feels the eyes in the crowded room rest on the trio. Marcus grunts and pants as he tries to extricate his hand from Elijah's tight grip. Marcus's hand, still in the vice-like hold, has turned blue. Elijah feels the satisfying cracks and pops. He hopes that he's fractured Marcus's wrist. That'll teach him.

'Let go of me!' Marcus shouts, twisting his arm from the

shoulder and kicking Elijah but he's like a girl. Elijah can't believe this weakling works in the building industry. What's he building? Doll's houses?

'Where did you get that watch from?' Bleats Marcus.

'None-a-ya business! What's it to ya?!' He tightens his hold and gives Marcus a hard yank.

'I know where it's come from! Oh fuck, how did you get it? Did you... did you...?'

'It's mine. Ain't sellin' it to pay rent, ya got it?' Elijah feels his blood rise. Now he's calling Marcus's bluff. Some insane pride has landed on him like a deadweight and squashed his earlier aspiration to sell it for rent money.

'What do you mean sell it?' Marcus is shaking his head. 'You can't sell it. It's a bloody fake!'

Elijah stares. Is this scum trying to pull his leg? His thoughts are cut short.

'Excuse me, hey, mate,' the pub manager's voice calls from across the room. He can hardly push through the crowds to get to the door. 'I'm calling the cops,' he announces, coming over, holding his phone. The tight space makes it a struggle for the pub manager to weave through the crowd. 'Break it up, and get out,' he says.

Elijah loses his attention. In that split second, Marcus has yanked his arm away, and taken off with his sidekick into the damp night. They stagger off, the mist so heavy that Elijah has to squint. He hears their running footsteps fading, and he's unable to tell which direction they are in. Dampened by the thick foggy atmosphere, the soft thuds disappear fast.

He grunts and pants as he struggles to run after the enormous amount of food he's swallowed. *Fuck. Where did they go,* Elijah wonders, scratching his head, eyes darting left and right down the street.

He looks this way and that for a minute or so. They're gone. Globe Road is dark. Not a soul on Sugar Loaf Walk. The van is gone. The yellow street lights cast a sickly shade of salmon pink on the mist draped around him — shifting, soulless, a grey-white blanket.

57
MARCUS

Marcus listens to his own short breaths as the seconds passed in the van. Sahil has driven as far as possible from The Camel as they could see in the mist. Their seatbelts are still fastened, though Sahil has switched the engine off. He doesn't know where they are. Maybe Old Ford Road near the Victoria Park Chinese Pagoda. Nowhere near Corfield Street. Sahil's forehead and temples glisten with sweat, his jaw clenched and grinding. Distant sirens blare and the lights of the city pulse in the distant, like amoeba on a screen.

'What was that about?' Says Sahil, finally, gritting his teeth. 'Are you going to tell me or do I have to ask?'

'I am NOT his landlord. He's got me mixed up with someone else.'

'Marcus, look. I deliberately did not hurt him when he pushed me. I didn't know if I should help you this time.'

'Great! Thanks,' adds Marcus sarcastically. 'You're my hero.'

Sahil turns and grabs the padded hood collar of Marcus's

puffs jacket. 'Don't. Bullshit. Me. Who is he? What's with the Rolex?'

Marcus keeps silent. He stares at the dashboard like he's reading the newspapers.

'Let's go,' Sahil said quietly, resigned, exhaling a long breath.

Marcus has paperwork somewhere. They are deep in the recesses of his eaves storage. The sloping ceiling had cages of documents. He has not cared about them or looked at them. They might as well have rotted away. Who has time to go through the detritus of admin? All he does is work to get his life back. Once he was someone. He was a top guy, someone they called Sir at work, someone whom headhunters read about on LinkedIn. Then following a panic attack, he had a nervous breakdown, and another. Now he has just been called 'slum landlord'. That has an ugly ring to it. Is that who he is?

His wife used to take care of filing, bills and dental appointments for him and the children. MOT for the car. Jabs for the dog. There was nothing that she did not take care of. He has only to take of one thing: himself, so that he could take care of them. He'd failed at that.

When Sahil has gone to bed, Marcus creeps out of his flat into the communal corridor and stairwell. He climbs all the way to the top floor, past Angela's flat, bless her soul. He presses the button to access the loft ladder. The steep pitch of the roof has given the building its ample storage cages for residents. He flicks on the switch which floods the whole space with the light from the industrial lanterns he installed himself. The place is bright as a ward. Marcus's wrist looks bad in this light. He has suffered a Chinese burn. Ironic, he and the assailant being Chinese. It's tomato-red but he is grateful it's only a sprain when he yanked his arm away.

In the cage assigned to Marcus, there are boxes of files he'd never looked at. Thick grey and black roof attic dust now covers the boxes. His mother had kept them locked in here before he inherited the flat. He had never got them out as he had a decent income, a family home in a good area, and a family before this... this life he now lives in Corfield Street with a flatmate. It seems unfamiliar to him. The image of his wife, the sound of her name now strange, like he had never met or married her. Her name is Shue Wen. It means thoughtful in the snow. Much more than he could say about himself. He hardly has a thought now. He survives day to day, hour to hour, sometimes with the help of Sahil, mostly without.

He finds a cardboard office box labelled in his mother's handwriting, when he brushes off the layers of filth:

Lam Poh Choy

There are a lot of other boxes either labelled cryptically as this was, or unlabelled. Possibly a decade ago, he had to help her move her things out of another storage unit. But he took no notice of them and assumed it was part of her job or work stuff. Why would he be looking in it?

Seeing her name brought tears to his eyes, and he presses at his eye sockets with both his dirty thumbs, black with dust from the eaves beams and floor that he has been crawling around in, as though the thumbs would push his tears, and the years, back.

Sahil called out, 'Marcus is that you? Are you OK?'

Oh shit. Shouldn't he be in bed?

'Are you OK?' he repeated. 'Marco?'

Marcus wipes his tears. It's the nickname that Sahil gave him. 'Polo,' Marcus replies. He lifts the lid of the box labelled Lam Poh Choy.

'I followed you. I heard the door shut, and it woke me. What are you doing here?'

Sahil has half-climbed the steep and long roof ladder into the attic of the building.

'Go back to bed, Sahil,' pleads Marcus. He feels gusts of cold air, and knows there are holes in here that need fixing. Those air gaps should be sealed and not allowed to get bigger or the attic would get wet and the items destroyed over time. He is meticulous about maintaining the whole building even if the interiors would never appear in Elle Decor or any of those namby-pamby social media posts with houseplants and pink Le Creuset cookware.

'What are you doing?'

'Something complicated,' answers Marcus, unable to describe what he's looking for.

His *is* a complicated job where he is a caretaker for the building, and handyman for the residents. They need him and he them. A well-kept, centrally-heated, double-glazed flat which does not leak and has A-rated energy efficient appliances is all you can ask for in this life, in this city.

'What?' Sahil answers, his hands gripping the edge of the ladder like he is about to haul himself out of a swimming pool.

Marcus removes file after file of stapled and photocopied documents, some so old the staples had rusted away and became brittle with touch, disintegrating like a sprinkle of black pepper. The papers are loose and have a lightness when separated.

'I'm coming up,' he says.

'There's no need. I'm going down now. Nothing to look at. Let's go.'

'What's going on?' Sahil calls out to him from under the loft access hatch.

'N-nothing. It is my mother's box of stuff,' he says truthfully, irritable at Sahil's nosiness. God, Sahil's as bad as bloody Angela now. 'Come on, then. Sahil.' He locks his cage, then scrabbles over to the access hatch. 'Help me get down this ladder quick. Hold it at the bottom. I have to get to Brompton Road tomorrow. Remember, I am working on Anjali's job?'

The flat would have cost something like 1.5 million Great British Pounds! What does Sahil think of it, of her? Surely he must have been surprised. Maybe not. Maybe he had always known that Anjali is from a well-heeled family and it is Marcus who's been in the dark. Marcus's life is so repetitive, monotonous and stupid. Even his buzzcut, dyed the yellow of his tiles, and huge designer glasses have done nothing to give him any sense of individuality. If anything his new appearance is just a gaudy parody of his dullard self. All that he had ever cared about had already been lost. He is a ghost in East London.

'I think I should come with you,' Sahil interrupts his thoughts. 'I— well— it's Anjali's flat. I—,'

'You want to work on it? But you may be living in it!' Something is weighing on Marcus. Not sure why it would be bad idea but it doesn't' seem a good idea either.

Sahil shrugs, glum. That makes two of them, and everyone else in London.

. . .

In his room, Marcus starts reading the one file he removed. His mother had left him the Corfield Street flat. But she was also the director of a trust which owns three other flats.

The Lam Poh Choy trust was set up for him and his siblings. He read the address quickly. It certainly rings a bell. Bullen House. The rental for that flat went to the trust. The long term tenants' name on the lease is Barry O'Keefe and Irene Chan. That's the name on the Barclays Bank card. Surely the thug will not give up. He would soon be tracking down the addresses of his siblings.

But why the eviction? The agency must've decided he was a thoroughly unsuitable tenant, maybe he had charges against him for his threatening others, he hadn't paid the rent, or all of the above.

He wanted to take the whole box downstairs but it would attract Sahil's attention, and he didn't need that right now. What if Sahil himself goes through the box and finds out about the trust? And the other flats, and that he was just another trustafarian who did building jobs to appear busy, a mummy's boy? Would that be an embarrassment? Anjali's family has provided well for her. She's not embarrassed. Hardly. She's rather proud of spending the family funds.

Marcus falls asleep, still wearing his glasses and clutching the file. His wrist aches from the sprain and wakes him up. He removes the Wahk Rahk watch to ease the swelling and switches off the lights.

58

NAFISAH

Friday 13th January

Nafisah is not expecting anyone except some deliveries of bulk sewing items she has ordered online from Temu. Zips and bias binding. When she peers through the Ring display, a bulky tanned face with a crooked nose appears, the slicked back dark hair showing off the widow's peak.

'Nafisah?'

'Yes, please come in,' she says to the door, as she pulls down a hijab hanging on the back of the door. She fastens it looking at the mirror on the wall behind the door before she undoes the chain. She swings the open door wider. 'The curtains, right?'

He ignores what she says. 'Nafisah, thanks for taking my suits to the police station. They got in touch with me.'

'I am so sorry about Angela,' her hand flies to her heart

and she shakes her head in sympathy. 'I couldn't even send a card or flowers. I did not know any of her family.'

'Don't think about it,' he reaches out his hand. 'I'm Barry O'Keefe. Angela's fr—,' he hesitates, 'Partner.'

Ah, so that's his name.

'I have the balance of the payment for the curtains. And I brought you a little something from Spain, where I now live.'

'You shouldn't have. Thanks so much. That is so kind of y—,'

'You're welcome,' he cuts in. 'It's no big deal. Angela thought very highly of you.'

Nafisah swallows, and takes a moment to think of Angela too.

'Please come in, please,' she gestures to the cramped living room and he sits down in the faux leather armchair without being asked.

'Can I get you a tea?' She offers.

'No, no. Thank you. You've done so much already for Ange and I.'

'Take your coat off. Wait here. Let me get the curtains.' She leaves him alone, and rummages around in the children's bedroom, busy looking for the curtains which have now been demoted from the front room Ikea 'CURRENT WIP' storage bins to her children's wardrobe, and where it is not given any more immediate attention.

When she returns, he's sitting in the armchair still, and his coat is slung over the dining room chair. He's wearing a kind of fine knit Italian jumper in green. 'I have the cash. And I have put a little more for your kids.' He says, tucking an envelope into her hand and squeezing her fingers shut.

'Oh! That's not necessary, Mr O'Keefe,' she tries to pull her hand away, but he shuts her fingers tighter.

'Nonsense,' he stares at her, meaning that he means it.

'Call me Barry.'

'Barry. You don't have to give me anything.'

He lets go of her fingers and waves in the air dismissively. 'Just don't worry about it. Ange would have done the same. The trousers, the shirts, they fit well and I may even come back with more hems that need taking up.'

'Sure! That would be my pleasure. Are you back — this time — for long?' Nafisah knits her fingers, trying to make conversation.

'I've come back for her funeral,' he sits back, making himself comfortable, crossing his leg over the other. 'Life is one long party, innit.'

'Yes. Yes, of course. I understand,' she says, though she doesn't.

'Tell you wot I'm gonna do. I'm getting that handyman arrested,' he enunciates Hand Dee Man like he is making a point. 'The building manager or whatever he calls himself. He should have fixed the bookcase. It's a menace. She has been on about it for months. He killed her. Guh.' His voice breaks into a sob.

Nafisah is stumped. 'It's awful,' she whispers. 'I couldn't stop crying after I found out.'

'As you know I have known Ange for far too long. And she has always wanted to, you know, tie the knot. We might even have done it this year when the weather's better. She never lived to see the summer.'

'She showed me photos of the midnight blue dress she wanted so badly made,' Nafisah adds, though in her conversation with Angela, Barry is definitely not keen, and has never proposed to her.

He sighs, almost chuckling softly. 'It's not to be,' he

shakes his downcast head. 'You see, I was married once. Bad idea.'

'Oh. Sorry to hear that,' Nafisah wonders what he means. 'Why?'

'She wanted it.'

'Angela?'

'Nah. Irene Chan. Walked out on her and my son. Couldn't bring myself to talk to her again. Met her while she was in hotel work and I was on security in the club opposite. We were going out. Then, she somehow convinced me to get married to her within 6 months so she could stay in the country. It was all so sudden. We rented a pretty basic flat through her employer, but what she really wanted was a baby. That's where the trouble began.'

Nafisah listens, sitting on the sofa, her arms folded. This can't be right.

'We couldn't have a baby. We had no money. I was too busy seeing Ange at the time. Then somehow, Irene got news that a baby's come up for adoption. Chinese. Perfect. Cos then it'd look like her. Ange knew whose it was; she was a nurse at the time. So we got this baby and Irene called him Elijah.'

Nafisah inhales sharply. She unfolds her arms and they drop to her lap. Those are her neighbours down the corridor of Bullen House. Irene who babysat for her when she needed cover, with whom she shared meals like Chinese and Bangladeshi potluck dishes, during weekends and holidays, and more than a cup of tea over stories of "back home". Unemployed hard-up big Elijah who was robbed two weeks ago and left with nothing.

'She completely doted on him,' the man drones on, but

Nafisah's attention is already rattled. 'She never looked at me again, so I thought, what'm I for?'

'Did you not...,' Nafisah shakes her head in disbelief. Does he think she would sympathise with him? 'D-did you not like being a dad?'

'Cor, yeah. At first, it was a laugh. We really did have fun. I did everything a dad did. Games, matches on the weekends, parks, Hamleys. bouncy castles.'

'Then what happened? Why did you leave them?' She doesn't sound too polite now but she speaks slower to keep her tone and emotion down.

'Irene is a devoted mum, an obedient wife. A real Asian girl. But she was not what I wanted. The more I tried to change her, the more we drifted apart. I wanted a passion-ate, intelligent woman, someone brilliantly funny. Someone I could have fun with and do "proper going out" in the evening. Dinner. Theatre. Cocktails. That kind of thing. Irene wasn't. Ange was.'

Nafisah is starting to find him tedious. Partly because she feels sorry for him but partly because she's loyal to her friend, Irene. Everything that he says is just not true. Irene was funny, warm, charming, just not to *him*. She did not touch alcohol, and would never spend a penny on theatre or fancy restaurants, and that's ok. Neither would Nafisah.

'The letters kept coming, too,' Barry adds.

'Letters? Letters from who?'

'The family abroad, can you believe it?' He throws his hands in the air. Nafisah is as surprised as he, that Elijah, is even connected with his birth family. 'Toys, socks, snacks from Singapore. The White Rabbit candy, haw flakes, Hacks cough sweets. Didn't touch any of it, nah. Irene and Elijah had them. The boy was her world, let me tell ya, I never got a look in again.'

That's what children are and should be. Your world. Nafisah creases her brow in thought. She rests her chin on her fist.

'Meanwhile, Ange was putting pressure on me to leave the family. I did, didn't I? And after I walked out, I moved in with Angela in Corfield Street. Then thought, know wot, it's too close to Irene and Elijah. Had enough. I got a job in a hotel in Marbella in Spain and started a security business from there. Made a fair bit. Never moved back here. When Irene passed away maybe 5 years ago, I started coming back more often to see Ange. I can't stay away from her for long.'

'Did she not want to move to Spain?'

'Nah. She wouldn't. She loves London.'

Nafisah nods. She can understand that. She would not want to live anywhere else either because she doesn't really want to start the whole process over. This is home, no matter what. Right here, in Bullen House.

'She would not move out, she'd always said. They'd have to carry her out, and they have,' he takes a second to pinch the bridge of his nose and squeeze his eyes shut. His voice cracks a little. 'I've always taken care of Elijah. Always. I send him money, even now. He calls me Dad. Breaks me heart.'

Nafisah blinks.

She hands him the bulky TK Maxx bags of curtains. When he leaves, she shuts the door. She takes her hijab off and hangs it on the hook. She thinks about it for a few seconds, then re-opens the door very quietly to just an inch's width. She watches as Barry hurries down the corridor and knocks on

Elijah's flat door. No reply. After waiting a few minutes with his head down, Barry strides to the stairwell.

59
STELLA

I am up early because I have had a really terrible night; can you blame me? The boy will drive me to my grave. He was up late making a hell of a racket in his room, and needs attention all the time. I've had enough of him.

Jean-Viv is so used to being tended to by her servants in Singapore that she cannot look after herself or her son. She has no idea that I cannot take on more than one ward. I explain as much to Richard. Fortunately he agrees that she should go.

I am thankful that it is my day off and aim is to get the £3,500 for my son. The closest HSBC to me is on the Fulham Road minutes from Fulham Broadway underground station. I pack my passport in my bag; I assume identification is required.

The door bell ring. Qamal must have arrived. Thank God. It's time for me to go.

I glance at the time on my phone. A text has come in yesterday which I hadn't seen until now. It is an account number and sort code. It's an unknown number.

> Plcld u put my rent directly into this
> account? It's the landlord's. There's no need
> to give me cash. And no need to come.

What the hell? He just wants me to pay his rent. How thick is his skin? His adoptive mother sure hadn't done a good job raising him. He hardly has any manners, if yesterday is anything to go by.

I only get to text him and reply to his texts. Young people don't engage in conversations. Only Uber drivers call, and that is just to tell you they're outside.

I will be spending my day off alone.

60

SAHIL

Sahil has never got into a van quicker. This is the only stage in which he is still a small part of decision-making, albeit with Marcus. He is a colleague too.

In the van, they remain quiet, each with his own thoughts. Marcus drives from Bethnal Green Road onto Shoreditch through the Barbican crawling in the London traffic, no more than third gear at any time. It will take an hour approximately at this time of day. He cuts across St Paul's then all the way on the Embankment. They enjoy a long view of the Thames, the joggers, commuters and dog walkers. Kiss FM is playing OneRepublic's *Sink or Swim*. He takes a left to get to Westminster, Victoria and towards South Kensington.

'You've overshot, Marcus,' Sahil informs him. 'I thought you're using Googlemaps. You've gone too far west.'

'Oh, I— I seem to be on— autopilot. I was heading to — for — breakfast. Somewhere I used to go to. A lot.'

'Feeling OK?' Sahil's immediate concern is Marcus's head injury. Has he had a turn? A flashback or an alternate universe moment? He's heard of these episodes after trauma. 'Do you want me to direct you?'

Marcus shakes his head. He stops at the lights on Old Brompton Road. He's staring at a shop window. Sahil follows Marcus's gaze. Unmistakable. It's the thug. He's wearing a beanie hat, standing outside the Sutton and Robertson's Pawn Brokers opposite Franco Manca pizzeria. After staring at the shop window, the thug tries to enter the shop, pushing open the glass door. It's shut, but the lights are on inside. When it doesn't open, he slams his fists on the door and backs off.

'It's him,' says Sahil, watching the thug march off in a straight line on the Brompton Road, swinging his arms.

'Let's follow him,' Marcus says, and the engine hits first gear and roars to life. 'I'll explain later.'

It *is* the first time that Marcus even acted in such a decisive way. Marcus *has* to be doing the right thing, hasn't he?

'How do you know where he's going?' Sahil asks.

Marcus doesn't reply.

The thug shoves his hands in his black puffer jacket pockets and they bulge like oranges. He heads west and takes a left at Onslow Gardens. Marcus turns left, and then right. Thank God for the snail pace traffic. The pedestrian they are tracking is in sync with the van speed.

Sahil's eyes glue themselves onto the target. He must not let the thug out of sight. Every so often he adjusts his Carhartt cap and checks the passenger side wing mirror. He has aged twenty years since the incident, living in fright, and the luggage under his eyes shows. The thug crosses at the

Fulham lights and waits at a bus stop. Marcus turns right, and finds a place to pull over.

Sahil opens the glove compartment. He sweeps his fingers from side to side in the detritus of Prêt paper napkins, chocolate wrappers, greasy Greggs paper bags and parking receipts for his "spare" £7 sunglasses from Flying Tiger which he promptly puts on. There is comfort in knowing that in Marcus's van lies his personal possession, dependable and prêt-a-porter, as if the glove compartment is *his* mini storage unit too.

Sahil and Marcus sit like brothers, in a tense yet amicable silence, and when the 414 arrives, the thug queues with other passengers and gets on it. Marcus sets off again, stepping on it at any junctions that he could, in order to keep up with the bus. Traffic lights on the way, and changing lanes frustrate and relieve him in an alternating frequency. Back home, Sahil doesn't drive although he has a licence. His father and uncles hire a shared driver who drives for members of more than one family. James Arthur has finished singing *Singers* and the DJ cuts in to remind listeners *it's Friday the 13th. What spooky movies have everyone lined up for the evening?*

The thug gets off at the Chelsea Football Club stop. 'Oh no,' groans Marcus, 'This is shit.'

'What's the matter?' Sahil manages to ask though he senses that he's not allowed to ask any questions. Marcus's mood is not great.

Marcus shakes his head. 'Jesus. There will be a bit of delay,' Marcus briskly replies, his breathing short. 'I have to turn back as there is only a pedestrian route here. No entry. I have to do 3 right turns to go all around the block. Damn!'

'What?'

'Nevermind,' Marcus snaps like an alligator, as he manœuvres the van round in a high speed 3-point turn, back on the Fulham Road. He takes a hard right at Hortensia, then another right at Kings Road.

'Hope you know what you're doing,' Sahil meekly adds.

'Of course I bloody know. Sorry. Sorry. Don't mean to bite. I *know* where he's heading. Let me just get there, please.'

Sahil blows out.

The van turns right and parks at the end of Rumbold Road. It's a quiet residential street without any traffic. They watch the thug head towards to the formidable double-fronted property from the direction of the Chelsea FC stadium.

'Marcus?' Sahil checks. Marcus decides to drive a few car lengths nearer to the opposite of the road, about 100 m or so away.

'Let's get out,' says Marcus.

'What about the parking?' Sahil, ever practical, reminds him. A penalty ticket is likely to be £70 or £80, whatever the going rate is now. He's beginning to think like a Londoner.

'OK,' Marcus turns to look at him, putting his hand on Sahil's shoulder. 'You can stay and do that on the app, and join me in a minute or so.' Without waiting for Sahil's response, Marcus jumps out and slams the door. 'But how long will you be?' calls Sahil, not knowing where Marcus is heading or what he's doing. But Marcus is already taking big steps crossing the street, keeping up to speed with the thug.

The thug raps on the brass pull-ring of the panelled door.

61

STELLA

Qamal is here. I practically run from the kitchen to the front door to let him in. When I fling open the door, my jaw sails open in incomprehension.

'It's Elijah.'

'Who's it?' Calls Richard, as if on cue. He is just coming out of the downstairs toilet. The flush goes.

'It — it's Elijah, whom I think you— already know— from yesterday?' My voice is shaky and trance-like.

'I don't think so,' Richard replies, shaking his head slowly, his brow furrowed. He would not look at Elijah.

'Richard,' I steady him as he staggers a little.

'Stella, please,' he pleads. 'Where are you going? Aren't we going out now?'

'No, we're waiting for Qamal. It's my day off.'

'Where's Boy?' Richard asks.

'He's left for school, and Jean-Viv has gone with him.'

'What... can someone tell me what's going on...?' he tearfully murmurs, all the while looking down.

'Richard, everything is fine,' I hold him by his shoulders

and look at him to make sure he looks back. I check his pupils as the dim grey light enters the open front door. Elijah does not budge. He is blocking most of the limited English winter light.

'I don't... think... so,' Richard remarks, irritably. 'I feel... terrible,' he almost loses his balance. 'Why is he here? Is it fixed? We have new valves?' He points at Elijah.

'It's fixed. But he's not... he's not the plumber.'

Elijah says nothing. He just stares with a strange expression at the old man: pity.

'Stella, I just saw my wife in her office. She's working.'

This is not the first time. 'She is gone now, Richard. You didn't see her. She was not in her office.'

'She...,' he gasps like he just caught a breath of air. He goes back to looking down at his denim broadcloth-clad lap. He absent-mindedly rubs the collar of his fine jersey knit shirt. He is so well-dressed thanks to me. Calvin Klein. Ralph Lauren. His late wife had bought him such awful clothes from Marks and Spencer on the Kings Road while she wore Jaeger, Hobbs and L.K. Bennett. And that meddling friend of hers Mrs Wong also bought him towels and Christmas jumpers from Sainsbury's Tu to "cheer him up" during the festive season. I promptly put all of it in the St Barnabas charity collection bag. Richard does not need cheering up. And certainly no more towels. I make him the happiest man on earth. He's told me as much.

'Who was it then?'

I don't answer.

'But I don't want a stranger in my house. Gen? Gen!' He continues, wailing pitifully at the direction of the street.

'Richard, let me please re-introduce you to Elijah, my son.'

I glance at Elijah, perplexed. The boy is now 32. He isn't even a boy. There is no resemblance to me, or his father. Unfortunately, he looks exactly like *my* dad. The hard, hooded Cantonese, not Hakka, eyes, the slope of the wide forehead.

Elijah grunts and nods perfunctorily. I address him.

'Elijah, we cannot leave Richard. We must wait until Qamal gets here.'

'Ain't got time for that. You got my money?'

'Pardon?' My heart sinks. 'You sent a text message that I have to do a bank transfer.'

'Nah.'

'What do you mean *nah*?'

'I'm here to make sure I get it from yew. We can go together to the bank now.'

I blink at him, not sure how I should reply, since it is quite a sudden change of plan. All to suit him.

'But. Mum. You said you would help me,' he growls.

'I would,' I reply. 'Richard needs to sit down. Richard, you must sit down if you feel a little unbalanced.'

Maybe Jean-Viv has taken a walk and not coming straight back after the school run. She would cover for me as it's my day off. Right now, I can't get out of the house. I am still wearing an apron and I am not ready.

Once I settle Richard in his chair, to which he demurs, I return to the hall, where Elijah is now looking bored.

'OK. Elijah. Look. I have a confession to make. I couldn't transfer it just like that this morning or last night. I — don't —,' I take a deep breath and let it out in a sigh. 'I am going to apply for a loan today.'

'What the fuck, mum,' Elijah says. 'Whatdjumean?' He adds 'mum' to every line to soften it, yet it sounds worse.

'I have to send all my money back home for my mother's fees in a posh nursing home,' I explain. 'How much do you think that costs? I can't just magic up £3,300.'

'What—? What does he need?' Bleats Richard. 'Does he need paying? If he's finished the job, he needs paying.'

My mind spins. 'Richard, please. I'm sorting it. OK?'

Elijah puts his hand on my elbow. I flinch, at first. 'Get it from him,' he tosses his head sideways towards the sitting room. I shut my eyes and shake my head vigorously. How? I can't. The thought that I have given him the watch already sends shivers through my spine.

'From today, I am gonna make sure,' Elijah says, in a lower voice. 'Nothing will come between us again. Mum.'

His first words of kindness. My heart wants to be believe him, but my head says 'Are you kidding?' My eyes fix on him, and my mouth quivers. I don't think anyone has ever loved me, or tried to, so hearing his words have brought some comfort to my bruised soul.

Jean-Viv was not exactly a good mum and neither was my mum, and look where they are now. Maybe this is as good as it would get for me.

But I wish Qamal would hurry. I look at my watch.

'Go on,' he urges, in an impatient whisper, 'You can ask the old boy. He probably has a stash under a loose floorboard in here somewhere,' His eyes dart to the ceiling. I need to put him off.

'Elijah,' I take a breath as I come back into the hall. This is not going to be easy, although I have practised saying it for months. 'It was my mother, your grandmother, who had been writing to you and Irene. You were taken from me when you were born. I was a foreign student in the UK and could not keep you. You went to a childless couple called Barry

O'Keefe and Irene Chan. Your name means the Lord is my God.'

He lets out a dirty little toddler laugh. 'Fuck. I am going. Absolutely fucking useless.'

I can't believe it. 'Why won't you wait for Qamal? He is not even late yet. He comes at 9,' Desperately, I inform him, pointing at my phone screen's clock.

'You never meant to help me. Mum.' His eyes fall. He doesn't trust me.

'What do you mean?'

'You would've sorted it out by now. You haven't made the transfer this morning, you haven't got money, you gotta get a loan—,'

'Of course. That's why I have my passport with me. I was just about to go to the ba—,'

'Yeah, yeah. Heard it before. Do you know anything about the cost of living crisis while you are swanning around in a castle with a living corpse?'

'Elijah,' I snapped with a shrill beat, like a bird about to hunt. His whole name pops out just as all 9 pounds 11 of him did from between my legs when I had been young and fit for birth.

My heart pounds. I feel quite sick. This is like an encounter with a stranger, which I suppose he is. I've come all the way to England to be mugged. I thought he showed me an ounce of kindness but it's only perfunctory, a means to an end. The boy will bite. I wonder where he got that from? No guesses. My father.

The doctor who delivered him was none other than the mop-haired paediatrician, Trudie Lam. Richard's wife.

62

MARCUS

Marcus shoves the door open, since it's ajar. He bursts into the spacious and dim hall with its crystal chandelier. The thug's back is to him. A tall and slim Chinese woman in a navy coat with brass buttons stands at the bottom of the stairs, facing the thug. Her face is white and scrunched up and her eyes wide like she is about to scream. She seems familiar. He has seen her recently, but it could have been anywhere, like in a shop. Before he can think it any further, the thug turns around and lunges at him.

'Elijah,' the woman screams. 'Elijah, NO!'

'Get out!' Marcus roars at him. 'Leave her alone!'

But Elijah sneers, he towers over Marcus and his serpentine hooded eyes dart between Stella and Marcus. 'Hilarious. Come awn and get me, if you can. You're just a washed-up handyman. Gotta a job to do 'ere, 'ave ya? Put up some shelves, eh? Or are ya a scum landlord?'

In a heartbeat, Elijah lunges at Marcus, sending them

both crashing into the back of the front door. It slams shut from the force.

Pain shoots through Marcus as he feels a punch connect with his jaw, but he fights back, yanking the hems of Elijah's tracksuit. As he tries to pull the bottoms down, Elijah loses balance and he falls backwards into the half moon antique glass hall table against the side of the grand staircase. Marcus crawls to standing, grabs a brass candelabra and aims it at Elijah. He misses.

Instead his swing strikes a blue and white Chinese porcelain vase. The sound of it exploding pierces the room as the vase shatters on the floor. Elijah pulls up his pants. Marcus knows he is no match for Elijah, being older, skinnier and shorter than his opponent. He is like a lizard taking on an elephant. One accurate blow from Elijah is all it would take to stamp him out.

The woman is now screaming, her hands in fists. She says *she's calling the cops, she's calling the cops.*

Marcus's head strikes the rosewood carved occasional chair, sending him to the floor. Dazed and disoriented, he cowers as Elijah looms over him in silhouette, ready to strike.

Elijah hesitates for a split second, but it is enough for Marcus to recover. Summoning his remaining strength, Marcus tackled Elijah to the ground. They roll across the floor, knocking over a coffee table in the process.

The woman lets out a piercing scream, rushing forward to intervene, but tripping over the broken crockery.

Marcus struggles, and manages to twist Elijah's arm, and

sinks his teeth into Elijah's thigh. But Elijah has grabbed the nearest piece of ceramic shard of the shattered vase, and as he raises his fist clutching it, a loud cry echoes through the room.

63

MARCUS

Marcus sees a frail elderly man entering the room, staggering pitifully. His palms clutch the walls as he approaches. His eyes fill with terror and confusion.

'What's happening? I hear all these voices.'

When he notices Marcus, he repeats, 'You're back!' He almost lights up, as his fearful face breaks into a small smile when he sees the short balding man. 'Always knew you'd be back.'

The old man looks around and whispers inaudibly. He shuffles to Elijah. 'Don't hurt him. Hurt me if you want.' His eyes are rheumy and filled with tears. Marcus is stunned for a second, mesmerised. Elijah does not drop the shard. He aims it even higher.

The woman turns to Elijah and screams, 'Run! Go! Go now!' She is covered in ribbons of blood on her legs where she tripped and fell.

Distant sirens wail in a crescendo as they approach.

The old man suddenly collapses to the floor.

. . .

Marcus takes advantage of the distraction and kicks Elijah who drops the shard and reels. Marcus jumps onto and pins the thug down with his arm behind him. He tosses a glance at the weeping woman, who rushes over to kneel beside Elijah. 'Who the hell are you?' Marcus asks, but does not look at her for long, instead turning back his focus onto Richie.

'Have you called the ambulance?' Marcus asks her. He looks up and down at the woman. She nods, flustered, shaking.

She is smartly dressed and Marcus would have assumed she is a visitor but she's wearing an apron. Marcus has so many questions that they drive him nuts. He repeats, 'OK, let's try this again. Who are you?'

'I'm... I am Richard Ho's carer. Stella.'

Marcus ignores the name Richard. He is reviled. 'How could you let this happen to him?'

The woman shakes her head, weeping. Marcus has already forgotten her name. 'You let a mugger in,' he adds.

'No. No! He's not...! He's not who you think,' she sobs hard, both her hands on the thug's chest, stroking him.

'That's even worse! Who is he?'

The old man could hardly lift his neck and look up, but his eyes move and meet Marcus's gaze. 'You are home. I can't believe it. Ah Zai ah, Alistair Marcus Ho,' Richie whispers almost to himself. 'He is home. My Ah Zai is back. My dear son. I am so sorry. Daddy is so sorry.'

Marcus checks his father's pulse, his eyes watery with tears, his voice cracked. 'I'm here, Dad, you'll be fine.'

64

GENEVIEVE

I head to a cafe after the school run. I need to get out of the house and to have some breathing space. It will set me back £4.25 but a coffee from a shop is worth every hard-earned penny. It's Qamal's day with my dad. Qamal seems very sweet and I have a burning redness in my cheeks when I see him, but I am not in the right frame of mind. I am very ashamed of my circumstances and feeling antisocial. I just cannot face him, and all the pleasantries in the hall or kitchen.

I open my laptop and as usual am crushed that there is no reply from The Republique. I also cannot find where I have saved the previous CV so I had to look in every folder. There is a document called *Letter to Eva*. I wonder if Auntie Evie knows this and if not, I should get it to her since it's addressed to her.

When I click on it, I am curious. I cannot help but start reading:

Dear Eva,

Leaving this computer for you. None of my children will need or want it. When you said you didn't have a computer, I thought you should have one. I have no need for it where I am now! LOL. You said you wanted to do online courses. Well. Now you can.

I started writing a memoir but I got a bit too sick to continue. Don't let the children know what I am about to tell you as they would be very upset. When I married Richie, I *already* had Alistair. The girls don't know. I was in Singapore, married to a consultant who was killed in a crash in Malaysia. Poor Alistair didn't have a dad.

I started dating Richie Ho whom I met when I was at a medical conference in Singapore at Raffles Hotel. He is a talented piano player, and a very clever and ambitious man. He was just playing the piano in a bar on Beach Road not far from Raffles, and his music captivated me. I just wanted to hear him play every day of my life. When I brought up the fact that I was a widow, he did not seem to mind and could not wait to meet my son.

I fell in love with Richie immediately and you can see why. We started the most passionate and crazy affair in my hotel room at the conference. He even pretended to be a cardiologist and my date at the dinners and events. Oh. Those days. I blush even now at the thought of it.

He told me that his dream was to run a hotel, a really special boutique hotel, where he could occasionally play the piano should he wish to. He wanted an audience, guests, fans, customers. Eva. I tell you. I wanted to make his come true. We got married very fast, shocking my parents, and made plans to emigrate to the UK under skilled migration. Mine.

When Alistair went to work in Dubai he started using his middle name Marcus, because they thought he was Muslim and that he was Ali Setar. It was one of his anecdotes. We were very close. Alistair and I got on very well. Better than the girls and I. Don't tell them this. LOL. I know you don't have sons, but a mother and her son's connection is really quite something. There is a reason why I am drawn to Virgin and Child sculptures such as the Donatello at the V&A.

Alistair met his wife in Dubai. She was in IT. A lovely girl from Malaysia. They had two girls and have only been back in the UK once, and that was before the pandemic. I think his wife was not keen. She wanted nothing to do with our family. Richie had always been a bit cold to Alistair because he is not a biological son. It breaks my heart —

I couldn't read anymore. I am blinded by the tears welling up. I shut the laptop lid and pack it away in its green mock croc bag, numbed by my mother's letter, not sure if I should be saddened or angered.

'Hi,' says a familiar voice behind me.

'Oh, hi Qamal!' I blink back the tears and give him my fake cheery voice.

'Are you OK?'

'Yes, fine.' I turn my head away from him. 'I am just heading back to the house now. School run.' I grin. I look ridiculous. He is the last person I expected to see. Here I am thinking I could get away from everyone.

'Me too,' he smiles and lifts his cup to show me. 'I just got my takeaway coffee. Shall we go?'

I reluctantly nod.

When we arrive back, something strikes me as not right.

There is a fleet of police cars and two ambulances parked outside.

The front door is open.

65

SAHIL

Sahil has been sitting nervously in the van, his fingers drumming on the steering wheel. He checks his phone and there's nothing from Marcus. When he creeps up to the front steps, he hears voices because the door is ajar. It then suddenly slams shut and the sound of glass shattering follows. He runs back to the van and calls the cops. He keeps glancing back at the mansion in case Marcus comes out.

Minutes pass. He is so nervous he has to switch off the radio. Who cares what Taylor Swift is singing? He pulls up the Ringo app and pays for parking. He may have to get out of the van after all. He needs to know what is happening to Marcus and to do something about it. It would not be the first time when he has to get Marcus out of trouble. He stands around the van, doing his pranayamas and counting exercises. Relief flows over him when he hears sirens and looks up.

He steps out of the van, waving as two police cars

approach. They screech to a halt outside the mansion and four officers quickly exit, assessing the situation.

'Over here. That house! Hurry.' Sahil points, recognising DI Beauchêne-Gill and DC Holden.

'You're Sahil?'

'Yes!'

'I thought so,' says DC Holden, nodding. 'Stay here.'

There's been a fight,' Sahil blurts. 'I'm coming in.'

'Please don't for your safety,' says DC Jenny Holden.

The two other officers led by the DI and the DC rush to the front door. Weapons drawn, they proceed cautiously.

'Open up!' DI Beauchene-Gill commands in a voice Sahil had never heard.

Sahil expects them to kick the door in but the door opens, and it is a tear-stained woman in an apron. Her legs are bleeding. She waves them in.

Sahil ignores them, his heart is pounding and he could not leave Marcus in there. He rushes into the scene after the officers. They are a bit busy to have noticed him slipping in. The expansive hall is chaos as he imagined from the violent struggles that he heard. An elderly man lies at door opening to the living room, unconscious. The woman is sobbing and kneeling next to the thug. Marcus is restraining Elijah, struggling to keep him subdued.

DI Beauchêne-Gill shouts, 'Police! Stay where you are. All of you.'

Sahil is relieved that Marcus can now let go of Elijah. 'Cuff them,' says DI to the two officers waiting. Two officers immediately secure Elijah, pulling him away from Marcus and handcuffing him. 'You're under arrest for assault and trespassing,' one officer declares.

DC Holden unexpectedly cuffs Marcus who twists away.

'Hang on. Why am I being arrested? Can someone tell me?' Marcus slurs, the swelling and injuries making him hard to understand.

Sahil's hair stands. 'DC Holden. This is a mistake, surely?' He demands, trying to establish eye contact with her but her eyes are on the cuffs. 'What's going on? What did he do?'

They do not reply. Moments later, paramedics arrive, wheeling two stretchers and carrying medical kits. They brush past Sahil, and politely tell him to 'Please get out of the way.' A pair go straight to the old man, and Sahil hears one of them saying 'Stabilise him for transport.'

Another pair of paramedics attend to Elijah. 'Head trauma. Possible concussion. Clean and bandage.'

Sahil is about to bother DC Holden again.

66

GENEVIEVE

I burst in with Qamal. 'What's happened here? Is everything OK?'

'Daddy!' I gasp when I see him on the stretcher strapped in.

'We're taking him in,' a paramedic steps in and speaks before I do. 'We've run a few tests and we think he may have had a stroke or a cardiac event.'

'What's happened here? It looks terrible.'

'We're looking into that too,' he replies, nodding.

No need for them to elaborate. I can tell it's robbery and assault. There are broken pots, and the candelabra's weight has damaged and cracked the marble floor. The octagonal table has been overturned. My mother's blue and white Chinese vase collection smashed. Blood drips trail everywhere and... I am shocked to see that it's Stella who's bleeding. She's weeping but calm, like she's in a trance. She won't look at me, and she sits on the third step from the bottom of the staircase, knitting her fingers.

'Oh my god!' I hear Qamal echoing my own thoughts.

'Stella! What happened?' He rushes to Stella and shakes her, but the paramedics tell him to stay away.

There must have been a robbery. Daylight robbery. Another stretcher is being carried out with a huge crewcut man on it, also bleeding heavily. I have never seen this man before. Is he the robber? Who is he?

I see my dad again and he's being carried out now. Oh, daddy! I choke. My fingers gripping his arm. Sweat is pouring from my forehead and neck. He looks so calm, just like he does when he is napping in his favourite chair. They have put tubes from his arm already.

'Madam, I'm DI Marc Beauchêne-Gill. This is my colleague DC Jenny Holden. Your father and the others are being attended to. We'll need to get statements, but first, let's leave the paramedics alone to get him to Chelsea and Westminster ASAP.'

I look hard at someone being led away to sit down in the now upright carved rosewood chair, my eyes widening.

'Alistair? Is that you?' I ask tentatively. I can't believe my eyes. He has been in a fight too. His jaw is swollen and bruised almost black and I cannot tell if he can even hear me because he does not answer.

'You're back from Dubai?' I can't believe my eyes! My brother has come back. I advance towards him but he backs off, squirming in the chair as the paramedics treat his injuries.

'Technically, yes,' he slurs, hardly moving his swollen jaw.

'Why are you... why are you arrested?' I glance at his handcuffs, from the corner of my eye, trying not to make it look obvious.

'That is what I am trying to find out,' a young Indian guy steps around the paramedics to get to me.

'And who are you?' I ask, curiously.

'I am Sahil.'

'Sahil?' I repeat incredulously. 'And you are?'

'I'm a good friend of Marcus,' he shakes his head and throws his palms in the air in a 'whatever' gesture. '*Alistair*. We were supposed to be working on a job today. But Marcus saw the thug and followed him here.'

His eyes dart to Alistair, whose wounds are being dressed now. The paramedic in his blue gloved hands is cutting the gauze.

'Probably need you to come back for X-rays,' he says to Marcus, giving him a closer look.

'How're you feeling?' Sahil asks, crouching next to the chair.

Marcus nods weakly. 'I'll be fine, thanks to you. You called them just in time. I know, 'Cos *she* didn't.' He lifts his eyes at Stella.

'I am going to check with them when we can see Daddy,' I say, my voice trembling. I start to fear the worst.

Sahil shows the paramedics and the stretchers out. He seems so efficient, organised. I wonder what he's doing here, and how he got here with my brother.

'We'll follow up at the hospital,' DI Beauchêne-Gill turns around and says to me. 'But we need to know what led to this incident. DC Holden, forensics. They coming?'

'They're on their way,' she replies confidently, her chin tilted upward.

67

MARCUS

Marcus trails behind him in a long beige corridor with blue accents. The place has recently been decorated, but not exactly in an attractive scheme — it still screams institution, with the harsh light and epoxy-sprayed aluminium skirtings.

'I just don't know what any of this is about,' Marcus manages to slur, the foam of his gathered saliva pooling and dribbling down his paint-stained Adidas hoodie. God, he looks like a real mess. No wonder they don't believe a word he says. He shuffles.

'We are holding you on suspicion for manslaughter of Miss Angela Fort.'

68

GENEVIEVE

Next to my father's bed at Chelsea Westminster where he has been warded, I am reading my mother's Letter to Eva from where I stopped at *Richie had always been a bit cold to Alistair because he is not a biological son. It breaks my heart —*

— to this day. Eva, we have been friends so many years and shared so many family events and festivals. It was so good to know someone from back home like you, who is in the same healthcare industry. Thanks to the Whitechapel hospital where we both worked, you as a nurse and I as a doctor that we even met many decades ago when the children were little. Cassie came along later. Without our network, I think our children would have lost their Asianness, however little that remains by living in this country.

Gradually, I see that Richie was not going to change in his attitude towards Alistair. When I was in the area after work one day, I saw in an estate agent's window that there was a very charming 2-bedroom flat for sale.

I don't know why it jumped out at me. But I viewed it that evening, and on the spot, made an offer. I bought my son a flat in Corfield Street, Bethnal Green. There is nothing wrong with parents taking care of their children, and I wanted to take care of Alistair because clearly, he does not even exist in Richie's eyes. He is my son, my only son. He will always have a home in London should Richie ever disinherit him. Richie does not know about Corfield Street. If he does, he will be very cross. Anyway, it's my money. I was earning a very secure six-figure income as a consultant and I may as well invest.

After the purchase, the estate agent recommended me another flat. He's like a tipster to me, since he knows I have money to invest but no time. Being a doctor is quite demanding. It was an ex-local authority flat that had come available and extremely cheap in the 1990s. They were practically giving them away as no one wanted them. It was something crazy like £9,000. I can't remember. It was in Bullen House. Naturally, I thought this would be another investment but this time, to avoid capital gains tax, my accountant and also the executor of my Will, advised me to put it in a trust fund. As an aside, do you remember him? Carlson Teoh. His kids and ours went to the same Chinese school on Saturday mornings.

The flat is in the name of an offshore trust that I set up, registered in the Bahamas. Your husband, Dr Robert Wong, is one of the trustees. When Alistair turns 40, the trust will be dissolved and the flat will be transferred to him. Why 40? I figured that is the age when he would have children and a family of his own. He will need the flat when he's mature enough to manage it for his own investment and for his family's future. Until then, the trust will manage it for him.

Both flats are rented out. Until one day —

I am interrupted by rustling and footsteps. The doctor and nurse have come into the ward. I shut the MacBook and return it to its green mock croc case.

'Good morning, Miss— Ms Ho?' The doctor says. He has a black beard and amber eyes behind thick glasses which I note are 'Karl Lagerfeld' as the words on the side arms tell me.

'Yes, it's Genevieve. Gen,' I say, regretfully with a yawn I am unable to stifle. Clearly the £4.25 coffee is insufficient for a day like this. 'Good morning.'

'I'm Dr Amir Farhad,' he says, not extending his hand. 'How're you doing?'

'I don't know,' I shrug, unaware of how I am or should be. 'I'm fine, I guess,' I bristle at the doctor's opening lines but I know I shouldn't.

'We've run the tests when he came in. Blood tests to check on clotting problems, blood sugar levels, and infection, and just his general health. We've done a CT scan too,' Dr Farhad lists more terms which forget.

I nod and reply, 'OK.'

'As you are aware, your father presented with an ischemic stroke, but as he was brought in so soon after, we've administered tPA, a clot-busting drug, thereby minimising the damage,' he says. 'It's going to dissolve the clot.'

'*That*... that sounds good... am I right?' I reply tentatively.

'Yes, *I* think it's good,' the doctor agrees, nodding his

head side to side as if weighing up the consequences. 'We'll see how he gets on over the next day or so.'

'That's great, I guess?' I am still unsure. Are my replies accurate based on his information?

'He'll likely need a period of rehabilitation. He might regain partial or full function, but he may also have lingering deficits.'

I bite my lip. My dad is OK. For now. That's all I can take in. 'I understand.'

When they had gone, I study the windowless room: my father's calm expression while he naps, the IV line feeding him, the heart rate monitor with its graphs, the cannula in his left wrist. I still have a few hours before picking up Jasper. I don't know what all these machines do exactly. But I know I don't want that job at Le Republique anymore.

69

MARCUS

'Why? You don't think I killed her, do you? That's insane.' What about getting treatment for his injuries? Had he not stopped the thug from attacking his father?

The DI bangs his fist on the melamine top. 'Firstly, you never dropped off the data key with the CCTV footage which we had asked for two days ago. Where is it?'

Marcus does not answer. 'I— I haven't got around to it.'

We asked the building management committee and another resident has provided it.

'Oh.'

'Yes, *oh*, indeed,' the DI mimics Marcus's exclamation. 'We have watched more than two weeks' worth. Guess what we've found. There is missing footage from December 29th and January 6th. Do you have anything to do with this?'

'It sometimes does not work.'

'What do you mean, *it*?'

'The CCTV. There may have been a power outage and it stops recording.'

'Do you have any proof of that, or shall I ask the residents?'

Marcus does not answer. He grits his teeth thinking about those two dates.

'Mr Ho. I'm warning you. The quicker you tell us what happened, the better.'

Marcus cannot tell him about December because he is protecting Sahil. Marcus had to remove the footage of the argument with Angela when she witnessed Sahil's accidental assault on Elijah. These thoughts are now racing and so is his heart.

'Mr Ho, I am waiting. My patience is wearing out.'

'I admit that I don't have the footage, and don't know why it failed to record,' Marcus says. It is a rubbish answer but it will do, until he gets a lawyer. He's in a corner now.

'Next, we have a witness. Someone found your wallet and handed it in on January 2nd at the Novello Theatre.'

'We've been through this,' says Marcus. 'I have never been to the theatre.'

'We know. A member of the audience found your wallet on the 30th, the night after the missing footage, and he left his name with the theatre staff who did not see the note or pass the message on.'

'Yes, you said, it was found at the theatre.'

'No.'

'No?'

'No,' he shakes his head adamantly. 'We have since been informed by the Novello staff that the member of the audience who found your wallet discarded in Corfield Street Park was getting on a plane. He had no chance to give it to the police. He was seeing a show and running late, so picked it up and left it at the theatre instead. You were mugged, weren't you? Why didn't you mention it?'

'Blimey. But who is this, and why is he in Corfield Street?'

The DI exhales. 'Barry O'Keefe.'

Marcus clamps his jaw shut. He swallows. The night becomes clear to him. Before Sahil came to his rescue, he handed over his wallet to Elijah. That wallet dropped out in the van; that is why Sahil did not find it when he emptied Elijah's pockets. But then, Elijah woke up in the van and found a wallet, Marcus's. Removed the very little cash and threw the wallet away. The next day or so, Barry O' Keefe, on his way to Angela's flat to take her to Mamma Mia, picked up the wallet and handed it in at the theatre.

He so wants to tell the DI everything, but where will he start? The tight-lipped DI, whose eyes are boring through him, may well be able to see through all the bullshit. Marcus begins hyperventilating and doing his counting exercises which Sahil had taught him. He has not had a chance to take his medication and Sahil knows. It's in the van.

'He is Ms Fort's lover, paramour, long term partner. We have interviewed him after her death. And asked him if anything unusual. That's why he told us that he found your wallet.'

Marcus listens.

'If you are not going to tell us why you hid the fact that you were mugged,' the DI continues, 'I am going to have to charge you. There's something not quite right, and we will get to the bottom of it. Once again, do you have the footage from those two days?'

'No,' Marcus says, shaking his head with sadness. It's true. He does not have it. It's deleted. That much he knows.

'Are you going to tell us or not?'

'There's nothing to tell,' Marcus replies softly.

Marcus is led away into a cell. He does not know how long he will be waiting, minutes, hours or days. It is just like in Dubai when he lost his job and then had his breakdown. Instead of standing by him, his wife took the children and he went back home. He kicked out the tenant in Corfield Street and has been living there since. Until Sahil moved in, he thought he was finished. Now, after all that, how could he turn Sahil in?

70

SAHIL

S ahil sits in the van. It is quiet now everyone has gone. The woman is weeping and has had to go in with Elijah. Genevieve has gone with her father. Should he go back to the flat before going to see Marcus? He wanted to stop DC Holden and DI Beauchêne-Gill but they were in such a hurry to ignore him and take Marcus away.

Sahil decides to take the van back to the garage unit. He has something there that he needs. The USB key with the CCTV footage. Marcus could not do this himself at first. For the first footage from the night of the assault, on December 29th, Sahil showed Marcus how to edit the film using his digital skills. It was quite an interesting activity for New Year's break when they were both not working.

But late afternoon on January 6th, only a week ago, Sahil did it for Marcus. This is because Marcus *was* the last person to see Angela, unfortunately, not to fix the bookcases but her washing machine cupboard which had now rattled and come undone from the spin dry cycle. The boiler pressure had been low too, Angela had complained to Sahil in the entrance hall. She thought engineering meant all kinds of engineering, including heating, ventilation and plumbing. He simply nodded in affirmation that he would pass on the message to Marcus.

Sahil knows that he is in trouble. Anjali and his parents will not forgive him. He prays for a good lawyer, hopefully Indian, and some decent court decision. He gets to the garage and uses his phone as a torch. He unlocks the metal storage unit with the key that is on the same key ring as the van keys. He rummages through the other odd items such as spare tools, keys to ghosts of previous apartments, magnifying glasses, discarded marker pens. He finds the USB at the bottom of the tray.

But before he hands it in, he will watch it first.

71
MARCUS

Monday 16th January

Marcus is in a blindingly light-coloured small room that is not really a cell. The interiors have been designed to look intimidating, austere, powerful. It looks like an ordinary windowless meeting room, except there is no other furniture apart from a table and two chairs, and no one in the room except Sahil and Marcus. Plastic cups of water are all the stationery that's on the table. There are cameras in every corner. Those are the only "windows" to the outside world.

Sahil rubs his forehead with his fingers absent-mindedly. He looks calm, at peace, and not the haunted doll that he has been for months. 'I have the footage. I am sorry; I know you were trying to protect me. You didn't want them to have the file. But now I have given it to them. I don't really care anymore.'

'Why not? Your family has sacrificed a lot to get you here.'

'I know. But I also know I did the right thing. He would've killed you.'

'What about Anjali?' Asks Marcus.

'What about her?' Asks Sahil back.

Marcus shrugs.

'She's fine with or without me,' Sahil replies. He leans back in the plastic chair, folding his arms, and it bows a bit. 'I told her there is a slight delay with the building works and she seems to accept my explanation that you're a bit busy right now.'

Marcus smiles.

'Your dad is doing well,' Sahil adds.

'Oh yeah?' Marcus sits up, his ears pricked.

'Yes,' Sahil nods reassuringly. 'I have been in touch with Genevieve, and Jasper. They are seeing him in hospital every day. He'll be out in a couple of days. He may not be able to play piano or talk properly.'

Marcus nods, not really agreeing or disagreeing. 'That sounds fine, doesn't it? What about that woman?'

'She is back in the house. She will clean up after forensics have been through the mess. Now. About the footage, Marcus,' Sahil hesitates to get Marcus's full attention. 'I have told the cops that I was the one who doctored the recordings on the day of her death because I *knew* you were the last one to see her when you were in there to fix her washing machine or boiler or whatever at 2:30pm. They put the time of her death between 1 and 4pm. You said you had to get to her in the afternoon, but you didn't tell me you had keys and you did NOT actually see her.'

'No, I did not see her,' Marcus sighs. 'They won't believe me. I do have her spare keys when she gave them to me just recently when she went abroad, to Spain or something, at

Christmas and I was her keyholder. She asked me to hang onto them for all those niggling jobs she started and stopped and started me on again.'

'Did you tell them you had keys and went in without her permission?' Sahil says.

'Yes, of course. Now it's much worse. Trespass,' Marcus looks solemn, at his folded hands on the table. He's resigned to this. He's said it over and over, to different personnel, the cops, his lawyer. 'I meant well. I thought I'd fix the shit before she got back from wherever she was. But THEY think I let myself in, got in an argument with her over all those bills, delays in her works and trespassing. They have no idea that she is the worst client. She keeps changing her mind and expecting me to pay for the materials and time wasted. And —,'

Marcus feverishly shakes his head, trying to erase memories of how she was so awful to work with. Sahil waves away Marcus's explanations. 'Pas de sweat. Marcus. I wanted to watch it with you, on my phone,' Sahil leans back again in order to reach deeper into his jeans pocket. 'Wait 'til you see this.'

The recording shows the front of the building just after 1 pm and Marcus has propped open the door open with a 10-litre tub of white undercoat paint. Marcus moves equipment, materials and tools into the lobby in more than one trip from the van. A woman in a coat and small-brimmed hat slips in behind Marcus at one point and he lets her pass without even looking at her. Sahil pauses the video.

'That's *her*!' Marcus exclaims, perplexed. The woman working at his father's house was at the scene?

'Yes. And she leaves the building a long time after you.

Look at the time of the recording. Marcus notes that it is hours later.'

'All this is great, but... we have no proof that she went into Angela's flat. There are no cameras outside Angela's front door. All she did was enter the building. So what?'

'It was a Friday. Angela was only found on Monday by her seamstress.'

'And?'

'And that night I went back into her flat.'

'You went to Angela's? Why the hell did you do that?'

'To check she was OK, of course. I knocked first before I entered with her keys that you kept safe with your own keys on the ring. You were asleep. The keys were on your bedside cabinet.'

'Oh my god, please don't tell me you discovered her body and did nothing about it!'

'No, I did not know. Because I did not even need to go into her flat! As soon as I knocked gently and waited outside her unit, I was standing on something hard and uneven on her doormat,' Sahil lowers his tone into a whisper. 'I was wearing those thin white hotel slippers of course, not shoes, as I did not want to make a sound. I looked down. And guess what?'

Sahil sits forward this time, to reach into his back pocket. He pulls out his wallet, folds it open and reaches in.

'We're going to get you out of here, Marcus,' Sahil's excited voice is reflected in his glittering eyes. It has been a long time since Marcus had seen any life in Sahil's dead and hollow eyes. 'Might even be today.'

Marcus's heart races. His flatmate's face is confidently beaming.

In Sahil's thumb and index finger he shows a small object. At least, the lighting in this room is glaringly useful. Tiny and very yellow with a green heart. A short fine thread of a chain dangles from a fishhook. It looks like an intricate jade earring set in 22K gold.

72
SAHIL

Sahil's evidence makes no sense at all for the cops. The earring, which he thought would clinch it, was dismissed. Marcus confirmed that the earring looks Chinese in design and style. It's jade after all. It is too much of a coincidence that the earring would belong to anyone else. Yet, it's true; they can't prove that it belonged to the woman in the footage.

'What? But it's Chinese!' Sahil's frustration grows in his outburst.

'With due respect, Mr Maitreya, this is not some Cinderella fairytale. We will not be chasing the missing earring,' DI Beauchêne-Gill sighs. 'The found earring could have been anyone's. It could've been Angela's! Have you thought of that? And the fact that the other earring is not in her flat is neither here nor there. What we will accept, however, is the missing footage. Thank you for that.'

'You're very welcome. I just want you to release Marcus. He meant well. He looks after the whole building. There is no way he will hurt anyone.'

The DI looks down and nods but in a thoughtful rather than agreeable way.

'We can see that the same woman, Miss Stella Choi, is in the video and left the building hours later. We will be bringing her in.'

'What about her phone?' Asks Sahil.

'There was no phone found in her flat. But we have Angela's number from Barry O'Keefe and will have to track her calls from the phone provider instead. That won't be quick.'

'What about witnesses?' Sahil feels like he is the inter-rogator, not the police. After all, he has helped with the investigation, hasn't he?

'There was a loud crash according to a neighbour, Phil Cross, of Number 6, but he says he heard it well before Marcus arrived, and that Angela did answer when he asked if everything was OK. We will be releasing Marcus now. We don't have any conclusive evidence to hold him.'

Sahil wants Marcus back, and for life to return to life B.E. — Before Elijah. Working on site, eating sandwiches, attending his classes, screwing Anjali. He had not realised he was living the dream then.

Now what has happened to that dream?

'However, we are pressing charges against you, Mr Maitreya.'

'Me?'

The DI grunts patiently. 'Yes, you, following your admis-sion. You're guilty of Assault Occasioning Actual Bodily Harm (ABH) under Section 47 of the Offences Against the Person Act 1861 and further more, you were Attempting to Pervert the Course of Justice. By moving and hiding what you believed to be Elijah O'Keefe's dead body, you were interfering with or obstructing the legal process, and tampering with evidence.'

'I didn't — this is just—,' Sahil splutters. He has no reply to these charges. How can they be fair? After all he's saved his friend, who has now got out scot-free!

'Your error was not the assault, but moving what you thought was his body. This shows intent. That means you *did* think what you did was a crime, and you were going to hide it. Why did you do that?'

'I don't know!' He grabs his huge mass of hair. Where are his brains in all that? 'I don't know! I thought he was dead.'

'Even so. And all the more! But your lawyer will advise later. We will have to keep you here until she comes tomorrow. Your actions were to protect yourself AND Marcus, so they may mitigate the assault charge. Let's see. We will wait.'

'But will I have to go home?'

'Well. As I said, we'll see.'

73
MARCUS

Tuesday 17th January

The alarm buzzes at 6:30 but he has already been on and off awake all night. Marcus dreamed of his mother, Dr Trudie Lam, carrying her box of documents, but instead of her name Lam Poh Choy, the label reads Sahil Maitreya and the box is covered in blood. Marcus's head is drenched in sweat which covers him in chills from the cold morning air. He shivers.

With his painkillers he can just about make it into Chelsea to work on Anjali's flat, though the doctor has ordered that he shouldn't. He needs more rest. But he is sick of resting. He had enough when he was in that detention cell. He has hardly slept because he has been thinking of Sahil. From hero to zero.

Now Sahil is at the mercy of publicly-funded legal aid which he may be eligible to receive due to his student status. Marcus wipes his icy sweat. There is no question he will hire a lawyer for Sahil if legal aid is unavailable. If this is a high profile case, Marcus could also look at pro bono firms. Is it? He is confused. He has gone through all this legal shit in Dubai when he tried to sue his employer for unfair dismissal due to his stress-driven breakdown, but he lost the case and ended up with even less. No job, wife or kids. If not for his mum's flat from which he had to evict the tenants, he would have no home too.

Marcus looks at the time again, even though he has just looked minutes ago. When will Sahil update him from the station?

He switches on his phone and his eyes are drawn to the News item on Twitter/X:

🟦 **BREAKING NEWS: Woman's Belongings Found Abandoned Near Dover Cliffs, Suspected Suicide** 🟦

This morning, police discovered a navy and red striped Tommy Hilfiger handbag, tan loafer shoes, and other personal belongings abandoned near the famous White Cliffs of Dover. The items are believed to belong to Stella Choi, a caregiver originally from Singapore, who had been residing in the UK.

A note was reportedly found inside the handbag, indicating that Stella intended to take her own life. The note revealed that all her earnings from her job would be directed toward her mother's nursing home fees. Authorities have yet to recover a body.

Search operations are currently underway, but the challenging terrain and rough sea conditions around the cliffs make recovery efforts difficult. The White Cliffs of Dover, while a popular tourist destination, have tragically also been associated with several such incidents over the years.

The police are appealing for anyone in the area or who has any information to come forward.

More updates to follow as the investigation continues.

PART FOUR
8 DAYS AGO

74
STELLA

Friday 6th January

As soon as Qamal has arrived and settled Richard, I put on my coat and am on my way. I may even buy cinema tickets for a local showing and surprise her. I have known my friend since our nursing school days. She is a fan of rom com.

The journey will take almost an hour and I call her to let her know I am coming. 'I'm not feeling great, so I don't want to do lunch.'

'That's OK, we've done lunch, coffee, theatre. We can just hang out. How about I bring you something?'

'Awww,' she coos gratefully.

I spend the morning in Aldwych at the Courtauld Gallery. My mother never thought I was artistic. She's right. I am a punter. A member of the audience, the public. I could never do any of this art but I appreciate it and every time I look at art, I think of my mother less. I have a cappuccino and lunch at the old-fashioned Crown Portuguese cafe on the Strand. I hardly drink coffee at work in Richard's house because I prefer the excitement of going out for coffee. How mundane to make your own coffee and gulp it.

I prefer traditional coffee houses, which make me feel like I am really in Europe, to nondescript modern joints like Caffe Nero and Paul's with their fake-old wooden furniture. I buy a toasted ham, cheese and avocado sandwich to take with me.

I get on the Central line at Holborn. It's so easy. Only 30 minutes. When I get to Corfield Street, I take in the grand mansion block building. I look up and down. It's the first time I've been invited here.

I slip in with a builder, through the front self-closing door propped open with a heavy large tub of paint, and climb the stairs.

'Hi Angela!' I chime with a little wave.

She is surprised to see me when she opens the door. Her eyes are wide.

'I hope you don't mind, Ange, the downstairs door was open. I didn't press your buzzer.'

'No problem!' She hugs me, and it is just like the old times. In moments like these, I cherish the experience I've had, living in the UK as a young person and learning so much in and outside my college hours.

'Look. I brought you lunch.' I hand over the posh brown paper bag, when she has shut the door.

'You needn't. Thank you. Appreciate it. I can't go out as I got a builder coming in later to sort out the boiler pressure and my washing machine cupboard. But enough of my nonsense. How has your week been?'

'Tough. He's like a toddler, I tell you.'

Angela grins sympathetically. I want to slap her. She is so fortunate not to have to work or to care for anyone. And to have some bloke pay for all her clothes, food, expenses and repairs. Still she complains all the time. All these months that I've been seeing her I've kept my irritation to myself.

'You know,' she takes the £6.50 sandwich in its brown paper bag and tosses it on her white marble worktop. 'I'm so happy you connected with me when you came to work in the UK.'

"Well, we *were* best friends,' I throw my hands in the air and break into a smile. 'Thank God for social media. Otherwise I would not have been able to track you down.'

'Sit down, please.' She fills, and puts the kettle on. She places a teabag each in two mugs. 'Tea?'

'Yes. Please. That would be great. You have a lovely place here,' I comment, my eyes darting around the room, decorated in emerald and gold highlights, with timber panelling and dark wood furniture. It would not have been cheap to do up a flat like this. I would know, since I oversee the ongoing repairs to my employer's home.

I sit at one of the velvet dining chairs in a brilliant dark green quilted seating. It feels divine on my bum. I hardly sit at work and when I sink myself into proper deep and expensive upholstery, I want to collapse into it.

She takes the sandwich out of the brown bag and sets it on a small white scalloped porcelain plate edged in gold.

'Angela, I wanted to ask you how long you were planning on keeping it from me,' I say suddenly.

'Keeping what?'

'I told you I came to the UK to look for my son, whom I've found out about nearly a year ago in my mother's stuff.'

She pauses. She looks away from me and says, 'Stella, you and I were students, and you asked me to help you. You could *not* keep him.'

'You knew someone from the adoption agency through the hospital. But why didn't you tell me you knew who he went to?'

'How would I know?' Angela blushes. She shifts in the plush velvet dining chair, her usual air of confidence faltering for a moment. She picks at the edges of the sandwich, avoiding my gaze. 'I was a student, just like you, Stella.' She looks up suddenly, with a pleading look.

'I kept telling you that I was writing to Elijah since I arrived and he never replied. I only had his address and photos of him as a child.'

'Stella, you were in a bad place then. You were too young. You had to focus on your studies, your career. You couldn't handle a child. I did what I thought was best for you, find him a good family, and quickly,' Angela says, her voice trembling, but she quickly recomposes herself. More lies. It's all rubbish.

'And look what happened? How could you? I trusted you, Angela. You were my best friend,' my voice, barely above a whisper, is breaking, as is my heart. 'You knew exactly where he was all along, didn't you? For a year you said nothing.' My hands start to shake.

'I was messaging you for months before they got my visa to work here, and I told you I am looking for my son,' I sound repetitive now. I know I just said all of that. But the words keep coming, like when I was with my mother. 'That has been my aim of moving to the UK.'

Angela exhales, placing the sandwich on the oak table. She stares at it.

'I found the adoption documents at my mother's care home. I told you his parents' names and that his name is... Elijah. O. Keefe,' I enunciate every syllable of my son's name. 'One day, about half a year ago, you mentioned that your partner is *technically now a widower*. I sympathised with you. I was so happy for you. You were not happy that he was married. I did not know his name or anything about him, because you always called him *My Sweet Honeybunch*, *My Lemony Cupcake*, *My Passionfruit Pie* and other stomach-churning terminology.' I made jazz hands befitting the sickening parlance.

Angela cringes, her face contorting into a squeezed rag. 'Those are our special names. Why are you bringing this up?' She whinges.

'Why? You were keeping his identity a secret from me. Luckily, I saw you carrying a Barclays card to pay for our celebratory drinks. It was in the name of Barry O'Keefe. You told me he was a bouncer in Marbella, but that you'd never move to Spain.'

'Not *bouncer*. A security services professional.'

'Oh for fuck's sake. Don't split hairs. There are not exactly many Barry O'Keefes in Spain. Once I found out about your wonderful partner who pays for our days out, it was easy. He has a business, so he is looking for new clients all the time, isn't he? His LinkedIn profile confirms his experience but not his connection to Elijah.'

'But —,'

'Let me finish,' I snap. 'I made a few calls to Marbella, and managed to get through to Barry himself in security services. I told him that I am a relative of Irene's, from Hong Kong. I just wanted him to confirm that Irene has passed away but Elijah is alive. He did. It's all true.'

Angela is shaking her head now, somewhat in a mixture of disbelief and sadness. 'Stella, I didn't know at first,' She pauses. 'After the adoption, I didn't think about him at all... but years later, I... I found out through a mutual friend in the NHS that... Elijah's foster family... they kept in touch with the agency.' Angela mutters. For a nosey cow that she is, she sure has been good at keeping quiet about important news while she is busy complaining about the other residents and gossip-mongering people's trivialities. How many times have I met up with her since arriving in London? Countless. I have seen her true colours now. 'I learned about him, about where he was, but by then, so much time had passed. I didn't think it mattered anymore. I didn't want to drag up old wounds.'

My eyes widen with rage. 'You knew he was out there and my son's father pays all your bills while I work my arse off morning to night. Just so I could see him one day.'

Angela flinches. 'You are doing great! You have a professional, independent life, and you are providing for your mother, yourself and your son. I didn't want you to ruin everything for a past you couldn't change. What is the point, Stella? What is the point?'

'But it is my right to know! Four words were all you needed to say. *Barry is Elijah's dad*. After all, you talk about Barry enough! His birthday gifts to you, theatre tickets, duty free perfume...,' My voice cracks and trails off when I imagine her lifestyle versus mine. 'Elijah needs me. And I need him. You don't. You have Barry.'

Angela stands up.

'Where are you going?' I ask. I am not even finished but I stand up too, the force of which knocks the chair to the floor onto its back. Forget the plush velvet seat. I have a certain height advantage and now is a good time to use it.

'I can't listen to this, Stella,' she snaps. 'I didn't even know you cared about the boy.'

'What the —?' I see red then. Alarm bells peal in my head. What the hell does she know about care? I have lived all my life first caring for patients, then my mother and now an elderly man.

Angela heads for the bedroom. 'I am not asking you to leave. I just need to take my meds.' She does not cast another glance at me. She looks completely remorseless.

I try to follow her into the bedroom, but she says, 'Won't be a minute, Stella, dearie.' She stops me before I enter her room. I glance a beautiful double bay window bedroom without curtains, an olive green quilted bedspread, glass bedside lamps.

I'm too busy admiring her decor to notice.

She is standing at her bedroom door holding a cricket bat with both hands.

75

STELLA

'What is that? What are you doing?' I ask in a tight voice, my brow knitted.

'Stella, please, you have to understand. I was trying to protect you. I can't find my meds. You probably should leave now.'

My breath quickens. There's no way I will turn around, turn my back to her and walk out. That's counter-intuitive. No way. The last thing I will feel is her blow on me. I am not that dumb. I take steps backwards, reversing into the lounge. The smart and lush green and gold room is a jungle closing in, the gold features like daylight cutting through.

'Protect me? From what?' My words hang in the air, thick with uselessness. I must not panic.

Angela's face darkens. 'I never meant to hurt you, Stella. I thought it was the right thing to do.'

She raises her arms and swings the bat down. I lunge forward, ducking, and it missed me. She takes a step back, and swings again, but tears are blurring her vision, whereas I have no more tears to shed. The bat is so close to my head that I feel the wind from its power.

'You hid the fact that Barry is my Elijah's dad because you were protecting yourself,' I shout.

'What?' She growls.

'Barry wants to have a connection with Elijah forever. He told me as much when I called him in Spain,' I say.

'No —,' Angela hisses, shaking her so head furiously she appears out of focus. I try to grab the bat off her, but she moves it away fast. I must think of more things to say to delay her.

'If I take Elijah away, then Barry will lose him *and* blame you. He might even leave you. You're only worried about losing Barry. Totally selfish but I can understand that. He pays for all this.' I rotate my head around to demonstrate what I mean by *all this*, but in fact, my eyes dart to the large bookcase near the edge of her bedroom door, stacked haphazardly with Angela's collection of sculpture, glassware, luxurious, arty knick-knacks and heavy books. She is so clever, isn't she? All these books on art and culture and politics. I slave from morning to night to a family who does not appreciate me, followed by meaningless TV-watching with my employer.

She never says sorry once. Yet her tears pour and she's howling. Who's this supposed *friend*? Why cry? My questions flit by like fireflies, but she takes another swing. This time I see the huge arc to gain momentum, like she's drawing an elegant circle. I dodge by picking up a large ceramic vase and cracking it over her skull, a surprising strength surging through me. As I remove it the bookcase moves forward. I only then understand that the vase is there for counterweight.

Angela also barely has time to register the movement before the massive bookcase tips forward. She drops the bat. She makes an ugly face full of teeth as she grabs my perfectly curled hair with her right hand. She yanks and a sharp pain shoots from my earlobe. I jump back and avoid the crash.

She gasps, stumbling backward in shock. The heavy wooden structure crashes down on her with a deafening thud.

The room falls silent, save for the muffled sound of my ragged breathing and the dull echo of books and ornaments clattering to the floor. All those darling, expensive, clever things — they are the end of her.

76
STELLA

I spot her hands and feet visible from under the sculpture of wood, books, art. I tug out her wrist, remembering our nursing days when we had to practise taking blood pressure and pulse counting on each other. Heavens. That was a while ago. I check. No heartbeat. I open her fist, and remove all the clumps of my hair that she's pulled.

Someone is knocking on the door. Damn. 'Are you OK? Angela? I heard a crash? It's Phil from No. 6?' An Australian voice calls out in a series of questions.

'Fine,' I answer. 'Thanks,' I say in a high-pitch Angela voice from as far away as possible from the front door — the bathroom.

I listen for the footsteps to indicate that the neighbour has gone away, and I am now able to get on with my tasks.

There are yellow Marigold rubber gloves under the sink. Something from back home. Made in Malaysia, the country next door to mine. It gives me a layer of comfort in my time of need. I pull them on. I spend the next few minutes checking, spraying and wiping down what I had touched apart from Angela: the edge of the bookcase and the kitchen sink unit from which I got the gloves.

This flat is small compared to the huge mansion I take care of. I put the unused mugs back, and threw away the teabags. I pack the sandwich back into the brown paper bag, meticulously picking up each piece of lettuce. No sense in wasting food. I wipe up each crumb from the oak table and marble worktop. I'm about to wash and dry the scalloped shaped gold edged side plate but on second thoughts, what's the point? I slide it into my bag too, along with her mobile phone. Saves time.

I am just about to leave at around half past two in the afternoon, but a pesky knock on the door comes. A voice calls out. Not again!

'Angela? I have been ringing your phone. It's Marcus.'

A pause.

'Coming to fix your washing machine cupboard?'

Another pause. He knocks again.

'Are you in? Hullo? Hullo?'

Such a nightmare then. There is a rustle of keys. Oh shit, *he has keys?* I keep the gloves on and enter the bedroom to be with Angela for the last time. I shut her door, lock it and wait an eternity until the builder has left.

On the Central Line home, I brush my hair gently where it has been mussed up by my dear friend. My hairbrush touches my left earlobe. There is no familiar chink of metal. Oh no.

My mother's jade earring from San Francisco. It's gone.

PART FIVE
FIVE MONTHS LATER

77
NAFISAH

She makes it in before the rain. Nafisah passes the barb-wired high walls and into the entrance lobby. She stares at each wall and equipment, not surprisingly it is her first time in the HMP Pentonville visitors' room which is run by a charity called Sturgeon.

She learns the protocol when she did the online booking: no food, drink, mobile phone or drugs. First she places her phone in a designated locker, and then is subjected to a body search and a dog sniffs her for drugs.

Just like at an airport, following the customary photo ID check, Nafisah is then registered onto the biometric system with a photo and a scan of her index fingers. She has not told her husband of her "day trip". She just figured he would go apeshit that she would even bother to see Elijah. 'He got six months for assault, what the hell are you doing trying to see him?' She pictures her husband throwing down the Metro on the coffee table.

But she owes it to her late friend and neighbour Irene Chan.

Sure. It's a prison. It's just a place for the free to meet the damned. And what the world needs now is more love, not less. The Prophet Muhammad, Peace Be Upon Him (PBUH) said, "Kindness is a mark of faith, and whoever is not kind has no faith".

Once the biometric records are done, Nafisah is given a day trip wristband, like at a theme park, for identification during the visit. It will be removed when she leaves.

There is a constant murmur, somewhat resembling a train station or immigration office. The dull grey walls and rows of plain tables and chairs buzz with the constant chatter, laughter, weeping and coughs of inmates and their visitors. She spots Elijah sitting at a table near the back, his face lighting up as soon as he sees her. The warden guides her to her seat. Despite the harsh environment, there's an air of hope around him.

'Thanks for coming to see me, Naf,' he beams. 'I really appreciate it.' He breaks into a big smile, and it has been a long time since she had seen his crooked teeth. But it *is* a smile.

'You look well,' she says sincerely, studying his appearance with interest.

'I do?' Elijah pipes up. 'I won't forget you brought me snacks and meals.'

'You can't not eat. In fact, if they didn't do a body search, I would have brought you some samosas today.'

'No need,' he shakes his head. 'Remember I was worried about being evicted? The irony is I have had free accommodation here for the last 5 months.'

Nafisah grins and throws her hands in the air in mock astonishment.

'I know, right,' Elijah concurs. 'I am going to be out next

week,' he nods and clamps his mouth with a kind of pride, maturity, resignation. 'They reduced the sentence because the medication I had been on after my mother passed away had a side effect of unmitigated rage and aggression.'

'They should have known that,' Nafisah sympathises, shaking her head.

'I know. But they didn't,' he shrugs.

She wants to ask what medication it was, but decides not to. He is well now, isn't he? 'And you're a first timer. You've never hurt any one before... before Alistair Marcus Ho. I read his name online. How has it been in here?' Asks Nafisah.

'Well, it's insane but I have had a positive experience. I am very used to being unfortunate, rejected, given a raw deal. That's my usual life. But they, *and I*, have discovered I am quite a good cook.'

'Oh, really?' Nafisah's ears prick up.

'I think it might be my mother's influence? Being Chinese? I never thought of myself as Chinese before,' Elijah runs his hand over his buzzcut absent-mindedly, already reminding Nafisah of confident chefs, just like Heston Blumenthal, when they talk about their origin story. 'I just think of myself as an East Ender.'

'Being Chinese can't go wrong,' Nafisah's voice lowers in anticipation of excitement. She jokes. 'People who love Chinese food will trust a Chinese chef, innit. What's next?'

'I am going to be a chef in training! I can't believe it! There is something called institutional cooking,' he chuckles self-deprecatingly. 'In 6 months after this place, I will be finished with the academy. I can work in offices, colleges, canteens. Cooking for the masses.'

'This is music to my ears,' Nafisah's jaw drops open. 'I'm so pleased for you. Congratulations.'

'Thanks so much. Are you sewing?'

'Oh yes, all the time. That is how I became involved in the first place. Angela's curtains—,' Nafisah starts, but before she can mention Barry's suit trousers, Elijah interrupts her.

'So ironically, being in here has given me a job. Remember how long I was looking?'

Nafisah nods. How could she forget his hardship, the mounting bills, the eviction notices. He had been too embarrassed to even let her in to his home after his mother passed away. When he opened his flat's front door a chink, the pervasive stale stench of egg-farts, acidic dairy odours of unwashed linen and the minty air of toothpaste and kitchen detergent swamped her.

When the visit is over, they hug each other. Nafisah feels tears prick at her as she says goodbye to Elijah, and a string of well-worn well wishes, *all the best, good luck, take care* and so on. His body is huge as a door and he blocks the daylight. She shuts her eyes.

As she exits final gantry, the security guards take her theme park wristband of her, she gets back her phone and umbrella from the locker and leaves the womb-like interior of the building into the cool, open air. It's still raining. She presses the umbrella button and it shoots open with a satisfying whump. Each step she walks, she walks free, back to Caledonian Road to catch the tube to Kings Cross.

78
SAHIL

T he evening sun is intense and casts long shadows. Sahil runs his hands over the smooth red leather with polished chrome accents. He chooses a barstool to sit on, from a long counter lined with them. The smell of freshly brewed coffee mingles with the scent of sizzling bacon and pancakes. He orders a Coke. A jukebox in the corner plays Van Halen's *Jump*, and before that more soft rock music from the 70s and 80s he doesn't recognise as he's too young to remember.

He's only been in the city a week, though this diner would be full of his colleagues since at the bottom of his tower block office carpark. Sorry, *parking lot*. That is what Americans call it and he might as well get used to yet more new terminology. His employer is a software firm headquartered in Austin's burgeoning tech district. The place is buzzing with the after-work crowd. Tech professionals in casual attire sit at tables with laptops open, sipping green smoothies as they work or chat with colleagues. Sahil blends in, wearing a casual yet professional outfit—Uniqlo jeans, a button-down shirt, and a lightweight Zara jacket. His eyes scan the room as he sucks his Coke from a striped straw in fluted glass.

He is still slightly jet-lagged as he has had no chance to recover since his Graduate Visa was revoked. He was eligible for legal aid due to his being an overseas student with his education paid for by three families back home.

After the trial, Marcus paid his £4,500 fine and Sahil was not allowed to stay in the country anymore. He is also not ready to return home because he needed another year's work experience post-qualification minimum. He considers himself very fortunate that through one of Cousin X's uncles, he has applied for a systems engineering job in the USA, in a city known for its vibrant tech scene, innovation, and culture. At last he is doing what he should have been doing in London, which is what he has trained in. No more building jobs for him.

The view from the glass windows overlooks the lively street outside, where the eclectic mix of Austin's downtown architecture is visible—modern high-rises interspersed with historic buildings, all under the clear Texan sky.

Sahil's smartphone buzzes beside his fluted glass. He glances at the screen — an email notification from his line manager about tomorrow's meeting. He also notices that he has had a WhatsApp message from Anjali. He quickly opens and reads it.

> Hey. I hope you are settling in. I've been on Hamptons looking at houses again, as is my hobby. Marcus's dad's house is on the market for £8.5million. My parents won't be making an offer. LOL.

What is this LOL? It's not even funny. He checks the time. It's 10 pm in London. He replies.

> I'm doing great, thanks. Hope you're well.

He always replies the same way. Blandly. He puts his phone away and hopes she does not reply. He won't be playing WhatsApp tennis with her.

Sahil looks out the window. Did he really break up with her so many months ago? It feels like only days. She said she would not forgive him for his "insane actions", yet she messages him every few days to see "how he is". Sahil is starting alone, in a new city in a new country. He does *not* want to go over and over the entire trial with Anjali. He's so tired of it, of her, of her Chelsea flat with all its remote control fittings.

Once he's settled in, he will pay Marcus back. He wants to do this as soon as he can, even though Marcus has said there is no hurry. With his inheritance, Marcus will buy a bigger property. He's already made contact with his wife and children in Dubai to reconnect with them and invite them back to London. The father's house will take almost half a year to sell, but Marcus will be keeping himself busy. He has hired an assistant and is in the middle of doing new jobs, always is, always will be.

As the evening progresses, the diner fills with a diverse crowd—students, artists, tech entrepreneurs, and musicians, all part of Austin's eclectic scene. He finishes the rest of his Coke. He is about to get up, pay and go. But a voice stops him.

'Sahil?'

'Yes?' Sahil splutters. He turns around. In front of him is the most beautiful tanned girl he had ever seen. She has glossy dark auburn hair and amber eyes, and Sahil thinks he must have been struck blind because he can't see anything else after seeing her. The countertop and barstools all fade to white.

'Hi, I'm MacKenzie. We didn't get innerdoosed today? We're on the same team working on the project starting tomorrow.' She has a southern accent, and says Ahm MacKian Zee.

'Project Sentinel?' He blurts out nervously.

'Yeahhhh. Did you receive the memo?'

'No,' he replies like a monosyllabic teenager. Damn.

She pulls up a bar stool and sits next to him. 'Now. Just in brief, Project Sentinel is a cybersecurity initiative aimed at developing a new security protocol for one of our firm's major clients, a global financial services company,' she continues, taking on a serious voice, which makes him feel quite weak. 'The project involves building an advanced intrusion detection system that leverages machine learning algorithms to identify and respond to cyber threats in real time.'

'Uh-huh,' Sahil replies, then shuts his mouth, aware it's an open cave.

'It's a pretty big deal for us,' MacKenzie continues, her eyes now twinkling in a mock-sly manner. 'If we can pull this off, it'll put us on the map in the cybersecurity world.'

'Mmkay,' he slurs.

Sahil takes a deep breath. He wants to say, 'Looking forward to it, yes! I've always been fascinated by AI and machine learning, especially in the context of security.' But instead, like an imbecile, he says, 'Yeah.'

MacKenzie grips him on the shoulder. 'You'll be fine. I've been with the company for three years, and this is the most exciting project I've worked on. It's a big opporchooniddy for both of us.'

'Mm-hmm,' Sahil mutters. She lets go of his shoulder.

'Perfect. You and I are gonna make a great team,' she says. 'I see you've had a drink. But can I getcha some'inna eat? A snack? Jever try Austin's Frito Pie? It's mandatory office initiation.'

Sahil grins like a dog and then covers his mouth with his hand. Luckily she misinterprets his shock and self-consciousness as fear of new food.

'It's a Texas classic,' she explains. 'Fritos topped with chili, cheese, jalapeños, and a dollop of sour cream. Not exactly health food, but it's comfort food at its finest. Did I mention that I am half-Indian? My mother is from Punjab.'

She breaks into a huge American smile, the kind you only see on Netflix. All lip gloss, teeth and eyes.

79

GENEVIEVE

After Daddy came home, he never got better. He got worse. He couldn't and wouldn't speak. He communicates with hand gestures with his good side and we adjust to his new rehab life, a physiotherapy schedule, appointments, outdoor time now the weather is better, visits from Marcus, and TV time. I look forward to supporting my father in my new role. From sommelier to daughter. I tell Jared at La Republique I don't mind doing stints three times a week when I have cover for daddy. But they decline. They need someone full time. I totally understand that. I once only hired full-timers too.

Sometimes my father accepts that Stella had gone. Marcus (as I now call him but sometimes I forget and go back to Alistair) and I decide not to inform him about her tragic death in Dover. Why twist the knife? Sometimes he still imagines her around, that she's just out for a short while, while the only words he says all day are 'Stella... where?'

The police have searched her belongings and lodgings.

They have found the earring which matches the one on the doormat at Angela's.

He pines for her, often looking in the direction of the coat rack where his and her Ralph Lauren quilted jackets hung like uniforms. He looks for her royal blue apron embroidered in gold with my sister's initials. He grips onto it in the kitchen and inhales her scent, until I hide the item.

I could not heal him, no matter how hard I try. I read to him, even horrified myself by playing on the piano some terrible Easy Piano Elton John arranged for five-year-olds. I learn Hakka recipes on YouTube and cook for him.

But nothing and no one could ever replace Stella.

He needs help with getting in and out of bed. Unlike Stella, I do not buy him new posh clothes and he knows it. Qamal is not great at dressing him. Daddy does not look like who he was. He is used to be so smartly turned out, primped and pimped up like a bank manager about to step onto a yacht for a weekend away, but he now looks tired, frustrated, wasted. Pyjamas with mix and match stained white shirts.

Qamal is now coming 4 times a week as Daddy is eligible for NHS home care since his stroke, which provides me some time off, although I do like to spend time with him, learning about being a care giver, and getting tips and advice.

I hire a cleaner for the house. She needs at least 6 hours per week. I soon become aware of the amount of cleaning involved in this huge house, on top of caregiving duties and appointments. It really is non-stop. I am grateful to crash in front of the TV. Forget the yoga. Just don't even go there.

Daddy doesn't get hungry much. Sometimes on his uncooperative days, he refuses any meals. He doesn't care if it was homemade Hakka food or Tesco's TV dinners. These are longest, shortest days, watching my father kill himself slowly. He no longer talks about Stella, or asks where she is. Marcus and I assume he must have now let go, and does not miss her much anymore.

One day, he talks. It's more than two words. He is in his wheelchair staring at the portrait of my mother over the gilt fireplace surrounds.

My father slurs, and I listen hard. 'I miss her. She is the love of my life. The only woman who made me happy.'

'Daddy? Who?'

He shuts his eyes momentarily. 'She should've taken me with her.' When he opens them, he glances at his knobbly fingers, the jade and gold signet ring on his little finger.

At nights, he sometimes still talks to my mother, who he claims is "in his room". 'Trudie?' He calls out, plaintively. 'Why are you here? What do you want?'

At times he has conversations in his bedroom with his imaginary wife, slurring with difficulty. 'No, not yet. I haven't eaten; how about you?'

'Trudie, don't bring that dog in here. He's covered in mud.' He chuckles.

My father passes away peacefully in his sleep on 18th June. I sort of expect yet don't expect to be so overwhelmed by sadness and unspeakable tearful bouts almost every hour, followed by periods of numb blankness. They don't tell you grief is like a disease, a sickness, a love.

Cassie flies back immediately from Riyadh. The busyness of the house and family arriving bring some comfort. I manage to even apply lipstick when we meet the Wills probate lawyer Henry Tummings in a grey office block in Pimlico. He's portly with little round glasses. He reads out my father's last will and testament.

The house in Rumbold Road goes to the three of us. He also had two other properties we did not even know about, a cottage in Dorset and villa in France, both rented out. Those would be split three-ways too. Marcus is looking forward to managing both, though I cannot see how he will divide his time. It will save on agency fees, that's all, he shrugs, agreeing with Cassie and I that he's not thought things through. I am relieved that I will not need to find work so urgently now, and instead will be able to focus on Jasper and his school, and look for a small apartment. He's started to enjoy drama and is performing in his first musical at the beginning of autumn. Theatre has been great for his confidence. I want to take him to the West End. That is what London gives us. I offer my services to Marcus. I may be able to join his team and do all his PR, admin and whatever else he needs to manage his projects and the rental properties. They will not run themselves, and I have plenty of experience in running my business in Singapore.

Henry reads out that Daddy has given the sum of £25,000 to someone called Elijah O'Keefe. I gasp.

'That's ridiculous,' snaps Marcus.

Cassie, lost in the pace of the conversation, butts in, 'Who's that?'

'Isn't that—,' I don't manage to finish my question, but Marcus finishes it for me: 'Yes, it is, but I don't understand when he decreed this gift and why? Surely it can't be on the day that Elijah broke into the house? Dad has never met Elijah before —,'

'Well,' says Henry Tummings, 'It's dated this year. Your

father has written a letter for you,' and he reads it off his screen:

Thursday 12th January

Dear Alistair, Genevieve and Cassie,

By the time you read this, I would be having cocktails in the sky. Please do not be surprised. I am leaving Elijah O'Keefe £25,000 which at the time of writing is quite a lot of money. Who knows what it's worth by the time I kick the bucket?

I have never met him. I only know of him through your mother. *Don't worry, dear, I've taken care of "it" for you,* she said, after he was born.

Alistair is not my biological son, though I have treated him like my own child, and if not, better than my own flesh and blood.

It's absolutely not true. Marcus grimaces and hangs his head. He clamps his jaw. I reach out and hold his hand. My father has been cruel to him, hence my mum having to protect Marcus.

I have only one son, and it's Elijah. He's been banned from ever seeing me.

When you were all little, and your mother and I worked non-stop, we put up an ad on the hospital noticeboard and interviewed for a part-time nanny. The candidate who got the job was a tall and slim nursing student with a swishing, long ponytail, *and* she was a girl from back home. I always prefer to hire *kakilang*, our own people. I absolutely fell in love with her, we had the most unexpected and irreplaceable affair in the hotel rooms at the Peony. I was already in my late forties and she was more than half my age.

Cassie buries her face in her hands. 'I can't listen to this,' she mutters. 'I feel sick. Just tell us the ending.'

'OK, I won't read out anymore,' grunts Henry, shifting in his plush office swivelling office chair uneasily. He looks up. 'If you like I can send it by PDF or print it now? Would you prefer to read it at home?'

'No, just read the damn thing,' says Marcus curtly. 'We will never read it otherwise!'

Henry blows out. 'OK. There's not much more,' he says.

Your mother knew of course. I don't know how. But she knows everything. She's very smart. Trudie delivered the baby, and had it adopted through the agency that the girl's classmate knew, found out who the adoptive parents were and paid £500 into the account of that baby every month until he turned 18. In return, I was not allowed to ever see him.

I had never met my son until today.

He came by and I thought he was the plumber. I have been haunted by Trudie's ghost ever since she died. Funny that. I didn't believe in ghosts either. I thought this must be one of her tricks. But as soon as Stella said he was *not* the plumber, I put two and two together.

That night, one of Trudie's collection of porcelain vases shatters in her study. We all heard it but no one went in to check, and Genevieve who sleeps like a log. The next morning, Stella found the clothes from Trudie's wardrobe scattered messily in piles all over the room.

My memory may not be great and I may be tormented

by Trudie, but the moment Stella walked in, I *knew* it was her. I showered her with plenty of cash and jewellery gifts over the entire time she has been here, because I want to make her happy *while* I am still around.

She is the love of my life. The only woman who made me happy. The mother of my son.

(Signed) Richie Ho esq.

(Countersigned)   Henry   Tummings   LL.B   (Hons) LL.M UCL

80

ELIJAH

Dorking, Surrey

The academy, housed in a charming, renovated manor house surrounded by lush green fields and woodlands, is where he has been training for a few weeks now. The 300-year-old stately building with ivy creeping up its stone walls used to be some rich aristocrat's house before it went into disrepair and dereliction in the 1950s from lack of income, funding and staff. See, poor people have nothing to lose and rich people risk losing it all.

Elijah, £25,000 richer from his inheritance, has used it to support his training and banked the rest of it. When he sees his own large ugly plates of meat every day with their claw-like toenails, he regrets those blasted hideous £450 Hanwags he ripped off Marcus. To think he'd got only £80 for them.

Elijah's main aim of starting and staying in the catering industry is getting three meals a day. He's huge, grown up hungry, worked hard for pittance, and frankly, he's sick of it. Poverty is a wise motivator.

· · ·

Elijah has never lived outside a city before. He is a Londoner through and through. He misses the roar of traffic, scream of sirens and the constant knockout odour of smoky fried food, drains and car fumes. The idea of growing one's vegetables was like going to the moon for him.

Being surrounded by the Surrey Hills, Dorking is a charming, picturesque town with a combination of history and scenic beauty. As London is not English, Elijah is still discovering what "*quintessential* English character" means. He is a tourist in his own country, on a kind of staycay, a renaissance.

At first, the silence and lack of any strong smells in his rented one-bedroom cottage gave him headaches every day. Fresh air made him sick. As he is now off medication, it takes him a while to acclimatise. The silence is not silent, and the absence of strong smells is actually the pervasion of subtly faint aromas.

Elijah's accommodation is just a short walk from the academy. His room has basic furnishings — a bed, a small writing desk and a wardrobe. All IKEA. It's tidy and functional. Elijah spends his evenings with his sketchbooks and TV watching after a long day in the kitchen. These are what he enjoyed as a child and still enjoy. He doodles or plays with his phone while watching TV. *You're not multitasking, are you?* His mother used to tease him when he lay on the sofa. Her voice, amusing but stern in its reproach, still talks to him occasionally, but it is now faint. He surprises himself when all the things she used to make for him, he now cooks for his class — traditional Hong Kong snacks. How he had taken for granted his own family's skills.

Elijah calls his father when he has settled in.

'Dad?' He waits with a certain ingrown fear.

'Elijah? Where are ya?'

'Just wanted to give you my new address, Dad,' his voice is shaking and he doesn't like it. 'Been 'ere a few weeks. I don't want any money.'

There is a pause.

'Son, I am so proud of you,' Barry says, and Elijah's mouth drops open. His dad is not ashamed of him?

'I can't wait to taste the meals you make.'

Elijah hesitates. He can't think what to reply. 'When are you coming?'

'I'm coming back from Spain in two weeks.'

'I'll show you around,' he grins, although his father can't see him. He is not ready to do a video call with his Dad yet, but by the next call, he sure wants to let Barry see his accommodation. 'I've learned so much. I'm in this 300-year-old building that's converted into the academy.'

'How's what's-his-name?'

Elijah chuckles. 'We are not allowed to talk about him. That's in the non-disclosure.'

Barry is asking about the world-famous celebrity chef who founded the academy which is in his name. He put in the money to modernise the building whilst maintaining its rustic charm. The main kitchen is a spacious, open area with state-of-the-art cooking stations, stainless steel countertops, and an assortment of cooking utensils hanging from the walls.

'You know what, Dad, we bake our own breakfast every day!' Elijah exclaims.

'No way! You've won the pools. There is no need to worry about your next meal ever again.'

The aroma of freshly baked bread and simmering sauces fills the air each morning. There are long tables for group work and a demonstration area where instructors showcase techniques.

'Remember when you took me out for breakfast on weekends? It was such a treat. Full English.'

'Yeah. I do,' Barry affirms.

'Well, it's not full English now. 'S all sourdough and French pastries.'

'Ah know. Gone all fancy now, have ya?' His father jokes.

Elijah WhatsApp calls his father a week later. He holds up his phone so Barry can see through the large windows in the Manor House which overlook the scenic landscape. Elijah opens the front door to show him the cobblestone path leading up to the grand entrance. He walks the phone around to the back of the building. 'OK, Dad, just showing you our a vegetable garden. We're growing fresh herbs, peas, beans, kale, chard...,' his voice trails off when he realises there are just too many to name. 'All used in our cooking classes.'

Classes start at 6 am every day. Discipline is not new to him: he has been an early riser with a rigid routine since HMP Pentonville.

'Is it quite international?'

'Oh, yes, my classmates are from all around the world. They are most definitely not local. No one is from Dorking,' Elijah laughs. There's a hum of activity when Elijah and the other students practise their creative and technical skills, chopping, stirring, and plating. The sound of sizzling pans and the clinking of utensils play a constant background rhythm. The academy's instructors have been impressed with Elijah's ingenious ability to cook a meal with very little or very cheap ingredients.

Barry says thoughtfully, 'Would you like to work in Spain? After you're done here.'

'Never thought about that.'

'I can get you a top restaurant or hotel job just like that.'

'Oh, really? I'll keep it in mind. I'd better go now. We're starting again.'

Elijah doesn't want his dad to see his over-enthusiasm so he ends the conversation. He *could* work in Spain or the UK. But he wouldn't like to decide yet. He has new friends now. He thoroughly enjoys being in a multicultural classroom. It's like London but in one room. Elijah spends his days immersed in learning, tasting and perfecting his dishes. He'd be sad when this course ends.

Elijah receives a letter one evening after class when he gets back to the cottage. The envelope on the doormat has a French postmark, and he feels a chill in the air when he sees his name and address written in a familiar handwriting.

Dear Elijah,

I know you must be surprised to hear from me. I know you miss me. I apologise that I have not been in touch. I had to leave the UK in a hurry. And with Trudie's passport. It was a challenge to look like an old lady, but white hair and her glasses fixed it. And an entire LK Bennett outfit from her wardrobe which has never been emptied.

All that is over. I have a new name and passport now. I never managed to pay your last two month's rent. I said I would help you. I will be coming back to the UK. I am working again, as an English-speaking nanny, with a rich family. I am learning French every day and I am almost fluent.

Have nothing to do with THAT family. Your birth father, Richard, was the only good egg, and the only man who ever loved me. Unfortunately, he did not know you. Thanks to him, I have somewhere to live in France now. I told him everything. He wept and said goodbye to me. He asked me to come back as soon as it is safe. He gave me the contact of an estate agent and close friend who manages his French property. If I ever needed a place to stay, I was to contact this agent.

The rest of them are not worth your time. That Jean-Viv is an appalling businesswoman and completely ungrateful daughter, after all I have done for her father and son. I even did her a favour putting her ex, Shiong or Benjamin or whatever he called himself (who hires conmen and women for his syndicate), in jail! I've helped to stop the conman from spending anymore of *her* money, which *isn't* hers anyway. It was her mother's. Trudie was as mean as Angela. They were in cahoots with my mother, taking you away from me.

I am so thrilled I have found you again, not for the first time in my life.

Until we meet again, keep cooking! Say hi to the celebrity chef from me.

Love,

Mum.